D0755445

DEAD PRETTY

Roger Granelli

Published by Accent Press Ltd – 2009

ISBN 9781906373580

Copyright © Roger Granelli 2009

The right of Roger Granelli to be identified as the author of this work has been asserted by him in accordance with the Copyright, Designs and Patents Act 1988.

The story contained within this book is a work of fiction. Names and characters are the product of the author's imagination and any resemblance to actual persons, living or dead, is entirely coincidental.

All rights reserved. No part of this book may be reproduced, stored in a retrieval system, or transmitted in any form or by any means, electronic, electrostatic, magnetic tape, mechanical, photocopying, recording or otherwise, without the written permission of the publishers: Accent Press Ltd, The Old School, Upper High St, Bedlinog, Mid Glamorgan, CF46 6RY.

Printed and bound in the UK

Cover Design by The Design House

For Phil Rickman, for all the help over the years,
for Ian and Chris for the writing retreat, and for Nige

Thanks to Eltham Jones for the germ of an idea

Chapter One

Mark thought Lena had left the cat's food out, but not long enough for it to reek. This was a more subtle smell, a butcher's shop smell of blood soaking into sawdust, cold and sweet, with something ominous at its edge, something that spoke of that journey from field to slaughterhouse, to butcher's slab. Lena liked to give the cat food that didn't come from tins, it was fond of liver, but there was no liver and no cat, not at first. Then Mark saw Danni, cowering under the settee, her black fur undulating as she breathed in rapidly, nostrils narrowed, eyes on fire, angry and fearful in equal measure. Though Mark had never much liked cats he clucked his tongue at her, but she retreated further under the recess, making a half-hearted hiss, that was more plea than threat.

Mark called for Lena but she didn't answer. She'd be upstairs, sleeping the afternoon away, as she often did after the Amsterdam trip. He poured himself some of the orange juice she'd left out on the kitchen table. It was too warm, the day was too warm and his last job had been too warm. It was time to chill out a little, spend some money.

The smell wasn't going away. Mark looked at the cat accusingly. The creature was desperate to get out and got up enough nerve to shoot past him, hurling herself through the flap in the door with a clatter and a strangled cry. He'd never seen it move so fast but the smell did not go with her and the cat's bowl was empty. Mark left his juice, thought of something stronger then thought better of it and went upstairs. He'd shower, and join Lena. Maybe he wouldn't even wake her until later. Maybe he wouldn't shower.

The smell was getting stronger. Not so sweet now. Maybe it was the weather. They'd sweltered for the last week, hitting thirty some days. He looked in on Lena, as he'd done so many times before. She was often asleep when he came home. They led frenetic lifestyles that collided occasionally, fought occasionally and loved occasionally, but it suited them.

The blinds were drawn and Mark's eyes took a moment to get used to the gloom. Lena was slumped on the bed, on her back in her usual position. She hadn't even bothered to undress. Mark would have turned and gone to the shower room if it wasn't for the smell. It was coming from here. It was coming from her. He switched on the light, stepped towards Lena, then stepped back quickly, almost falling. Mark stared for a few seconds, but didn't want to believe his eyes. He turned away, opened the blinds, then the window, and leant on the sill for a few moments, blinking and breathing like the cat, filling his lungs with air in an effort to calm himself. Kids were chasing a kite in the park opposite, a few people walked dogs. An ice cream van was approaching, and the kids forgot about the kite when they heard its chimes, leaving it to lose shape and fall silently to the ground. The van was playing a snippet of Italian opera. It felt like an age before Mark could turn back to the bed.

There was not that much blood, not as much as you might expect, and what was there had congealed into a dull red paste. Lena's eyes stared past him, as blue as the sky, and fixed on eternity. Her stomach had been ripped open, and other organs were visible. They glistened slightly. All the cheap horror films Mark had seen as a kid reared up before him. He'd watched videos with singular dedication, smoking and drinking away the wasteland of his youth. They had been substitutes for school, seen so many times that gore meant nothing, just paint on the screen. It meant something now.

2

Mark began to swear, a litany of rage as he steadied himself on a bedpost of that ridiculous four-poster Lena had insisted on, until he could look at her again. Her face was unmarked, if it had registered horror when she'd died someone had smoothed this from it and there was no sign of a struggle. Her top had been opened carefully, as if someone had calmly undressed her, and she'd let him. Mark was not sure how long he stood there before he touched her face. His senses had almost shut down, but he felt his eyes becoming wet. He stretched out a shaking hand to touch her skin and it was as cold as a church wall. He drew it away quickly. A fist was grabbing at his guts, trying to push its way out and make him like Lena. He pulled at his shirt and ripped open the top buttons, but it was still hard to get his breath. Mark looked around. Everything was in its place, neat and tidy, like Lena had always kept it. Nothing unusual except a gutted woman on the bed. His woman.

Mark sat down on the bed, gingerly, as if he didn't want to cause Lena any more hurt. He wasn't sure what he felt, it was a mix of rage, shock, disbelief, and maybe self-pity too, that old demon he'd all but conquered by putting his life back on track, and his past in its place. Mark looked around a bit more, but there was no sign of a break-in. Nothing had been touched. Nothing.

They'd think it was him. He tried to keep this thought out of his head but it jostled for first place amongst all the other emotions. His eyes kept going back to the wound. It was fixing itself in his mind, making a home there, becoming a permanent image that could be viewed any time in his private hell. He gently closed Lena's blouse and began to tidy her long hair, a genuine dirty blonde, smoothing it into the style she liked. Then he closed her eyes. It took two attempts and he kept his own shut.

His mobile rang, his new blues ring tone, *If You're Looking For Trouble*, and Mark answered it.

'I'd get out of there now if I were you,' a voice said, 'they'll think you did it.' The voice had a slight accent which he couldn't place, then it was gone. Mark had no reason to run, but the voice put his own thoughts into words. His past would scream out his guilt. Mark Richards, delinquent thug, serial burglar. Then they'd find out about his baby brother. He'd be news again, all across the country – again. After years of quiet, of something approaching a life, his world would be ripped apart. He was being stupid, his world was already ripped apart, Lena lying cut up and very dead besides him.

Mark went to the bottom drawer of a cupboard and took out a tin box. His passport and money were in it and hadn't been touched. He put this stuff into his pockets and was almost out of the room before he forced himself to look back. He couldn't leave Lena like this, found and abandoned in minutes, so he went into the other bedroom, brought a blanket back, and placed it over Lena, as if to cover up her pain, and his confusion. Mark was not confused about the white hot angry grief that was beginning to surge through him.

Very few people knew the number of his private mobile, but the voice did, and it knew he was here, so that meant someone was watching him. It might be the voice of Lena's killer, it might be inviting him to run into the arms of the police, but he had to get out, to get away and think. He stumbled towards the door, seeing Lena smile again, seeing her snarl, the complicated Lena of a thousand scenes, the tender lover of more than a few. So beautiful.

Mark heard sirens and began to run, out into the sunlight of the block's back yard, up and over the rear wall like the cat he'd always been, then down the alleyway and into the bustling street on the other side, his head blown apart. He'd gone straight since he turned twenty, that was the crazy fucking part of all this. His reward.

He slowed down, and tried to walk calmly into the adjacent street, where he went down the steps of the underground and got on the first train that pulled in. His head felt like the shaking tube, hollow, rushing, digging deep into the belly of the earth. It was mid-afternoon of a lazy summer day but it wasn't that full. Tourists mainly, inquisitive faces, some happy, some tired and lost, but none running away from a butchered partner. Someone was staring at him, a woman, Japanese maybe, one of a group that looked as if they'd been welded together. Was he talking to himself? He hadn't done that since the old days. Mark looked away, down at the floor, then at his reflection in the dirty window glass. It merged with the walls as the train rushed past. A snatch of anguish here, a wild eye there. A desperate face flashing back at him every time.

The police would be tapping him into a computer any minute. His past would arrange itself neatly and stop at the last young offenders' home. It wouldn't take them long to track him to the agency, to find out what he did. He'd have to get out of the city. Kelly would help, as long as Mark didn't mention Lena. That would be too much for that Irish runt.

Mark got off after two stops, and walked the rest of the way, trying to merge with other people, to put all his self-imposed training into practice. The life long ability to fade into shadows, to lose himself into the night, all the stuff he'd played at when he was a kid was now real. Kelly was in the Queen's Head; he always was at this time, in a corner, his table a mess of betting slips, piled cigarette ends, and a few empty half pint glasses. Kelly thought he saved money drinking this way. There were a few others in there of similar stamp, and no one else.

Kelly was sinking into an alcohol and no-wins fug when Mark tapped him on the shoulder.

'Jesus, Mr Richards, don't do that, man.'

Kelly had lost a little of his brogue. Now it had merged into a strange mix of south London and Donegal. The Irishman scanned him shrewdly as he sat down.

'Where's the fire?'

'Go and get me a drink. A large one.'

Mark found a crumpled ten and threw it at Kelly.

'And get yourself one.'

'Large one?'

'Whatever.'

He came back with two large shots of Jameson's and a small jug of water. Like many drunks, Kelly was meticulous in his preparation, and messy afterwards.

'I want you to get me a car,' Mark said.

'What's up with you? You know I don't do that no more. I'm always too pissed to drive for a start.'

'You've never been too pissed. You could drive asleep. You probably have.'

Mark was calming a little. At least outwardly. The last hour was starting to become dreamlike. He'd wake up in a minute, sit up in bed sweating, swearing, then see Lena besides him in that deep sleep she'd perfected that always mocked his own fractured napping. The last few years with her had been an interlude, a time that had almost got him believing that change was possible, believing in things like normal, ordinary, and almost daring to believe in *happy*.

Mark felt the wad of notes in his chest pocket and wondered how much to give Kelly. His chosen helper was not much to look at, and there was probably even less inside. Kelly was a wasted little man, maybe fifty, but he'd fucked himself up so much he looked far older. A bit of red fuzz was left for hair, watery grey eyes were set too close to his nose, which was small and sharp, and amazingly had never been broken, and his teeth were just a decaying memory. There was always a certain smell about the man, nicotine, whisky and sweat combined for the Kelly trademark, plus

6

the overcoat that was always with him, even on a hot day like this. Watching Kelly mix water with his drink Mark realised how alone he was, again.

'I want something fast, but not showy,' Mark murmured.

Kelly studied his drink and sighed.

'Water, never ice, that's the trick with Irish.'

He raised his glass against the window light, which the sun caught for a moment in the fuliginous air, making the liquid burnt orange. Kelly gazed on it with a moment's reverence and downed it.

'Look, Mr Richards, what's going on? You never asked me to rob no car before. A bit of following people, getting you the odd name, but never robbing.'

Lena flashed into Mark's mind, open and bloody, he couldn't keep her out. He fought to stop his hands from shaking and drank his own drink, quickly, so that it seared and kicked at his empty gut. She'd eaten pasta for lunch, he thought, before almost coughing up the drink.

'What's the matter, Mr Richards, I ain't never seen you like this. You look like you bin to hell and back. Been on a bender, eh?'

'Nothing's the matter.'

'You're spooked, that's what you are.'

Kelly said this with a certain satisfaction. Mr Richards, with a body opposite to his in every way, and a lifestyle to match, was shaking, and wanted a car. Kelly felt important.

'Must be something bad for you to be like this. Wanna car that blends in, eh? Well, I don't know.'

Mark took hold of Kelly's arm, which felt like a stick in his powerful grip.

'You *do* know. You used to nick cars for fifty quid, and change the number plates.'

'That was years ago. Fifty quid, you must be joking.'

Mark looked at Kelly's charity shop pick-and-mix outfit.

'I'll give you two hundred if you get me one by six.

You'll have plates in that hovel you live in. You'll have kept some, just in case.'

'Look, I don't want no bother, Mr Richards.'

Mark put three twenties on the table.

'The rest later. I'll come round to your place at six.'

He worked his thumb through the roll of the money as Kelly watched, his eyes sharp flints, his body on greed alert.

'You owe me, Kelly.'

'Yeah, I know, but ...'

Mark dug his fingers into Kelly's arm, making him gasp.

'You owe me.'

'Okay, okay.'

'Don't fuck up and you'll have enough to bet on everything that runs tomorrow. Get going.'

Mark helped Kelly out of his chair and left with him. It wasn't much of a plan. The police might pick up Kelly any time that night but they wouldn't get much out of him, or the Queen's Head. It was full of people who were deaf, dumb and blind. Kelly would be shaken when the news hit, but fear would be added to it, and his tongue would lock up even more. If it didn't happen like this there was nothing Mark could do about it.

Chapter Two

That voice on the phone. Mark could hear it echoing in his head. *They'll think it was you*. The accent was Dutch, maybe Slav, one of those bandit territory places, but he'd never had contact with anyone like that, and Lena, what connection could she possibly have, for Christ sake? Lena, a full-time model and part-time student. Her never-ending Open University degree, women's studies, which had gone on for as long as he'd known her. Mark had made no real enemies in London, as far as he knew, or anywhere else, for that matter. The childhood stuff in Wales was of no interest to anyone here. Yes, his two-year-old brother Shane had gone missing from the garden of their council house, yes it had fucked his mother up, it had fucked him up, and the fact Shane had never been found had kept it fresh but no one else cared about that. It was the Richards family tragedy, history he had to live with. And he had, in his way, keeping out of trouble, doing bailiff work, sometimes providing protection for Z-list celebs, and lately private dick stuff. Checking out on a few missing people, and the odd shagging-away husband for an agency up town.

Mark had met Lena on a celeb minder job. She'd just finished a photo shoot and noticed him hanging around on the fringes of a function, looking tough and uncomfortable in his suit. She'd picked him up, at least that was how it seemed at the time. He'd been flattered enough to ignore his usual suspicion, though he did think she might have been a high-class call girl. She wasn't and it had worked, and lasted, until a few hours ago. None of it made any sense, but he'd have to make sense of it. For Lena, and himself.

Mark hadn't thought of Shane for some time, but finding your girlfriend butchered focused the mind on such things. Mark saw his mother Julie's face that day when Shane didn't turn up. The way she looked at him. The way she accused. He was on the phone, talking to his fence, Shane was in the garden playing, then gone. For good. A disappearance to end all others. The locals gorged on it, everyone had a take on what happened to Shane, every talking head wanker the media could dig up had its say, and most of the talk involved Mark. Julie no longer thought he'd had anything to do with it, they'd come that far at least, but in the pit of his guts Mark could never really be sure.

Tragedy had created space, and this had stretched to distance between them. When Julie heard about Lena all the pain would sharpen up again, and old doubts flood through her mind. The police would be down to see her pretty soon, sniffing around for him. Valley Boy running home. At least Julie wasn't on that estate any more, she was twenty miles away, down on the coast, in a flat, and working in a TV factory. A new start, away from the tongues and the looks, and the awful celebrity. The media would bring Shane up again, of course they would. He could hear the voices getting into their stride again - *ripped his girlfriend open did he, that proves it must have been him with the kid. Aye, I remember Mark Richards, a crazy bastard, Psycho Eyes we used to call him around here. I'd bring back the rope, I would.* Then the nationals would piece it together and he'd be famous once more, for another long fifteen minutes.

Mark walked around until six, keeping off the main streets, going into a few parks, watching all the people going home, like he had only a few days ago. Like him, Lena hadn't had much of a start in the world. Her father was just a yellowed black and white photograph, and she had never bothered with her mother as soon as she was old enough to get away. Lena had a brother somewhere in the Midlands –

Tony, he'd have his address in the small book he always carried. Thank Christ he did, for everything else was in the flat. Mark had only met Tony a few times. The man was nothing like Lena, Tony was a man in his mid-thirties with big hair from another age, who looked like a cross between a pimp and a hairdresser, complete with rings and false tan. Lena never said much about him, which was one of the things Mark liked most about her. They shared a mutual reticence about the past, it had helped draw them together. They were a new beginning for each other and it had worked, in its way. When she went off on modelling jobs Mark never asked too much.

Mark felt his eyes becoming wet again and brushed them with the back of a hand. It was the first time in years they'd performed like this. The last time was on that beach in Shetland. He'd been sent there as the final part of his young offenders' stint. They did things like that then, gave twisted kids the chance to try the life of the rich, as if a new way of life could be caught, like a disease. It was an outward bound course, a problem, one-parent, shattered family kid mixing with public school boys, crazy, but it took him to a beach near Lerwick, which was fresh, open, and empty. Flat sand and shingle stretching up to a big sky which might have been another planet for him. He'd learned to row and had seen whales, seen them swimming around the boat, seen them dead on the beach, washed up for no apparent reason. He'd cried then, for himself, and his whole cracked upbringing, he'd cried about the state of the world, and his own dark place in it, which also seemed to have no apparent reason. He cried for his missing baby brother, that more than anything. Now he did so for a woman, dabbing at his eyes and wondered if it had been love.

If Kelly cocked up there was no plan B. Mark's mind was in no state to think of one. It was hard enough keeping that image of Lena out of it, he wanted to see her laughing in the park over the road, trying to brain him with a frisbee, he wanted to see her the only time they been on holiday; Paris, a place she knew well, which enveloped him in winter chill, strange light and long nights. He wanted to see her like this, but shades of red cut into him whenever he tried.

Mark stood in the alley behind Kelly's place. All seemed quiet. Kelly had a bed-sit, on the second floor, not much more than a rancid squat. Downstairs was a boarded-up shop. Mark went up the back stairs and knocked his door lightly, thinking how easy it would be for Kelly to grass him up, for the Old Bill to open, and the rest of them rush up the stairs. Would he resist? He wasn't sure, but old habits died hard.

There were no police. Kelly opened the door to a crack and squinted through with his stubbly, weasel-like face. Mark pushed past him.

'Did you get it?' Mark asked.

Kelly nodded towards the window with his head. In the street, amongst the bent and busted bangers was a Mondeo, not too old.

'What do you think I am, a fucking rep?' Mark said.

'I know, Mr Richards, but I used my head, see. Millions of these buggers about, you won't stick out, like, and I had some 'Y' plates that are the right year for it. It's a good car that is, a good workhorse and it's gotta full tank.'

'Where are the real ones? I don't want you keeping them.'

'In the river.'

Mark doubted that they were. Number plates were collateral for Kelly.

'Key?'

'These will be OK. Got a good collection of Ford.'

Mark scoured the street. It was full of crap and a few people coming home from work but empty of police. Not much action at all, really. A few Rasta sweating and smoking on the corner, and a fat git slouched against the doorway of his video shop, probably wishing it was winter and pissing down, so that he might get a bit more trade. Kelly's room stank. It had been innocent of a real clean since Kelly had moved in. Mark knew the smell, he'd been in so many places like this, they permeated his life from its earliest days. It was the smell of failure, that 'going nowhere' sourness that was so hard to get rid of once it attached itself to you. It was the deadliest virus he knew.

'My money, Mr Richards?'

Mark took the notes from his inside pocket but stayed Kelly's reaching hand. It seemed pathetically small inside his own.

'Don't go blowing this like a fool, I'll know if you do.'

'I won't, I didn't get where I am doing anything stupid like that.'

Mark's eyes swept past him to Kelly's few square feet of nothing and would have laughed if it wasn't so tragic, if his girlfriend had not been cut up that morning. She'd be on some slab somewhere now, a bored pathologist going about his business one more time. Not that he felt any better than Kelly, not this day. Kelly would never have a killing pinned on him.

'What will you say, Kelly, if anyone comes asking about me?'

Kelly jumped to his cue.

'Nothing, Mr Richards, you know I'm good for that. Always good for that.'

'And if someone says they saw us in the Queen's Head?'

'Not much chance of that, but if they did, well, I always drink there. We was just passing the time of day, like.'

'Good.'

Kelly squirmed under Mark's stare. He let him take the money. As Kelly pocketed it Mark wondered who else would be coming around, and what tactics they would use.

Was anyone after him, too? How could he know? Lena was dead and he didn't know why. He had no motive, no names, nothing was taken from the flat. He felt his body tense as he thought of catching up with her killer. Muscles were tightening, his hands flexed, six foot two and fourteen seven of perfect shape wanted a result. Kelly edged away from him, five foot four of hopelessness in piss-stained trousers, but Mark felt more kinship with the man than anything else.

'It's OK, Kelly,' Mark said softly, 'nothing's going to happen to you, as long as you keep it shut.'

Mark took the keys and went out quickly. It wouldn't do to keep the car long, but it should get him to Coventry, to Tony. It was all he could think to do. Lena had seen her brother quite recently, when she'd been working in Birmingham. As he thought of it now he remembered her quietness that following week, almost introverted, which wasn't like her. That was his show.

The Mondeo had a full tank, and an air freshener hanging on the dash that immediately activated his hay fever. It was a two-litre job, its interior pretending to be something grand but it went well enough, which was all that interested him. Mark drove off, imagining eyes everywhere. He threw the air freshener out of the window and headed into the tail-end of the London rush hour. He was on the M1 in half an hour and drove at a careful seventy, keeping the windows shut despite the heat. He passed fields with crops the colour of Lena's hair, lush with summer growth. He'd only been this way once before, when he'd driven up with Lena to be introduced to Tony. Mark hadn't really been interested but it had seemed important to her at the time.

Mark tried to fix Tony's location in his head; it was a terrace in one of the Coventry suburbs, not unlike the ones of his Welsh valley, but on the flat in the middle of a city, not stuck at crazy angles on hillsides. He was tired, so tired it didn't so much creep up on him as zap him. If there was an opposite to an adrenaline rush he was feeling it now. Every sense told him to pull over and sleep but he couldn't afford to. He turned on the radio, and searched for news. Nothing yet. He kept it on, enduring the useless music until the next newscast.

The sun was lowering in the western sky. Mark headed towards a deepening red, cut with the odd feathery vapour trail of a plane. He was one of thousands of cars heading home for the weekend, but maybe he'd be unique on this motorway, the only one running from a killing. He had a sudden flashback to the flat and blinked it out quickly, but not before the car swerved a little and someone behind honked. There were sunglasses in the glove compartment, amongst a few CDs by people he'd never heard of and a photograph of a couple with two kids. Everyone looked happy. How had one of Lena's favourite songs gone - *happy, shiny people*? He put the glasses on and felt calmer as he turned onto the M6. Coventry wasn't far away now.

Again nothing on the radio. The news was full of vile stuff, but not his vile stuff. Iraq was kicking off again, a kid had been found dead in Yorkshire, some football star was being paid too much attention, all the things that usually passed him by. Now they were more real. Lena was part of the game now, tomorrow she'd be added to the mix, just one more statistic, but one that belonged to him. Every one of the news items shattered lives somewhere but it wasn't yours so you glossed over it, dismissed it in seconds before re-engaging with your life, the one that could never be touched by anything like that. Lena was officially part of the world's mess, as Shane had been.

Iraq made Mark think of his last job. It had involved a guy who'd been working there. One of many picking over the corpse, looking for a quick return. Some sort of important engineer. He'd been cheating on his wife, and had set up a girl in a flat not far from Lena's, so the agency had asked him to do surveillance. It was a poor job and he'd used Kelly to do most of the watching. He'd just taken a few photos at appropriate times. The man's wife was a looker, more so than the mistress, but Mark had realised some time ago that these affairs had many dimensions, power, excitement, thrill, doing it because one could. They rarely made any sense. The wife sobbed in the office and told him she'd never really believed it, until he spread the photographs out on the desk. They always used black and white for this work. Cutting out colour seemed to tell the truth more. The woman had a kid away in a boarding school somewhere who loved his dad. Each time Mark did a job like this he wanted out.

Cloud was building up around the sun as it made its farewell, yellow on red. As Mark passed a place called Harborough Magna the nine o'clock news came on. Again nothing on Lena. It had been half a day now, this lack of news didn't add up. He couldn't think why this should be, but then it was hard to think at all. At least the need to sleep had gone. Energy had kicked in again but he needed to eat. He pulled off into a services. He was only miles away from Tony now but he had to take time out, to try and get some thought processes going. The guy might not be there anyway.

Mark sat in the car park for a while. *Try to think, you stupid bastard.* He hadn't seen Lena much in the last few weeks. She'd been in Amsterdam, he'd been busy helping to destroy a marriage. He tracked back, to last Christmas, when they had gone to that cottage in the Cotswolds. Her idea. It was like on a postcard, she'd said, but it had been cold, cold enough for a dusting of snow. It was the kind of England she was always searching for, log fires, hearty people, polite people, no crime, no filth, the kind of world he had no experience of, maybe the kind that had never existed, but if it was an illusion, he'd enjoyed it. They'd walked back from a pub, Lena's face radiant in the cold, his own happy, shiny person. We'll have all this, one day, she said, waving a hand over the cottage and its large garden. I know we'll have the money. He'd smiled, and let her dream. Then Mark moved on, month by month, looking for anything unusual, anything different in her behaviour. There was nothing. No reason and no sense to this, yet what she'd said about having money stuck in his mind.

Mark's two positive years with Lena had balanced out everything that came before, offset the kiddy crap, the teenage crap, that extreme and illegal journey from fifteen to twenty, the years of trying to find out who he was. For a crazy moment he thought of phoning his mother, the only other person he'd ever been close to, but for her, his news would be a mainline back to Shane.

Mark went into the services' rest room, he couldn't think of a bleaker or more lonely place to be at this time. It smelt of stale piss and ineffective cleaning agent. He didn't like what he saw as he stared in a mirror. A man who looked a lot older than thirty, but finding Lena like that had put another ten years on him. There was now a grey threat at the edge of his hairline. There were few photos of his early childhood. He had just one, of a crop-haired, bony kid, with an unsmiling face and hard eyes, perfect for any social documentary on the deprived. It still was. A hard man's face now, rugged good looks, Lena calls it. She didn't like 'pretty' men. A scar-free face, with surprisingly good teeth, none knocked out, or twisted. *Lena calls it.* Present tense, Mark. Dead people don't do present tense. Girlfriends with their stomachs ripped open don't do any tense at all. If someone hadn't come in he would have punched the glass. It was an old teenage trick, a last resort when everything exploded in his brain. The pain in the fist was like a charge that settled him down again, his problems smashed away, for a while. A small man in a suit looked at him strangely, then tried to make himself invisible when Mark returned the look.

He walked into the restaurant. At this time it wasn't very busy. The odd trucker, sitting in his special pen, dog-tired and wishing his journey was over. A few families, mothers trying to control over-tired kids on their way back from somewhere, fathers' arms folded in resignation. Lena had talked about kids, someday, sometime. She was older than him, by two years, and had dreaded hitting thirty. Forget forty, fifty, bus pass time, thirty is the one, she'd said. He'd never thought much about it, and had slipped past his own milestone a few months ago. Despite Lena, a part of him still felt that time was to be served, not enjoyed.

Mark ordered a plate of grease, which tasted as if it was on overtime. It might have been adequate in the morning, an overpriced surfeit of cholesterol washed down by caffeine, but now it fell into his gut like lead. He chewed, he swallowed, it was necessary. Lena would have been horrified. She was a vegetarian, almost vegan, and had begun to work on him in the last few months. He'd just about given up red meat, apart from bacon. You're doing well, she said, for a man.

Mark could see the motorway through the restaurant window, a police car went by, then another, chasing someone. His hands tightened on the cutlery. When he'd got back from Shetland, about to leave his teenage years, he'd told himself that he'd never run from anything again, and he hadn't. Until now. He raised his eyes and saw the large red lips of a model on a poster on the wall. For a moment it was Lena, the wounded part of her, almost the same red, the same openness. He pushed the rest of the food away, making a clatter that turned heads, but not for long. People had their own thoughts and worries in the tiny piece of world they inhabited and this place was perfect for indulging them. It reeked of isolation, the restless routine of people endlessly passing through. Transient thoughts. That most of all.

One of the first things Mark learned as an investigator was how little people really noticed you. You thought they did, if you tripped on the pavement, walked around with your flies open, had a pulsating spot on the end of your nose, but they didn't. Ask ten people to describe a suspect and you'll get ten different answers, and each one sure. The world was too fast to notice, let alone care. Unless you were on the run from a killing, from gutting your girlfriend, an evil fiend who will sell papers and make people watch the TV. They'll notice *me*, Mark thought, they'll have a field day with me.

They'd be rooting around the old estate again, shooting off their quick words, and everyone would have a story on him. Lena had taken him away from Shane, she'd brought him out of that dark Richards place, made him talk about it in terms other than denial and despair. Here was someone who actually seemed to care about who he was, what he thought, where he'd been and even where he might be going. He was never sure why she was with him, she'd always earned more than him, and he was hardly Mr Security.

Mark saw Shane that last day in the garden, playing around in the sand the council had left. Spooning it up in the air, hair cropped like Mark's, but Shane's a blond fuzz to match his blue eyes, his mother's eyes. He hadn't been much like his father, one of the many creeps his mother had fetched up. Mark had loved the little sod, he hadn't realised how much until he was gone, and he'd loved Lena. At least he thought it was love. He'd never been able to solve Shane's mystery, the kid had vanished and had stayed gone. He'd put his brother into every horror situation he could think of, each one churning his guts, like a steel hand in there, twisting. The hand of fate, hah hah. Keeping the wound open, and always fresh. No, he couldn't solve the

19

mystery of Shane but he'd solve Lena's, by Christ he would. At least he knew *her* end. He knew nothing else, understood nothing else, and didn't yet know how to go about changing this, but he would find out, and put things right. Finish it.

Chapter Three

Mark left the restaurant and drove on. He was on the Coventry ring road in minutes. It was like a mini M25, but without the traffic. At this time on a warm Friday night most people had got where they where going or were going nowhere at all. He tried to remember where Tony lived. Lena had driven up that time she had persuaded him to come. Mark didn't even know what Tony did. Something in advertising, Lena said, which could mean anything. The man didn't look like Lena. Tony was like her mother, she said, but Mark had never seen her parents. They'd never got around to visiting. Neither of them wanted to get into families. Her parents were from Lithuania originally, Lena had told him, but Lena was born and bred a Brit, yet another accent seemed to force its way out when she was in temper, an echo of her ancestry perhaps. It was one of her quirks that marked her out as different, quirks that he liked. He liked the vagueness of her background, it made him worry about his own less. When they met he'd been a private island, 'keep off' signs bristling all over him, deliberately isolated, cut off from others, emotions kept in check, and hiding his past. All the things he'd learned to do to survive. Slowly, and very cautiously, Mark had opened up to Lena, and in her gently persistent way she drew his past out of him. She was the only person he'd ever told about Shane, but Lena had never said much about herself. Now Mark realised how little he knew about her. She liked the fact he didn't ask questions, and he'd left it at that. Now he wished he hadn't, now he thought she might have had reasons for her secrecy.

Mark drove into rows of terraces until he recognised

Tony's street. For the showy man he was, Tony's house didn't seem right. It was in a street of identikit homes, places for people on the first rung of the ladder, or maybe the last. A few were boarded up. Tony's Merc was probably worth more than most of them. He was driving one the last time Mark saw him, proudly showing off the number plate to Lena. He'd arranged the letters to almost spell his name. Tony still had the car, which made it easier to find the house. Mark drove past it a few times. All the old instincts were kicking in. Ducking and diving, feeling the eyes of the pigs everywhere. Working for the agency had been perfect for him. He'd stayed on the right side of the law, just, but now Mark felt like a roaming kid again, with a chip on his shoulder the size of the world.

There was a light on in Tony's front room, Mark could see in as he passed. Tony was there, on the phone, maybe making arrangements to come down to London. Maybe telling the police about his sister's boyfriend. Mark still wasn't sure what he was doing here. Telling Tony how he'd found Lena, and how he'd ran, might not be the best action, but the man was his only real link to her. He needed to tell someone he hadn't done it, and he needed someone to share his grief.

Thought processes were slowly returning and Mark realised how stupid he'd been. There was practically no chance of finding out what had happened and if he went back now at least he could be involved in her funeral – they'd let him do that, even if he was chief suspect. Lena had never believed in an afterlife, or any type of ceremony, not even marriage. If anything ever happens to me, have a good drink, play some music, and get on with your life, she'd once told him. He'd thought it cold, but knew she was only reflecting his own beliefs. He wondered who'd be there, certainly more police and press than friends. Neither of them really had any. It must have hit the news by now.

Stories like this were the real stuff of life. Not politics or sport or some film tart's new boyfriend, but pain, suffering, someone going down in the most brutal way. They spread it over the front page, for people to enjoy their mock horror over their fucking cornflakes and buttered toast.

Mark was getting angry, which wouldn't do. Getting even was much better. He realised revenge was uppermost in his mind. It was blocking out any other feelings and he didn't want to think about the good times with Lena. There'd be time to do that later. She was another Shane. Two bolts from the blue to shoot him down. Yes, revenge was good, a counterbalance for the hurt, but he didn't even have shadows to chase. Lena was dead, but he had no motive, no suspects, and no ideas.

After a final drive past, Mark parked about fifty yards away from Tony's house. The daylight was almost gone and street lamps were coming on, pink slashes turning to orange amidst the gloom. There was a pub on the corner, and Mark felt the urge to go there, to sink a few large whiskies so quickly that they'd light a fire in his chest. Maybe there'd be an echo of the old illusory courage he'd tried to get out of bottles when he was a kid. He hadn't needed this type of support for a long time, but it wouldn't do, sitting at a bar when Lena's story might be flashed onto any TV. They would have got hold of a photo of Lena by now. Her agency could provide hundreds, to suit every occasion. That would stop punters in mid-sip at their local.

Get a load of that, Dave, wouldn't you like to go home to her?

No, not now, Carl, don't you know what happened to her? I read it in The Sun, *in work, done like a kipper, she was*

Is she someone famous?

Nah, just some model, foreign, I think.

Mark saw movement in the house. It was him, picking up

something near the window. The guy hadn't changed much, medium height, stocky turning to fat. Tony still had big hair and a T-shirt with a *fcuk* logo on it which summed him up. Mark decided to go round the back, there wasn't any reason to, just old habits kicking in. He knew there was a yard there. Maybe Tony was the type who forgot to lock his back door. There'd been lots of houses like that in the valley, he'd rarely had to break in anywhere.

A double-glazed door opened for him and Mark was in the kitchen. Tony was on his mobile, he could hear him moving around the room. He was talking in a foreign language. Mark stood there until the talking stopped, then moved quietly towards the living room. He had seconds to decide how to play this. Mark was surprised Tony was still here and he was even more surprised that he knew anything other than English. The talking stopped, as Mark stood in the doorway watching Tony fiddle around with his TV remote. The set was his main feature, a yard or so of colour on his wall, but the sound wasn't on. He'd turn any second now. People always sensed when they were being watched, some sooner than others.

'Who the fuck's that?' Tony shouted, snatching up an ash-tray.

Mark stepped forward into the room as Tony stepped back.

'What do you want?'

Tony blinked hard.

'Mark? It is you, isn't it? Where the hell did you come from? I almost had a turn then, you stupid bastard. Why didn't you ring the bell, like everyone else?'

Tony put the ashtray down and smiled with relief. He stuck out a hand.

'What you doing here, mate? Is my sister with you?'

'No, she's not.'

Mark hoped his voice was steady, and that his features

were under control. This made no sense. How could he not know about Lena?

'What's wrong, pal?' Tony said. 'You look as rough as guts. I'll get you a drink. Whisky, isn't it?'

Nothing was right about this. Tony was the kind of man who liked to call strangers mate, pal, squire, but he was not a friendly man. He should be going off on one for him walking in the back way, someone he'd only seen a few times in his life. Mark wanted to blurt it out about Lena, to get rid of some of the burden and confide in someone, but something held him back, the same sense that had made him come in the back way. Tony handed him a very large scotch.

'Good stuff, that is. Ten year malt. Sit down, mate, before you fall down.'

Mark did feel unsteady. He clutched his drink and sank into a chair. A large image of a woman perched on Tony's shoulder as he also sat down. A woman on the TV who looked a little like Lena, but not enough to make Mark jump. She was on a talk show anyway, not the news. He thought of Lena alive, he wanted her to be alive, need surged through him, for the clock to be turned back, for the day to start again with him getting into bed with her, smelling her tired hair and waiting for her to wake.

'Mark, you're miles away, mate. Look, what's up, you just appearing like this? You on a job up here, or something?'

'Yeah, that's right, a job. I thought I'd call in. Sorry I came round the back. Force of habit.'

Tony's mouth opened into a wide grin, his whitened teeth matching his ridiculous tan.

'Checking out some sap on a dirty weekend, eh?'

'Something like that.'

'So, how you been then?'

'OK.'

Tony was afraid of him. Mark could recognise fear very

25

quickly. Sometimes it was masked with aggression, but when it was there he knew. People had often been afraid of him, but usually they had a reason. Tony had no reason, but this brash, showy, guy was sweating badly now, and the more he smiled, the more he sweated. Tony smelt like a woman. He'd overdosed on expensive aftershave that still managed to smell cheap. Attempts had also been made to control his wiry black hair with gel. He was obviously going out.

Mark drank the whisky as calmly as he could, watching silver beads gather on the backs of Tony's hairy hands. The man had an olive complexion, more south Europe than north and Mark could see nothing of Lena in him. He'd been disappointed when he first met the guy. Lena had been trying to draw him out of himself at the time and thought Tony might be useful for this but the look on his face when they met put paid to that. Tony's way of talking was strange, like an actor who was poor at accents, and didn't know which one to adopt. In one evening he'd gone through a mix of south London, black country, and something else, something indefinable which spoke of his past. Mark wished now he'd talked to Lena more about her background, but she had always pushed his questions away and got him to talk about his own life.

Tony fingered an oversized medallion that hung from a chain around his neck. It was a gold coin which had been re-shaped, and another one matched it on a little finger. The clusters of hair on his hands were quite moist now. Mark wondered if the guy was acting, if he knew about Lena and was waiting for the police to get here.

'You look as if you were about to go out,' Mark said.

'I was. I am. A hot date, you might say.'

'Huh huh. Well, don't let me keep you. I'll come out with you. I should have phoned when I was up here, but you know how it is, in my job.'

'Yeah, sure, don't worry. I know, Lena insisted you call in, didn't she? How is my lovely sister? Haven't heard from her lately.'

'She's been working a lot.'

'Nice to see her so successful.'

Mark found it hard to keep his voice even. He finished the whisky and felt it burn. He wanted it to, it gave him something else to concentrate on, for something was wrong here.

'Well, shall we go then?' Tony said. 'I've got to get across town. Are you going back down tonight?'

'Yes, I'm all finished here.'

All finished. Only Lena was finished. Nothing else had started. He'd stolen a car and ran. No plan, no ideas, just rabbit action, and a surreal kind of action at that. You find your girlfriend cut up, a voice on the phone chills you, starts you running, and you head off for your one contact. At least Tony was the only one Mark knew about. If Lena had others she'd never shared them with him. He'd taken work calls for her sometimes, that was about it. They'd both been very private people and now it was costing him.

Tony put out a greasy hand which Mark felt rather than shook, for it fell through his own without hardly touching it. Mark watched Tony drive off in the silver Merc with TON 1 on the plate, and walked to his own illicit vehicle. Tony glanced back once and Mark saw him put his mobile phone to his ear. He turned on the radio in the Mondeo and searched for news. A calm, well-modelled voice took him through the world horror show. Blood in Iraq, Afghanistan, Israel, Africa, the world was dripping in it; someone had stabbed a policeman in Leeds, politicians were being politicians, but again, no Lena. Nothing about a woman who'd been found butchered in a London flat. No comments from shocked neighbours about how she'd been a lovely girl who was always quiet and very friendly. Nothing at all.

The last few hours had been useless, Mark wasn't even sure which way he should point the car. He wished it could drive him out of this nightmare but the tightening in his guts told him it was only just starting. He drove out of the city and stopped at the first services on the M6. It was the same one as before. It was almost midnight, not a good time to phone Kelly, but the man answered, on the mobile Mark had given him a few months ago. Kelly was stumbling about somewhere, going in and out of signal, his drink-sodden voice inquiring cautiously into the phone.

'Kelly, stop moving around and listen.'

'Whosat?'

'Richards.'

Kelly's voice steadied.

'Mr Richards, good evening to you, sir.'

'Yeah, sounds like it's been, for you. Listen, and I want a clear fucking answer. Anything been happening around the flat? After I left?'

'Happening, Mr Richards ?'

'Don't go vague on me, Kelly, you do that with other people.'

'Sorry, I've had a bit to drink, like. Nothing's been happening. It's been a quiet as churches round here today, Mr Richards. I was just remarking on it to the lads in the Queen's.'

Mark thought for a moment. Even pissed up, Kelly was reliable for information such as this. Police should have been all over the area. Cordoning it off with their blue and white ribbon, bringing in the men in white suits, all the usual rituals when a body is found.

'You still there, Mr Richards?'

'Yes.'

'Uh, you still got that car?'

'Never mind about that. Listen, you keep that phone on, and don't even think of telling me you've lost the charger.

Put it next to your head when you crash out. I might need you.'

Mark turned off his phone before Kelly could respond. He knew he'd do what he was told, no matter how pissed. Fear and greed always worked a perfect pincer movement on Kelly.

A plane was going over above, it was low, about to land somewhere. It fought against the motorway noise and won, for traffic was thin now. Planes had been one of Mark's favourite sounds as a kid. Especially if they were really high up and he could hardly see them, just trace their vapour trails with his keen eyes, and hear the faint drone of engines as they tracked across his section of sky. He'd be on the hillside somewhere, hands behind his head, maybe rare sun on his face, watching them until the trails spread into white feathers, to be taken by the clouds. The planes were a comfort, they spoke of other places, other possibilities, things he might do one day. They meant people escaping, like he escaped to the hills, which were right for him, which understood his need to get away; within minutes of having been amongst people he could walk alone. Since he refused to fly, Lena would never have understood this childhood fondness. The one job he'd done abroad, in Holland, he'd had to drive and take the ferry, making things awkward and annoying the agency by the time taken, but it was that or nothing. He couldn't get his head round the thought of being in that small capsule, many thousands of feet above the earth and completely helpless. His system rebelled against the thought of putting himself into anyone else's hands so completely. Lena had started to change that.

Mark went into the services, needing to freshen up. This was part of his territory now, he'd become an urban man, something he'd once despised. He'd grown used to rush and bustle, it was where the work was. When he first started working as an investigator they often sent him around the

29

country looking for people, it had amazed him how many people were hiding. Society had a secret inner layer of dodgers, everything from murder to debt, and service stations were the points on his search map. Their grim food, the ability they had to match the worst of his moods, had always told him how alone he was and how like the people he chased. Worse off, maybe, for he needed them, and they could certainly do without him. Then he met Lena and when he moved in with her his perception began to change. Night time places didn't get to him so much, usually they told him he was on his way home, job finished, and their plastic emptiness made the journey sweeter. He'd had someone to go back to, but she was gone and Mark was back to the original thoughts. In the rest room he threw some water into his face, and heard someone throwing up in one of the cubicles.

Mark went back to the car and turned the radio on again. Still nothing. He found some music, nothing he could recognise, but that wasn't surprising, for he'd never taken much interest in it, old or modern. It was one of the traits that had marked him out years ago. When the kids on the estate had gone on about the latest band, they were met by blank stares and lack of interest on his part, but what played was good for this time of night. A cowboy crooner wanted his woman back. You're not alone there, mate, Mark thought. All the adrenaline had drained out of him. The shock of this day was turning to tiredness, he felt like he'd never slept and it was hard to think straight, or think at all. The motorway was practically empty now but blue lights were approaching rapidly. He tensed, and wondered where Kelly had got the false plates from, but the squad car was past him, travelling on fast.

Mark hit the edge of London at first light, the pale yellow light of late summer that forecast another hot day. He parked up the car. The police would run a check on the plates and find they were from something stolen years ago.

He went into the first café he saw open, and had more coffee and grease. There were a few truckers eating with him and one guy who looked like he'd been clubbing all night, maybe gone straight from work for he had that kind of suit on, fat, blue tie still around his neck, but at a crazy angle, as if it was attempted to garrotte him. He fingered it nervously as he ate. The man was about Mark's age and ate the same breakfast. Their eyes met briefly, his registering consolation, the solidarity of the lonely, the loser. That sad git thinks I'm like him, Mark thought, that we've both been on the pull and failed, that we are on our own, then was guilty to be even thinking like this less than a day after he'd found Lena. Anyway, he *was* on his own. Never more so.

There was an overhead television in the café, turned on even at this time in the morning. The local news came on. Lena would have to be on it. She'd *have* to be the main story. But again nothing. Mark was baffled. She couldn't still be there could she, her murder undiscovered? That thought chilled him to his stomach. He'd heard sirens approaching, but they were always present on London streets. His panic, and the voice on the phone, had directed them to the flat, and he'd run away without waiting to find out if they were coming for him or not. The voice knew what had happened, the voice knew he was there. The voice wanted him to run.

The headache that had been threatening all night began in earnest, he felt it kick-start a vein above his right eye. It began to throb, insistently, like a finger tapping against his forehead, then the pain spread until it had all of his head in its grasp. A band tightened around his skull and tried to crush it. He tried in vain to cast it off, he tried in vain to think of a plan but there was only sludge in his head, and at its core a pain that he could scarcely dare acknowledge. He had to keep it under wraps until all this was over. The headache might turn into a migraine, which was the last thing he needed. He had them three or four times a year, when all he could do was shut down his body and wait for them to go. He'd been lucky with the work for they usually came on when he was inactive and waiting for Lena to come back from a job. He didn't like time on his hands, too many thoughts jostled for position in his head. Mark bought a large bottle of water from the man behind the café counter.

'Know how you feel, mate,' the man said, 'I was the same at your age.'

Mark walked through north London suburbs. The sun was out now, but not yet too warm on his face. Early morning people were about, milkmen, a postman delivering letters to affluent houses in leafy streets, people walking to the nearest tube. He joined them.

Mark went straight to Kelly's. He needed somewhere to think, and maybe sleep, even Kelly's squalor would do. He knocked the door for some time before Kelly appeared. A night-before smell appeared with him. Booze, curry and strong body odour. Kelly smelt like a pub at ten in the morning. Despite the weather he stood and shivered in his thin vest, his ribs standing out like the bars of a cage. He sniffed the morning air and blinked in the light as he scratched his stubbly face; he'd never looked more like a weasel. Mark pushed past him into the bed-sit. More smells greeted him, even more pungent.

'Christ, Kelly, how can you live like this?'

'Like what? You gimme a start, Mr Richards. This is early for me, like.'

'You amaze me.'

Mark brushed junk from the one chair and sat on it. He was dog-tired, even in this festering den sleep threatened to overwhelm him.

'Wassup?' Kelly said. 'First the car, now you here. Not your style, Mr Richards. Look, I don' want no trouble. Don' mind doing the odd favour for you, but I don' want nothing heavy - and you look like it's something heavy.'

Mark went straight to the window and tried to force it open, an action it wasn't used to. It had stuck fast with layers of paint.

'Careful, Mr Richards, don't bust it.'

'It's been quiet, you said.'

'Yeah, nothing happening here. Why, what you expecting to happen?'

'Never mind.'

'You still got that car?'

'You know better than to ask me questions. Don't worry, it's not outside.'

Mark took in the nine stone waste of space that Kelly was and felt embarrassed that he'd had to turn to someone like this. Loners always had a price to pay, at one time or another, and his was now, and he was as far away from a plan of action as ever. Tony came back into his mind. There were something badly wrong there, and Tony's farewell was ringing bells in his head. He sounded a bit like the voice on the phone, but maybe this was desperation talking, and the thumping pain in his head.

'You OK, Mr Richards? You look like you had a better night than me.'

'Get dressed,' Mark said. 'You might think of getting washed too, if you can remember how.'

'Leave it out, Mr Richards. Look, I don' want to be doing nothing today. As I said, it was a bit of a rough night, like.'

'It was your usual night, and you *will* be doing something today. I just want you to sniff around a bit. You're the best for that and there'll be a few quid in it.'

Kelly stiffened a little with pride at what he thought was a compliment. Mark had learned that praise was almost as useful as threats with Kelly, especially if linked with money. He threw a twenty at him, and it was caught and hidden in one action.

'Come on then, get your arse together.'

Twenty minutes later they were out on the street. Mark saw their reflection in the shop window under Kelly's place. It looked like he was in charge of a funfair gimp. Kelly, about half his size, struggling to keep up with him, his wiry red fuzz standing up brush-like on his head. The overcoat made him look like some nocturnal animal hurrying to get underground before it got too light.

They cut through the small park opposite the flat and stood by the railings. Mark could see their front door. He still thought of it as *theirs*. Kelly was right, all was quiet. There was no young copper standing guard outside, fidgety and bored, no activity at all. The nerve over Mark's eye went into overdrive. He wanted his eyes to close, but if he shut them he saw images of Lena. A freeze-frame history of yesterday took over. Finding her, finding her like that, the voice on the phone, his flight. His ineffective action since. He felt sick, and held onto the railings.

'You're not well, Mr Richards. I'd get some kip if I was you. Your missus home, is she? Cracking looking girl, she is.'

Mark's hands screwed up into fists, an echo of the childhood rages he thought he'd conquered for good. For a moment he wanted to smash Kelly, and toss his pathetic body over the railings. Sensing danger, Kelly stepped back, ready to bolt.

'Look, Mr Richards, what we doing here?'

Mark breathed deeply and regained control. He searched for the key to the flat and put it in Kelly's hand.

'All I want you to do is to go over the road, let yourself in, look round the place, then come back and tell me what you see.'

'Wha' for? I don' get it.'

'You don't have to get it. Just do it.'

34

Mark helped Kelly on his way. The man didn't want to be part of this but was more afraid of Mark than the situation. If he found Lena, Kelly would be out of there like a shot, puking on the road, and thinking Mark a killer. He should find Lena, the dead didn't get up and walk away. Things were going on here Mark didn't understand, but everything he'd learned over the last ten years told him she wouldn't be there. That voice on the phone had wanted him out. It had known he'd run, the stupid knee-jerk reaction of the kid from the wasted estate. That estate, and his time on it, was still in his blood - *they'll think it was you.* That had been enough for him to take off, minutes after finding Lena, the one woman he'd ever really cared about. Mark Richards, the street-wise hard man, had left her, and ran out blindly, and nothing had been gained from it.

The sun was well up now, and it punished him. It told him that this would be another long day, and so would the next, and the one after that. All of them would be long, until he found out why Lena had been killed and who had killed her. Until he put things right.

Kelly was not inside the flat for long. He came out calmly after a few minutes. Mark knew the answer but asked the question anyway.

'Well?'

'Nothing, Mr Richards. Everything was OK there. Tidy, like. Letters on the mat by the door. Look, I don' know what I'm s'posed to be looking for anyway. You never tell me nothing. Lovely place though, innit? Can I go now, I gotta get a bit of breakfast.'

'Give me the key back.'

Mark pulled Kelly close to him as he handed over the key, and went through his pockets. Kelly squirmed like an eel, saliva escaping from the stumps of his teeth but he did not dare pull away.

'Leave it out, Mr Richards. I'd never nick nothing off

you. 'Specially with you stood outside.'

'You can't help yourself. None of us can.'

'You don' half talk funny sometimes. Look, why don' you come down the café? You look like you can do with a few coffees.'

'No, I've got things to do. Off you go.'

Mark held onto Kelly's coat as he tried to turn.

'One last thing. What have you done today?'

'Today? I haven't even got up yet, Mr Richards.'

'Okay, then. Keep your mobile close and keep it on. I might need you in a hurry.'

Kelly almost stood to attention as he listened to Mark's instructions, like a soldier in some ragbag army. Then he winked, nodded, tidied his ragged overcoat and was gone, fading effortlessly into the street.

Mark walked across to the flat, and let himself in. It was not easy to push the front door open, and he stood on the threshold for a moment, shaking. That smell had gone, but another had taken its place. A light fragrance had been sprayed around, he recognised it. Jasmine, Lena's favourite.

Mark picked up the mail at his feet, one for him, and three for her. Nothing important. His hand tightened around a bill, and started to twist the envelope. It should have been the neck of whoever had been here. His shirt was starting to stick to his back, his forehead was damp, and the nerve was active. It wouldn't let him go, not until this was over. Maybe not even then. The temperature had been pushing thirty for days, as a poor summer went out with a bang. Much too hot for him, even on a good day, and this wasn't one. Lena loved the sun, and laughed at his nanny warnings of its dangers. She tanned easily, while he stayed in shadow whenever possible. They shared a small rooftop with other tenants, but it had become Lena's private suntrap. She should be there now, waiting for him to bring her up something cold.

He threw the letters down and managed to go into the bedroom. Slowly pushing the door open, he expected anything. The vein was really letting him have it now, pulsating, and pounding in time with his heart.

The bedroom was empty. Someone had cleaned it up. Last year Mark had attempted his first DIY, stripping the bedroom of carpets and sanding down the floorboards. Lena had wanted it this way and it was better for his dust allergy, but a carpet would have been much harder to clean. The bed was freshly made, and the sheets drawn tight, hotel style. They were new and he didn't recognise them. He'd made it easy for them by running, given them the time to do this. Mark decided it must be *them*, not *him*. He sat down on the bed, then sank down. He wanted to immerse himself here, where Lena had died, but wasn't sure why. Need maybe, not reason. Grief not action. He found it hard to get his breath, and his eyes were threatening to lose control again.

His eyes searched the room, everything was where it should be, but as the sun came through the blinds he saw something on the lampshade, a red speck on the yellow shade. He knew it was blood, her blood. He stretched out and rubbed at it with a finger, and particles came away. They'd missed this, or maybe left it for him to find. To make the last day real.

Chapter Four

Lena's removal could mean anything. Mark's gut reaction that he might be blamed did not hold up now. He'd ran for nothing, and relied on someone like Kelly, which had given them time to take Lena away. He'd performed how they'd expected, like a rat on a wheel, and the thought tortured him.

He could hardly call in the police. They'd think he was barking, then they'd start checking up on him, and might think something else.

The phone rang. It put a charge through Mark and it rang many times before he decided to answer it. It was someone from Lena's modelling agency. She hadn't turned up for a job. He said she was ill. He was surprised he could keep his voice so calm, though his guts twisted with each word. It seemed a betrayal. When he put the phone down he pressed 1471 to make sure it was the agency number. It was, but he couldn't trust anyone from now on.

He began to go through drawers and cupboards. All Lena's stuff was in place. All his. If anyone had looked through this they had been very careful. Lena had been butchered, maybe left for him to find, or maybe they hadn't expected him to come back when he did. Her killing was a savage act that made no sense and spoke of madness, perhaps hatred, emotions that always had causes. There was no time to grieve or let anger take over, only time to get even.

Most of the stuff in the flat was Lena's; Mark had never been an accumulator but Lena had more than made up for this. He was surrounded by her, all the bits she brought back from her trips, the endless clothes, some never worn. One day we'll have a house, she told him, there'll be lots more space then. Mark picked up a doll from Amsterdam, its mute, glazed face looked up at him, with fat beige cheeks, fatter blue eyes and lips the colour of blood. She was always bringing kids' stuff like this home.

Lena had come into his life out of the blue, and had been taken out of it just as suddenly, yet she had seemed so normal, childlike at times, someone who needed looking after. Only normal girls didn't get killed the way she did.

Mark had made enemies in his job, lots of them, but nothing to warrant this. Not remotely. His working world was peopled with marriage cheats, small-time fraudsters, debtors, inefficient tricksters in the main. Sometimes the agency told him a caught-out husband was up for it, but not if they ever met. He'd never had to use what he'd learned as a younger man. His physique and aura had always been enough. He dealt mainly with the middle-classes anyway, they were the people who could pay, and they were the most predictable. To think a cheating husband with a grudge against him could track him down and do this to Lena was ridiculous. It was crazy to even go there but he was desperately seeking answers, any answers.

Mark took one of Lena's dresses from the wardrobe, the blue one she'd worn in Paris, his favourite. They'd gone on Eurostar. You won't have to fly, she said, it'll be great, and it had been, a weekend that stretched into four days. His first time abroad and he'd enjoyed all of it, to his surprise. It was a trip that confirmed their relationship, and moved it forward. He'd been amazed that he'd managed to keep her for more than the usual few weeks, and alert to the fact that maybe his life was going somewhere, that someone could look at him with something other than fear or contempt. He was still an outsider, that would never really change, and maybe he didn't want it to, but with Lena he no longer felt a complete loner, he felt he could be a part of the small world she created for him. He could go out and work, then come home to someone. What other people did.

The dress still smelt of the Guerlain he'd bought her in Paris. She'd told him how to pronounce it and laughed with surprise and pleasure when he'd bought some for her. Lena had had an ease with languages while he struggled with his own. Closing his eyes Mark saw her body form up in all its glory, he didn't want this image but Lena forced her way in. He saw the minor imperfections in her skin, the mole on her lower back, the colour of her eyes that seemed to change from blue to the palest green in different lights. He clenched his eyes tighter, opened them again, rubbed at them, but she was still there. His mind was playing tricks, it had every right to. Mark let the dress fall from his grasp and allowed exhaustion to take him.

He woke a few hours later, disorientated, his head still full of insane imagery, and the nerve still with him. It started up again as soon as he was conscious, throbbing out its message against the side of his head.

Something was moving in the room. Mark prepared to spring up, his hands clenched into fists, then Danni appeared, inches from his face. They'd always shared a mutual disdain of each other and the cat had never been this close to him before, not even when he fed her. Now she was face to face with him, studying him inquisitively. She was confused, maybe traumatised by what she'd seen, maybe even willing to turn to Mark for succour.

If only you could talk, mate, Mark muttered, as he reached out and ruffled Danni's head.

She did not spring back, hiss or scream, her usual reactions to him, but accepted the fondle. Danni came nearer Mark's head, sharing the pillow with him and started up a cracked kind of purr. Lena had brought the cat in one day, declared her Danni, and that it was now part of the family. She'd actually used the word *family*. Danni had been hanging round in the street outside the modelling agency, and she'd adopted it, much to Mark's disgust. He was glad of the cat now. Danni was warm and alive, and she needed him.

Mark moved Danni away, got up, and opened the window. It was hot and stuffy in the room and well past midday. He looked down on the park, which was full of the kind of green you only get in a British summer. Lush, thick and safe. It looked safe anyway. He knew better. The park had filled up, kids and mothers mainly. Excited laughter drifted across to him, the ice cream van chimes again, a woman's anxious call to her child. For a moment Mark was taken back to his youth, when he had always got up this time, if not later. He felt ashamed he'd dropped off like this, sleeping so soundly a day after Lena had been murdered. He should already be on the trail of the killers, but he did not know where the trail began, let alone what lay at its end.

Danni was looking for Lena, sniffing around, eyeing the bed suspiciously, and eyeing him suspiciously, now that he was up. The cat was ready to bolt again, and Mark was envious. Danni could leave, latch on to another sucker, Lena fading from her memory in days. She followed him into the kitchen and whined for food. Mark fed himself also, some tuna he made into sandwiches with the remainder of the bread, washed down by orange juice and two cups of strong coffee. Eating also made him ashamed. He wanted to hunt for her killer or killers, and feed on the adrenaline of the chase, not bother with food and sleep. The need for revenge welled up in him, he didn't care how bloody it might be, he just wanted to give it back to someone, and could not see any further than this. Mark doubted there *was* any further than this for him. He was not quite thirty yet it seemed as if he'd lived a long time.

There'd been two good years with Lena, but before then, a trail of wasted childhood, struggle, alienation, losing a brother and being banged up. He could count out these events in his mind quickly, counting out his past was like counting money, it passed easily through his hands. It had always seemed him against the world, until Lena came into his life. Now he was back to square one. Maybe this was what he was made for, all he was good for, maybe Lena was just a dream, a device to trick him into thinking life might be better. They'd called him *Psycho Eyes* when he was a kid, sometimes he'd hated it, usually he'd liked it. It fitted his rages, and marked him out on the estate as someone not to mess with, but it was a title he always felt he had to live up to. To assume the role of the hardest kid on the block, to go about wasting his life while other kids, the ones who feared and even respected him, did better. Looking back, he could see that he'd only ever been a one-eyed king of a blind and useless kingdom.

The kitchen was full of Lena. She'd often watched the small TV here, smoking the occasional cigarette, knowing that he hated it, but unable to stop completely. There were several photographs of her pinned on their notice board and one of them together. A night shot, the Eiffel Tower looming behind them, lit up like it was hung with stars. She'd liked images and collected a lot of them. Lena had always seemed dismayed there was so little visual stuff from his past. No baby shots, just a few badly composed kid mug shots his mother had taken, not much else. The police had the best ones, on file. He'd stolen lots of cameras from the houses he burgled but had always sold them on for peanuts. Even then, he sensed his life did not warrant much recording. There was one good photograph of Shane, which his mother had paid to have done. Mark took it from a drawer and looked at it now, at the two-year-old who looked so little like him. Blond, blue-eyed, falsely angelic, butter melting in his hair, but never his mouth. He'd been his mother's new life at the time, someone to start again with, someone who would at least be hers in his early years. But he was quickly taken away, like all her transient pleasures, and his disappearance was never solved. The wound was still open, it always would be, and Mark felt it dig at him now. He put Shane's photo alongside one of Lena's and for a weak moment imagined Shane as their child. He wondered if they'd have got that far. They'd never talked about it, but he thought about it now. Danni cried out, as if sensing the strangeness in Mark, then she was gone, speeding through the cat-flap without a backwards glance. If she had any sense, Mark thought, she'd be gone for good, done with this place and the horror she'd seen.

Mark thought of going down to see Julie, his mother. It had been a long time. They'd patched things up as much as they could after losing Shane, but it would be a visit at the wrong time, for the wrong reasons. He could never unload Lena on her, it would take Julie further into hell. If she hadn't stopped blaming him for Shane at least she had stopped thinking he had anything to do with it, but Lena would start it all up again. It would be another bloody tragedy coming from him. Julie had met Lena once, about a year ago. He had taken her down to the Welsh coast, at Lena's insistence. Julie was living near Cardiff now, a housing association flat that seemed to suit her. She was anonymous there, her past had not travelled from the estate with her. Shane would always be part of that hill-top dwelling place and she'd never go back there. Mark hadn't been back either. They'd both moved on, as much as they could. Julie had also done with men, as far as Mark knew. There'd been plenty in his childhood, his upbringing was bound with a chain of them, a succession of pathetic 'uncles' that had dropped in and out of his life. Mark doubted Julie would ever bother again, she could never take another chance, though she was still under fifty. It seemed like neither of them had ever been young, maybe there'd

43

been no time for it in their lives. Grim survival did not do young very well.

Julie was quite isolated now. She'd been distant from her parents as long as he could remember, which meant there'd been no grandparents for him. Julie's mother had never come to terms with Julie's early pregnancy or her choice of men and when she moved to the estate their relationship became even more distant. Mark had grown up thinking this was normal. Julie's father had died a few years back but her mother was still around. Mark hadn't seen her since Shane went, and doubted that Julie had. A difficult line of communication, stretched by guilt and blame, finally snapped with Shane. It made no sense to go down there, it hadn't made sense seeing Tony. Mark wasn't sure if he was playing for time, or just pissing into the wind.

Julie had been impressed with Lena, and a little surprised that she was with Mark. They'd all drunk too much, and the two women cried over Shane. How do you stand it, Lena asked, then cursed herself for the drunken stupidity of her question. Because we have to, Mark told her, we've always had to. 'Hang on to her' was the last thing Julie said to him, 'if you can'.

He couldn't. Mark needed a drink. He needed a drink badly, he wanted to lose himself in it, to punish himself with booze, so that his thoughts might be wiped out for a few hours. He saw no need to go undercover now. If he was being watched, so be it. He didn't know what the fuck was going on anyway, so any development would be welcome. He put the rest of his money back in the tin, it was probably safer in the flat than on him, especially if he got drunk. He went to the Queen's Head, even Kelly might be company this night. The Irishman's watering hole was a Victorian pub, and little in it had changed in a hundred years; no one had thought it worthy of a makeover.

Kelly was there, he was always there, watching the

racing on the telly. If he was nervous to see Mark he didn't show it.

'Sit down, Mr Richards. I just won sixty quid. That nag there, Poison Whisky.' Kelly dabbed a finger at his newspaper. 'Had to bet on that, didn't I? I've drunk enough of the stuff in my time. Eh, do you want me for anything, Mr Richards?'

'No.'

'Shall I get us some drinks?'

'OK.'

Kelly was buzzing. He's enjoyed the last few days, Mark thought, it's been lucrative for him. Now he thinks I'm his friend. Now he thinks that I want to drink with him. Well, he's right on the second count, I'm that desperate. Kelly brought back two pints and two large chasers.

'Get that down you, Mr Richards. You're going through a bad patch, I can tell. Dunno why though, with a piece like that Lena. Where is she anyway, ain't seen her for a while. Eh, you 'avn't had a fight, 'ave you?'

Kelly's thin face broke into a grin, each tooth trying to outdo the next in crumbling decay. Mark drank the whisky first. One quick gulp and it was down, searing his chest like hot iron. He was barely aware of Kelly's rambling talk. It was humid, almost fetid, in the pub. The oppressive air of the underclass. Mark remembered the books he sometimes looked at in the houses he'd targeted, the ones with lots of pictures in them. This pub reminded him of a book he'd actually taken from the house of one of his school teachers, that weed who taught history. An old book full of dust, and lots of little sketches by someone called Hogarth. It was from another time but the people he drew were in here now. Same wasted, wizened faces, darting eyes, people at the bottom fighting for any scraps that might filter down, kept going by boozy dreams. Though it was risky, Mark had kept that book in his bedroom for a while, cutting out the

45

sketches and pinning them on his wall. Somehow they made him feel better.

Another race was taking place and punters offered encouragement to their nags. It was the nearest most of them got to energy. Smoke gathered in grey clouds shot with fresher blue near the open windows, to be forced back into the room by the outside breeze, forced back into the coughing lungs of the drinkers. Kelly's world was Loserville, but Kelly was by no means the most hopeless inmate. Mark scanned the ravaged faces and lost eyes of the late afternoon drinkers and knew this world of lager breath and piss-stained trousers was just a taxi ride away from some of the richest places in the world. Mark sighed and rubbed at his eyes. He wanted more sleep.

'Mr Richards? I said you haven't …'

'Yes, I heard you, Kelly. No, nothing like that. Just working a lot lately.'

'All the bloody country is working too hard, if you ask me. And getting nowhere. Know what some kid said to me the other day. Life is shit and then you die. Makes you think, eh?'

Mark knew that anyone in the pub could be watching him, working for a few quid in the way Kelly did for him. Well, they could watch him get drunk, with a derelict. Kelly hadn't stopped talking and Mark re-focused on what he was saying.

'Aye, she's a lovely girl, all right, that Lena. A real stunner. All the boys in here say that, when they see her passing. Nothing out of order, mind, outta respect for you, like, Mr Richards.'

Out of fear, more like, Mark thought.

'She don't look nothing like that Tony though,' Kelly continued. 'He looks more like a wop to me.'

'You've got a good memory, Kelly. You only saw him that once, that time I brought him here.'

46

'Nah, I seen him the other day. He was outside your flat. Didn't see me, like. You musta missed him. Come to see his sister, did he?'

Mark dug his hand into Kelly's arm, making his drink spill on both of them.

'The other day?'

'Ow, don' do that, Mr Richards. Yeah, that day you wanted that car. In the morning. It was early for me.'

'Where was he? Exactly?'

'By them railings near your flat. Just waiting like. Someone picked him up in a motor, nice one too, one of them Lexus things. You're hurting my arm, Mr Richards.'

It was taking more than a few seconds to sink in. Was Tony the voice? Lena's own brother? It could have been him, the accent was similar. No, this was crazy. Mark knew he was shaking his head, denying it to himself. Kelly had gone very quiet, not daring to pull away from his grip.

'Mr Richards, my arm.'

Mark loosened his grip.

'You're absolutely sure about this? You saw Tony the morning I asked you to get me that car?'

'Yeah. I was going to go up to him, say hullo, like, but he wouldn't have remembered me, would he? Anyway, he looked like a man with a lot on his mind. He looked like you do now, Mr Richards.'

Mark tried to think. He had to fight against lager and whisky to focus on what Kelly was saying. Drunk or half sober, Kelly was usually reliable for this type of information, especially when he didn't know the significance of it. But Lena's own brother? He thought back to the other night in Coventry, his instinct that the man wasn't surprised to see him, that somehow he'd been expecting him.

'Why the fuck didn't you tell me this earlier,' Mark said, 'when you got the car?'

'I only just thought of it. What's the big deal anyway? Didn't your missus tell you her brother was down? You *have* been having a row, haven't you?'

'I've got to go,' Mark said.

He pushed Kelly away, spilling some more drink. Faces turned to look at him, and any one of them could be his enemy. Mark pushed a ten at Kelly.

'You stay here and have a few more. And keep that bloody mobile on.'

'Sure, Mr Richards, you take it easy.'

Most of the light had faded into summer dusk by the time Mark got back to the flat. The mothers and children in the park had been replaced by older teenagers, kids from the local estate. Some of them passed him, one flicking a small ball of spit from his mouth with his tongue. It went close to Mark, but without any real chance of it hitting him. He'd grown up with kids who played this game, he'd played it himself. It was perfect to wind up adults. Charged with Kelly's news Mark had to fight hard to not react, to get hold of the kid and crush his face, and maybe his friends too. He walked towards the group, and they stopped giggling. The spitter tried to remain defiant and hip but wanted to run, Mark knew the signs. *I know what you're thinking, pal, you're thinking, fuck it, I've picked on the wrong dude, but you can't let your mates see it.* Mark breathed hard, controlled his fists, and walked away, the banter starting up again as the group rolled towards the park, hesitantly at first, then getting louder, more confident. The spitter shouted *wanker* as Mark entered the flat. He hated turning the key in the lock, and, whatever happened in the next few days, he would not be staying here again.

He packed a holdall with enough stuff to last him a week or so, took his money and his passport and the Paris photograph of Lena and himself, and the only one he had of Shane. As an afterthought he packed the Dutch doll. He wanted to have something of Lena's with him, something innocent. A year ago he'd handed in a handgun in a police amnesty. Now he wished he hadn't. It came his way in his first year as an investigator, and he'd never had any call for it, but there was always an idea in the back of his head that it might be useful one day, if his life blew apart again. It had. He had no idea what he might be dealing with in the next few days but he knew it would be hard, bloody, and probably final. Mark would have to manage the way he always had, on his guile, and instinct to survive.

The plan was simple. One dimensional. Find Tony and take it from there. He knew it wouldn't be so easy this time. The thought that he'd had the guy in his hands rankled. If only Kelly had mentioned it before. Mark tried to stop his thoughts racing. It still didn't mean that Tony was involved. Maybe Tony had left Lena before she was killed, maybe he'd knocked in vain on the flat's door, with Lena already dead inside. No, Tony was part of it all right. Every part of him told him it was so, the fifteen years he'd spent amongst lowlife told him it was so. That spitting kid was right, wanker, stupid fucking wanker. Mark stood in the doorway to the flat swearing at himself for at least a minute. He'd have to do better, much better. As he walked out into the night he drilled this into his mind.

Chapter Five

Mark watched Kelly approach his bed-sit. He was coming back from the pub, staggering in a diagonal line, trailing chips behind him, like someone seeding the earth. He dropped more than he ate. The Donegal man was surprised to see him.

'Christ, Mr Richards,' you waiting for me? I've seen more of you in the last few days than the last bloody year. What *is* up with you? You can tell old Kelly.'

A glare from Mark was enough to kill the question.

'Let me in,' Mark said.

Mark steadied Kelly as he struggled up the stairs. He made a few attempts to stab his key at the lock before Mark took it from him and opened the door himself.

'Thanks,' Kelly muttered, 'I often get the shakes this time of night.'

'You often get a shitload of beer. Is there any of that money left?'

'A bit. My lifestyle is very cheap, Mr Richards.'

Kelly was puzzled, but also pleased by Mark's presence. He fussed around the room, looking for clean glasses and fresh drink. He found the drink, but clean glasses were a step too far.

'I don't want a drink,' Mark said.

'Oh, right. Uh …?'

'I want to stay here tonight. I'll be gone early.'

Kelly giggled, spitting out the last of the chips.

'Kicked you out, 'as she? Things must be bad if you want to stay here. Why don't you go to a hotel up town, man like you.'

'This will do. Don't mind, do you?'

'No, course not. I only got the one bed though.'

'I'll be all right in the chair here.'

'OK, cheers, Mr Richards. Uh, do you want me to make you a coffee or anything?'

Mark glanced around the bed-sit. If it was a café it would be closed down on the spot. It summed up Kelly. Dirty, unable to cope. Life is shit and then ...

'No thanks.'

'I'll get my head down, then.'

Kelly didn't bother to take off anything but his overcoat and shoes, to Mark's relief, but he realised it acted as a barrier against the worst of his smells. Kelly was asleep in a minute. In two, the man soon began a fractured snoring, as his body fought against another night's abuse. Mark noticed the rattle in his chest, like a dried pea stuck there. Kelly had spent many nights outside in his time, and his chest knew it. This guy thinks I'm his friend now, Mark realised, that I've turned to him in a time of need. A few days ago the idea would have been laughable, the few times Lena had seen Kelly she'd likened him to a reptile. Yet tonight Mark could relate to him, his early life had been peopled with Kellys. Unsavoury, unsanitary, crazy people, challenged in a multiple of ways, but each having a kind of life to live, away from the mainstream. People like him.

Mark got up and moved his chair nearer the window, the sound made Kelly turn over in his sleep and mutter something incoherent. It was late now and nothing much moved in the street, other than a few drunken stragglers shouting their way home. Mark was too wound up to sleep, so he tried to think. He'd been trying to think since he'd found Lena but his mind was still fazed. Ideas did not seem able to penetrate what seethed there. Too much anger and shock had to settle down. Maybe it never would.

The weather was changing. It was warm but a light

drizzle had got up. Mark watched it drift noiselessly against the window and slowly dribble down it. He wished he could open Kelly's ruined sash, to smell the mustiness of long dry stone being rained on. He'd always loved that smell, there was something calm and permanent about it. A car drove slowly down the street, the first in a while. Someone didn't want to go home, or maybe it was some sad git looking for a woman. It was looking for something, but it wasn't a woman. The car cruised slowly past each shop, he could see the driver craning his head to check the numbers. It stopped outside Kelly's, then pulled over to the other side of the road a bit further down. It was a Lexus. All gold.

Kelly had thin and ancient net curtains, which were useless for any concealment so Mark got up and stood by the wall, opening a crack in the curtains. There was someone in the back of the car, someone who lit up a cigarette. He saw the flare of a lighter, then the speck of red glow. It was only for a few seconds but Mark's eyes were 20-20 and it was long enough for him to recognise Tony.

They must be looking for him. Unless they wanted Kelly for information. Tony got out of the car. Like Kelly he wore a coat more suitable for the winter, and he pulled its collar up against the rain. The driver got out with him. A large man, Mark's height but thirty pounds heavier. He knew they were coming up. Action was being delivered into his hands, very quickly. At least one thing had been sorted. Tony was as guilty as hell.

It was better to let Kelly sleep. He'd only panic and get in the way. Mark let himself out of the flat quietly, taking the sawn-down baseball bat Kelly kept by the door. It had always amused Mark, to think of his puny nark trying to wield it, but it was a solid weight in *his* hands, and quite comforting. He ran his hands over the splintered wood, feeling each imperfection.

Mark had to gamble that they would come in the back

way, that's what he would do. He went down to the first floor and buried himself into the recess by the back door. The landing light wasn't working, which was good. The big guy came in first, Tony behind him. Mark had learnt many years ago that it was better not to wait in situations like these. He charged Tony with his shoulder, sending him sprawling, and hit the other man as hard as he could. He doubted if he'd have the time for another blow, but there was no need for another. He heard something crack, it might have been the bat, it might have been the man's head. The man groaned once and fell down quite calmly, sixteen plus stones sinking to the ground. Tony was struggling on the floor, calling out for his mate and trying to get something out of the overcoat. Mark knew what it was and why he was wearing the coat. He kicked Tony in the side of the head, and pushed a foot down hard on his hand. Tony squealed and relaxed his grip on the gun. Mark took it from him and slapped him a few times to keep him safe.

'Hello, Tony,' Mark whispered, 'looking for me?'

Mark looked at the gun. A Smith and Wesson 38, squat and snub-nosed. He searched the big man, who was spark out, but he wasn't carrying, probably thought he didn't have to. Mark appreciated this. Only wankers, wimps and juveniles used guns these days, professionals had long since sought other ways. He'd probably fractured the man's skull. Maybe he wouldn't make it, but Mark was not concerned. There was no time to be. He found the car keys in a pocket, took them from him and hauled Tony to his feet.

'Come on, we're going for a ride.'

'Mark, for fucksake, are you crazy? What have you done to Angelo?'

Mark put the gun to the side of Tony's head. The man wanted to shrink away from it, but didn't dare move.

'Keep your mouth shut, Tony, if that's really your name, and you'll live a little longer.'

53

Mark thought of taking Tony up to Kelly's but it was better to keep the Irishman out of it. If the police found the big man, Kelly really would know nothing. He'd snored all the way through this.

He'd take Tony back to the flat. It was fitting, though a few hours ago he thought he'd done with it for good. Mark pushed Tony out into the street, the Smith and Wesson heavy in his pocket. They got to the car. There was no one else around and Mark doubted if there'd be anyone else watching him. Too bad if there were. He pushed Tony into the car.

'You drive.'

'Look, Mark …'

Mark slapped him to the side of the head again. Tony whimpered, a desperate kind of sound.

'I told you to keep your mouth shut. Drive, nothing else.'

'But where we going?'

'The flat. Lena's flat. Your sister's flat.'

Tony was about to say something else but stopped himself, and did what he was told. They were there in minutes.

'Park farther down,' Mark said.

Tony still had the hair gel on. It glistened in the streetlight, his eyes glistened too, with fear. Mark gave him the key to the flat.

'Walk in front of me and open the door. If you decide to get brave I'll kill you.'

This was like a film unfolding. Nothing was real. Nothing had been real for three days. Mark was acting on pure instinct, not knowing where this was going, not knowing why it had happened, but realising that now he had a chance to find out. He pushed Tony into the main room.

'Sit down there,' Mark said, pointing to the sofa. Tony was sweating, worse than in Coventry. Beads of sweat pimpled his forehead, which he dabbed at with a pudgy hand. His eyes flicked around the room, and towards the door.

'The big guy, what's his name, Angelo? He isn't coming, Tony. No one is coming for you, it's just you and me.'

'Look Mark, I dunno what you're thinking, just give me a chance to explain, man.'

'Where's Lena?'

Mark watched his eyes and recognised the guilt they registered before Tony could get into a role.

'Lena? I haven't seen her for ages. All we were doing was …'

Tony stopped when Mark produced the gun.

'Smith and Wesson. Pretty old. Not a stable piece, I'd say.'

Mark leant towards Tony and pressed the gun against his forehead.

'Mark, for fucksake.'

Mark curled his finger around the trigger and smelt Tony's alarm.

'This is going to be a long, long night,' Mark said. 'I want you to start at the beginning, I want it all, Tony.'

Tony was desperately thinking for ways out. Sweat pimples were turning into acne.

'I don't hear anything,' Mark said.

He brought the gun down hard on Tony's knee. As the man reared up he hit him to the side of the head, the same side he'd kicked.

'We don't want to be doing this,' Mark said, 'this thing could go off at any time.'

Tony howled, and as he slumped down Mark moved behind the sofa. It would be better if the man didn't see him, didn't know what was coming.

'Come on, Tony, stop whining. That's just a slap. If you're afraid of someone else there's no need to be. You'll be dead anyway. You'll never get out of this flat, like Lena, so you only have to be afraid of me and the pain I can cause. Think of the now, us here, this is your only chance to keep breathing. Your only one. Tell me everything and I might let you take it. I'll know if you're bullshitting. I always know.'

A thin line of blood escaped from Tony's gel. The man was unaware of it as it merged into his false tan.

'You smoke, don't you,' Mark said, 'have one before you start, it'll help you think.'

Mark tried to modulate his voice. If he could keep it together he'd try to play good cop, bad cop. If he could.

Tony took a pack of cigarettes from a pocket and lit one up. Mark took the rest from him. For the first time since his hillside childhood he took another from the pack, and lit one for himself. Tony breathed heavily, trying to grab a moment's relief from this ordeal. Mark sucked on his smoke and felt his eyes water.

'Why do you ask about Lena?' Tony said. 'What's going on?'

Mark pushed his cigarette hard against Tony's neck. The man squealed and tried to get away, only to receive another blow from the gun. The line of blood was joined by another, red tram-lines down his cheek.

'Wrong start, Tony. Look, neither of us has the time for this. Especially you. You better move things along or I'm going to put a round in the back of your head and go looking for your friends.'

Tony started to cry. Mark was expecting it. There was nothing else for him to try.

'I can't, man, they'll kill me. You don't know what you're dealing with.'

'No, but you know what you're dealing with here, right now.'

Mark put his mouth close to Tony's ear. He dropped his voice to a whisper and held the cigarette an inch from Tony's eyes, while touching the other side of his head with the gun.

'Your own sister, Tony. What did you think I'd do? Walk away from it? Forget what happened? And why was she cut up like that, what could she have possibly done to deserve that? It was you, wasn't it, on the phone to me when I found her?'

'I had to phone, to get you out of the flat. They made me. They didn't expect you to come back then. You'd never have found her.'

Even at this stage, Mark wanted there to be another explanation. For Tony not to be involved, for people not to be as evil as this. Mark dropped his voice even lower.

'Now we are coming to it. I think you'd better tell me about *they.*'

He hit Tony on the other knee. He felt the need. Again the man tried to spring up, but Mark pushed the gun into his throat and Tony sank back down. There didn't seem to be any hope left in his eyes now. This was good.

'You're involved with people who've killed your sister. What does this make you, Tony?'

'She's not my fucking sister, man. She's no one's sister.'

There was a silence for a while. Tony dropped his cigarette on the sofa, and it started to make a brown hole. Let it burn, Mark thought, let the whole place burn.

'Tell me, Tony.'

Tony started to rock slightly, holding his knees with his hands. Fear was fighting fear. Mark hadn't expected him to hold out so long, but understood it. Whoever killed Lena that way could not be sane. Tony was muttering *fuck it* repeatedly to himself, like a desperate mantra, trying to lock out Mark and take himself into ostrich mode. Mark brought him back by picking up the cigarette and pressing it against the side of his neck again. The squeal turned into a scream.

'Lena was a courier,' Tony shouted, 'a mule, she'd worked for us for a couple of years.'

'Carrying what?'

The *fuck it*s started up again.

'Carrying what? Come on, Tony, we're almost there.'

Mark moved to face Tony now, pressing the gun into his face. The man was starting to smell bad.

'Come on, Tony.'

'Diamonds. Whenever she went over to Amsterdam. We used her modelling work as cover. She got well paid, there was no need for any of this to happen. No need for this problem, man.'

'I'd call getting her stomach sliced open more than a problem.'

'I didn't have no part in that, Mark, I swear to you I didn't. I told them Stellachi was crazy, that there'd be problems with you, but they don't care, man, they don't care nothing about stuff like that. They just wanted their goods. Lena got greedy, and tried to cross them.'

Mark slapped him with the gun again. It was instinctive, and it kept him from pulling the trigger. Tony's face was becoming messy. His eyes glassy.

'For fucksake don't kill me. I'm only the message boy, sometimes I fix up the odd thing. I should never have been anywhere near the flat. They wanted me around because I was the go-between for Lena.'

'Don't even think of moving,' Mark said.

He went to the window. The street was empty, the faint edge of dawn challenging the orange lights, the loneliest part of the day. There was no way of knowing if Tony was telling it straight, but his fear was not phoney. There'd always been plenty of money in the last few years, modelling pays, Lena said. Though he'd never seen her in any of the major magazines she read, he'd just accepted it. Now Mark wondered if any of it was true. He wondered if he'd been a convenient pick up, to be also used as cover. He turned back to Tony, who was now lying face down on the sofa, blood from his head wounds seeping out steadily.

'Don't go to sleep on me, Tony. Where are you from? Don't tell me fucking Coventry.'

'I'm a British citizen.'

'Where?'

Mark was shouting. *Psycho Eyes was* coming back. Explosive teenage rages that he'd thought had drained from his system long ago were taking on adult form.

'Albania,' Tony muttered.

'What?'

'Albania. I got out fifteen years ago. I was what they call an asylum seeker now. Flutura came later.'

'Who?'

Flutura - Lena. She's Flutura Proli. She changed it to Lena Stolitz over here, when they got her a British passport. Same as me, Tony Stolitz.' Tony sighed, and seemed to calm down a little. 'Flutura,' he said quietly, 'it means butterfly.'

Mark thought of butterflies, on his native hillside in spring, orange, black and yellow, fragile wings blown around helplessly by the wind, but still getting where they wanted to go. Sometimes a fancy one would settle close to him, and he'd be amazed by its patterns. Getting fewer and fewer each year.

'What's your connection with Lena?'

'I knew her when she was a kid. I knew her family. I helped her when she got here.'

'Yes, you really helped her, didn't you.'

Mark thought of hitting him again. Tony tensed for the blow and tried to curl away from him, but Mark stayed his hand. Each sliver of information he extracted from Tony was a knife in the heart for him, and if he struck Tony again he doubted that he would stop. The man's face was already like raw steak. He knew Tony had slept with Lena. Too much fucking knowledge.

The cigarette started to burn Mark's fingers, and he stubbed it out quickly. He picked up the other one and put that out too. Tony was opening up now, talking for his life.

'Things was tough over there,' Tony said. 'We had nothing. You people here don't understand how rich you are.'

'Who are you working for?'

'People from the old place. I was introduced to them when I first got here. They helped me, set me up and stuff. I just done favours for them, take a package here, take something there. When Flutura came over, they got her modelling work. They could use someone classy like her, someone who would be travelling around a lot. Like me, she was desperate to stay here, and when you are desperate, you do anything. They fixed it all, the passports, the jobs, even English lessons. We were in paradise, then they wanted a return.'

'You were living with Lena?'

Mark felt his throat dry up, he could hardly get the words out. Tony was weighing up the safest answer. Truth or lies might kill him, but Mark knew the answer anyway. It was another shock for Mark, that Lena could ever touch this gelled-up, oily snake. He brought the gun closer again.

'All right. Yeah, for a while. They wanted it that way, and you don't say no to these people.'

'Were you with her when she met me?'

'No, I swear. That was nothing to do with anyone, just you and her. We'd gone our own ways by then.'

'Why was she killed?'

Tony breathed in deeply, coughing up a little blood.

'Stay put,' Mark said, but Tony wasn't in a state to do much else.

He went to the kitchen, wet a towel and brought it back.

'Clean yourself up a bit.'

'Thanks.'

60

'Why was Lena killed? Like that?'

Tony started muttering to himself, holding the towel and rocking again.

'Fuck, man. I can't …'

'You can. You're almost there, Tony.'

Mark rotated the old fashioned circular barrel of the gun. It was more like something from the American West than a modern weapon.

'Where the fuck did you get this?' Mark muttered.

He pushed out five bullets, left one in its chamber and spun the barrel. Again it felt like he was acting out a film he'd seen so many times – *make my day, punk,* but this was real.

'What you doing, man?'

Mark pointed the gun at Tony's head and pulled the trigger.

Tony yelled and put his hands in front of his head. The trigger fell on an empty chamber.

'Don't they play this game in Albania? That's not too far from Russia, is it? You like to gamble, don't you, Tony, you just won at five to one. It might be in the spout this time.'

Mark rotated the barrel again.

'OK, OK. Lena changed when you came on the scene. She wanted out, then she got greedy, like I said. Some of the goods went missing the last time, but they thought it was at the other end. Someone in Amsterdam paid. But this time more went and it had to be her. Lena wanted money for a house, she wanted to get a place with you. In the country. She'd always wanted that. I told her she was crazy, you can't do that with these people. They never let you go, but she wouldn't listen. She was always so confident.'

Mark couldn't believe Lena had done all this without him being aware of anything. Streetwise Mark, alert to everything at all times. What a joke. He would have stopped her if he'd known, got her away. Mark felt Tony was telling

61

this part straight, but he wondered what else had gone on over the years. Maybe he'd never know, but he did know what Lena had done with the diamonds, and how they'd got them back. Her death was no ritual slaughter or the act of madmen, it was business, of the bloodiest kind. These men did not care to wait.

'I didn't think they'd do that,' Tony said. 'They told me afterwards it would be a lesson, for all the others. I was sick, Mark, I swear it.'

Mark heard the chink of bottles outside. Milk was being delivered to the shop a few doors down. Another day was starting.

'They didn't get them back,' Tony muttered.

'What?'

'The diamonds. They didn't find them. They are worth half a million, maybe more. You could buy Albania for that. They won't stop looking, that's why Angelo came for you.'

'They think I might have them?'

'Why not? Who else could she have given them to?'

'Do you think I have them?'

'No.'

'I want some names, Tony.'

'What good will it do? For you or me? This is a big organisation, man, they make money from everything. Drugs, girls, smuggling, phone scams, Internet scams - the Internet is the new heaven for making money. My people think that God sent it for us. Some of my people have always been like this. Albania is ...'

'Yeah, I know. Bandit territory.'

Tony nodded. 'You can't touch them, man. We'll both die.'

'But you a bit sooner than me. Anyway, what do I have to lose now? I might have killed that guy with you already.'

Tony shut his eyes and thought for a moment.

'All I know is that things are run here by Agani, Alex

Agani. Everything goes through him, he deals with the people in Amsterdam. He works for them. A lot of the money goes there and comes back as diamonds. I don't know what happens after that, you have to believe this. I just took them from Lena and passed them on.'

'And Angelo?'

'Agani keeps him around as a minder. He likes hurting people. There's another one, even bigger. I don't even know his name. Angelo calls him the big man.'

'Angelo didn't do too well just now.'

Mark knew brute force impressed Tony, it was impressing him now. Brute force for brutal minds, it was the first law he'd learned. Mark turned off the light. The sun was up now, low over the opposite rooftops, spraying the room with silver light. Mark phoned Kelly's mobile. It rang for a long time before he answered it. Kelly's voice was shaky, the alcoholic waking up dry, with a tongue like a cloth. The fact he'd answered at all was a result.

'Oh, it's you, Mr Richards. See, I didn't turn it off. Jesus, what time is it?'

'Time for you to be up. Get your arse in gear, stick your head out of your door and look down the stairs.'

'Uh?'

'Do it now.'

It sounded like Kelly was falling out of bed. Mark heard a few *fuckit*s, and a general stumbling around.

'I don't get it,' Kelly said. 'There's just the fucking stairs, they ain't going nowhere, are they?'

'Lock your door and go back to sleep - and keep the phone on.'

'All right, I got it on the charger, just like you said, Mr Richards. Uh, do you need me for anything else? I could do with a few more quid.'

'I'll get back to you.'

So, it was Kelly and himself against what sounded like

Albania's version of the Mafia.

'Why do you live in Coventry?' Mark asked.

'They wanted someone in the Midlands. We are doing a lot of stuff up there.'

Mark noticed Tony had changed from *they* to *we* again. He'd been talking for his life, trying to put distance between himself and his friends, but he was one of them, and no better. Maybe he had played a direct part in Lena's death, maybe he hadn't. Mark knew he could never be sure, and it was the only reason Tony was still alive.

'Where does this Alex live?'

Tony started to sweat again. The room was heating up and it had been a long night.

'Look Mark, don't even think of going there. You'll get yourself killed and what good that's gonna do?'

At this moment Mark felt that this might do a lot of good, if he could take a few with him. The idea of the big sleep used to fascinate him even when he was a kid, when there seemed to be no future, and life had the taste of burnt paper in his mouth. Then Lena came along.

Mark threatened with the gun again. It seemed as if they had been playing this game for a lifetime.

'Ny' burrr i madh,' Tony murmured.

'What? Speak English.'

I said he's a very big man. An important man.'

'Aren't they always,' Mark muttered to himself. 'Where, Tony? It's the last time I'll ask.'

Tony sighed.

'One of them penthouse jobs. Greenwich way. Look there's always two or three guys with him, they come over all the time on false passports. Alex sort of trains them up, then they go all over Europe. The States too now.'

'Write down the address,' Mark said. 'Make sure it's the right one because you're coming with me.'

He pulled Tony up with his free hand. Looking at the

man, smelling him, he knew he didn't need the gun any more. He put it in his waistband, then dragged Tony to the bathroom and sat him down on the toilet.

'Stay put until I tell you to move.'

Mark dashed a lot of cold water in his face, then drank a glass of it. He was coming into a second energy surge. He'd go all day now before he dropped. Then sleep would have to take him, if he was still alive.

Tony's lurid shirt was made more so by the blood that stained it. Mark let the man wash himself then took him back to the living room. He looked for a shirt for him and told him to put it on.

'We don't want to attract attention, do we?' Mark said. The shirt was black and too big but it calmed Tony's appearance.

'For fucksake man, get away, while you have a chance. What you done to Angelo won't be forgotten, they can't afford to let that go, but if they can't find you it will pass.'

Mark wondered what had happened to Angelo.

'Look, can I have some coffee?' Tony asked,' I can hardly walk.'

'OK. Make me some too. All the stuff's in the kitchen.'

Mark sat by the window and watched Tony through the open kitchen door. The man was playing for time but coffee was a good idea. Tony looked at the knives in the kitchen but what little nerve he had was long shot.

Tony brought out two large mugs. He could have thrown them in Mark's face, but he placed them carefully on the table. Tony had at least told it straight about being a fixer, this man was no soldier. He'd let others deal with the situation now, and try to save his skin.

Mark took in the scene outside. People were opening shops, shutters going up, delivery vans arriving, a few early joggers out in the park. Shopkeepers were hosing down their fronts, the day smelt clean in the early sun, clean and fresh.

All days start with a lie, Mark thought.

There was little chance of revenge, and even less of resolution. Mark wondered if Lena had been working that time in Paris. There would have been plenty of chances for her to slip away and collect something. His past with her could no longer be trusted, memory was being adulterated.

'Come on, Tony, we're out of here.'

Despite the weather Mark took a jacket with him, he needed it to conceal the gun.

They were on the street for less than sixty seconds, hardly time to feel the sun on their faces, when the car hit them.

Chapter Six

Mark couldn't believe he hadn't seen the Lexus in the street. It came from behind a van with Angelo at the wheel. Mark moved quicker than Tony, which saved his life. Tony took the hit full on, bouncing up over the car's bonnet to land a few yards behind it on the road, quickly turning a patch of it wet. Their eyes met for a second, but Tony's did not register anything, and were filling with blood. There was a screech of brakes from other vehicles, and a woman screamed somewhere. Mark heard others shout out and saw the Lexus speed away around the first corner. Angelo's skull had obviously not been broken.

Mark had been struck a glancing blow, just enough to push him into the gutter and make his shoulder throb. He felt for the gun and it was still in place. Traffic was stopping, people were rushing towards Tony. Someone approached Mark.

'You okay, pal?'

'Yes. Help my friend.'

And Mark was gone without another look back, pushing through the gathering crowd into a side street.

If they wanted Tony dead it meant they expected him to sing. They were right, but for Mark Tony hadn't said enough. Maybe he could have got more out the man. Mark realised how cheap life was for these people. They had killed two of their own very easily. A few minutes ago he thought he'd had one vital element on his side, surprise, but he was behind the game, way behind. His situation had gone from hopeless to impossible, just like Tony said. Even so, he'd keep to his plan, such as it was, and get over to that address in Greenwich. Maybe it would be an endgame waiting for him, maybe not, but at least they couldn't know where he was going and Angelo hadn't hung around long enough to know if Mark was out of action or not.

Mark took the Jubilee line and got off at the North Greenwich tube station. This wasn't a part of town he knew very well. He checked out the usual mix of summer traffic and milling people, all on a mission to get somewhere, a thousand pairs of eyes, and anyone might be looking for him. The police might want to know why the man with Tony had disappeared, but Tony's end would be put down to a hit and run, not murder. The holdall had given Mark some protection against the car; what was left of his life was inside it.

Greenwich was a large station, concrete columns reared up inside a huge underground space, and glazed blue tiles were everywhere. It had been built to impress, like the Millennium Dome nearby. This had always struck Mark about London, or any big city. They were always on the move, buildings being pulled down, springing up, projects failing with millions lost, but always others to take their place. Ever-growing stone plants. So different from his hillsides, which only changed when wedges of forestry were cut down to leave gaping, exposed spaces, naked gashes in the masses of trees. Glimpses of what the hillside were once like.

Mark looked at Tony's scribbled address. Anyone might be living there, but it did exist, for Mark found the street in a few minutes. It was in the money end of Greenwich, a million quid's worth of converted warehouse, the penthouse on the top, Tony said, which would make things even harder. Mark remembered coming here with Lena once, he'd wanted to see the Cutty Sark, Christ knows why. He'd had his bellyful of the sea in the Shetlands but it had been in one of her magazines and it was in their early days, when trips around town had been a novelty for him, especially when it didn't involve spying on someone. They'd gone on to the Observatory, where his lack of knowledge had shamed him. He couldn't answer any of Lena's questions but it didn't bother her. 'You can read lots of books when you're an old man,' she'd said, laughing at him in that way she had, it was infectious, never mocking and made him feel so good.

Mark fixed Agani's place, as he leant against a wall a hundred yards down the road. It was overlooking the Thames, one of several warehouse blocks, new money spin offs from 80s Britain, Mark's growing up time. There'd be financial people from the City here, maybe a few soccer players, small time rock stars, conmen, and silver spoon merchants, but Agani was probably the only murderer.

Getting in was the first problem, staying alive the second. They'd have electronic entrance doors, maybe even someone manning them, but Mark had been here before, many times. There'd always been somewhere to get into, from his earliest days. He saw a pub further down the road and walked down to it. It was surprisingly full for the time of day, city types stretching out liquid lunches. He went into the toilet and tried to freshen himself up, slicking water through his short hair, putting on the jacket, and making sure the gun was secure in the inside pocket. He needed to look as if he belonged in this part of town. Mark thought about having a quick drink but thought again, it was too much like the last wish of a condemned man.

He walked quickly back to the warehouse block, his eyes trying to check everywhere at once. There was not much traffic about and no sign of the Lexus. They probably had it off the road by now, fixing the mess Tony had made.

It was a question of hanging around until someone went into the apartment block. That might be Agani himself, for Mark had no idea what the man looked like. He could not afford to stay outside for long, there was little cover in the modern design of the place, old streets were much better, full of the nooks and crannies of his trade, but his luck was in. A car pulled up outside, he saw a man in a suit kiss the woman driver, get out and go towards the entrance. If it was possible to move fast nonchalantly Mark achieved it, a lifetime of experience served him well and he got close to the man as he punched numbers on the door's security system.

'Nice to see summer's arrived,' Mark said, in the best voice he could muster.

'Yes,' the man answered, 'better late than never.'

He did not pay Mark much attention, he was still smiling back at his girlfriend. Mark let him go ahead into the lift near the entrance, then took the stairs, which were discreetly positioned behind a service door. He left the holdall at the foot of the stairs, if it was gone when he came down it was gone. If he came back down.

For a big man he'd always trod softly, and he did so now, making barely a sound on the stairs. It was four flights up to the penthouse. He got to the top floor and looked for a way up to the roof. He wasn't sure what good this would do him but it was worth checking out. Always know your ground, one of his golden rules. The door to the roof was locked but it didn't matter, for someone was coming up in the lift. There was just enough angle in the corridor to hide himself. Two men got out of the lift, talking in a language he didn't recognise. One was very large, and the other was Angelo.

It was an instinctive action, he'd always acted like this when the chips were down. Mark came behind the men very quickly and put the gun against the large man's head. He froze, but did not make a sound. A pro, Mark thought, like me. Angelo turned to recognise him and cursed under his breath.

'That's right, mate, still alive,' Mark whispered. 'I'll take his head off. We're going inside, quiet and easy.'

Angelo found his English.

'You're a madman, coming here. What the fuck you think you gonna do?'

'I could kill you, for a start. I should have last night.'

Angelo rubbed the back of his head in memory. He wanted to get his hands on Mark, to punish with his fists, to kill him with his hands.

These might be the men who had killed Lena. Mark felt the adrenaline kick in again, he was surfing on its rush, not sure himself what he might do, but if he was going down in the next few minutes these two were coming with him, he was certain of this. It was impossible to search them without losing his edge. One yes, but two was too dangerous. He'd assume they were carrying.

'Open the door,' Mark said. 'If either of you make a sound, or speak a word that's not English I'll kill you.'

'He don' speak English much,' Angelo said.

'Tell him what I said.'

Mark kept the gun hard against the big man's neck. He'd held one or two before but had never used one. It was not complicated. Pull a small piece of metal and someone died. Angelo turned a key in the door and Mark nudged them in. Very quietly.

It was a large room, more than thirty foot long, and one other man was in it. He sat at a desk by the window, smoking, and talking on the phone, in Dutch. Mark recognised it from his one job in Amsterdam. The man had a dressing gown on that looked like a woman's, a reddish pink colour, almost like another layer of flesh. He was small, very dark, about fifty years old, and wore glasses with heavy frames. This must be Agani, but he was not what Mark was expecting. This guy looked like a cross between an accountant and the doorman of a clip joint. Agani said something to the men without turning around, and continued to talk animatedly into the phone. If there was anyone else in the flat Mark knew the odds would lengthen. Not that they could be much longer.

Mark gestured to Angelo and his friend to sit down. Agani finished his phone call, looked at something on his desk and stood up, stretching and looking down onto the street. Only then did he turn to see Mark and the pointing gun.

Agani's face was quizzical, not frightened, but he glared at Angelo for a second before the mask came back. It said, you can't harm me, you are nobody. This was the man who'd ordered Lena's death and these were the men who'd carried it out. Mark saw her on that bloody bed and wanted to pull the trigger. He wanted it badly. A quick pull on the trigger, just increase the pressure of his curled finger a fraction. Agani first, one round in the head, quickly, before the others could react, then just empty the gun into them as they came for him. He was breathing very hard, trying to stop the shake in his hand. An inner voice talked to him.

It won't do, you stupid bastard, you'll find nothing else out. You'll spend the rest of your life behind fucking bars, never knowing what really happened, never knowing who Lena really was.

'What's the trouble, my friend?' Agani asked.

That almost did it. Mark fought hard to control himself and everyone in the room knew it. Angelo and the big man were weighing up their chances but they did not step between Agani and the gun. They wanted to live, maybe at the expense of their boss. Any real loyalty and they would have been at him before this, chancing that one of them would survive.

'Don't do anything stupid,' Agani said, 'we can work this out.'

His voice was soft, lacking the flamboyance of Tony, but there was more of an accent in it, and it was used to giving orders, having its own way. Mark found his own voice at last and hoped it didn't come out as a desperate shout.

'Do you know who I am?' Mark said.

Mark cocked the gun. Its click seemed to make the room jump a little.

'Don't do it, man,' Angelo said. 'You are out of your depth.'

'And you are close to dying. All of you are.'

Agani looked at Angelo.

'This is the man, the Mark Richards.'

'I thought maybe so.'

'Sit back down,' Mark said to Agani. 'I want you all to put your hands on your knees. Dig into them. I want to see your hands go white. If they don't, or you move, I will kill you all.'

'Can I tell him?' Angelo asked, pointing to the big man.

Mark nodded.

I want to kill you. I want it so bad I can smell it. Taste it. If it's revenge, it tastes like iron, like blood. My throat is dry and bitter with it. I have retribution in my hand and I want to use it. Anything to take the pain away.

Agani was a cool bastard, Mark had to give him that. The man knew his life hung by a thread but faced up to him like he was a business contact, with a proposition. Mark knew it hadn't always been like this. Agani had learned to do it. Even if the guy looked like a ponce in a men's clothes shop, Mark recognised a fellow traveller, someone born piss-poor and hating it, not so much from the wrong end of the tracks as beyond them altogether. Agani would have started with small time thieving, then built up, until success was plucked from his mean life. He'd probably done his own killing in the early days, maybe there were others like Lena in his past. This was an Albanian version of a scally from the old estate, but for ripping off motors read drug shipments, for fists and boots in the streets read throat slitting, for getting your girl pregnant read selling them. For a finale read

73

cutting up a woman.

'Well,' Agani said, 'we might as well talk.'

'Did Angelo tell you I was dead?' Mark said. 'That I went the same way as Tony? Or did you think I'd just crawl under a rock? Go away somewhere and blank Lena from my mind?'

Angelo's hands tightened further on his knees. Maybe he *had* thought Mark was dead. He would only have had time to see him spin into the gutter.

'Never mind, mate' Mark said, 'at least you got one out of two.'

'Mr Richards,' Agani said, 'you're upset. Not thinking straight at all. It's understandable. Such a pity you came back to your flat when you did. All this … unpleasantness could have been avoided. And Flut … Lena, she was such a silly girl. She had a good life here. She was a British citizen. Why is it that some always want more?'

Mark rushed forward and clubbed Agani to the side of the head, knocking him onto the floor. Angelo and the big man thought of doing something but the gun was back on them in seconds. Agani moaned, and spat out a string of foreign words with his blood.

'Shut up,' Mark shouted. 'I only want to hear English. Get back in your chair.'

Agani did so, but was groggy. He almost said something else in his own tongue but stopped himself.

'Can I get a handkerchief from my gown?' he managed to ask.

Mark nodded. Agani was bleeding freely. He dabbed at his wound gingerly. Mark had also caught his cheek with the gun butt. It was turning purple.

'I haven't been hit for twenty years,' Agani said quietly. 'I'd almost forgotten about such things.'

'You haven't forgotten shit,' Mark said. 'Only now you pay men to do this stuff for you. You're just a lowlife ponce, a dago woman killer.'

Agani dabbed at his head again, and winced, yet a thin smile crossed his face.'

'Tony said we'd have trouble with you.'

'Look,' Agani said, 'Mark, can I call you Mark, this is getting us nowhere. We can make a deal.'

Mark tried to keep a lid on this. Angelo was right, he *was* out of his depth here, and holding a gun on three international killers. He backed against the wall, and wanted to sink down it, but he kept the gun steady, and pointing at Agani's head. The nerve was letting him have it again, jerking him to its tune. Tap-tap, tap-tap, on the side of his head. His personal Morse code but it had few words. He allowed his eyes to flit to the window for a moment. The sky outside was a serene soft blue. It matched Agani's furnishings. Everything was toned down here, soft pastels, polished boards, and an oversized white leather suite. Lena would have approved. It looked like a woman lived here, though Agani's red, patterned dressing gown was effeminate enough.

'A deal?' Mark said, trying to tone down his voice and sound like a man in control.

'We are men of the world, you and I,' Agani said. 'What happened to the girl was unfortunate, but we can't allow our own to steal from us. There was no need for it to go as far as it did, and I have said that, but some of our people have too much of the old ways in them. They are not civilised, like us. They thought she'd swallowed the gems and should have waited. But waiting is hard to do for Stellachi.'

Stellachi was a new name, but Mark did not react. He wanted to ask questions, but he knew Agani would just spin him a line, until he dropped his guard. He was seeing the horror again, the smell of that morning was still in his nostrils.

'Mark,' Agani said softly, 'stay with me now. Keep it

together. I can set you up for life. Angelo tells me you are good, there's always room in the organisation for someone like you. You know this country.'

Mark shouted, at least he thought it was a shout, but he wasn't sure what came out of his mouth, but it turned into a kind of low-throated scream that shook Agani. His mask dropped for a moment. Mark's body knew what it was going to do, even if his brain didn't agree. He fought to control the gun in his hand, but it had a life of its own. It stayed cold in his grasp, fighting against his sweating hands, alive, and wanting action. Agani got up from his chair and waved a calming hand. Their eyes met for a long second as Mark pulled the trigger. The gun reared in his hand and the round took the top of Agani's head away. His skull detached at his hairline and what was inside sprayed itself on the wall behind him. Red and grey on white. Agani stayed upright for a few seconds, his body shaking out its life, like a decapitated chicken in an Albanian farmyard. He was dead before he hit the floor, and looked small and ridiculous, as he curled up in his gown on the hardwood floor. Ridiculous and very bloody. The big man wanted to get at Mark but Angelo restrained him. Maybe this saved their lives. The discharge of the gun had been thunderous but now the room was very quiet. A crazy calm in the aftermath of a killing. Mark too was still. For a few precious seconds he felt a tremendous peace, so tangible he thought he could wrap it around him, and let it take all this away. Bring Lena back. He wanted to close his eyes, which would be the end of him. Maybe he wanted that too, but not yet.

Angelo was shaking his head, but there was no panic in his voice.

'Wrong move, my friend,' Angelo said. 'What are you going to do now? Shoot all of us? What then?'

These men were not that shaken. The brain of their boss was a new wall decoration but, like Agani, they were not pleading wrecks. They'd dealt with death many times before, and had been close to their own before. Maybe so much so that their own mortality had become blurred, and fear muted. One of them might have cut up Lena, maybe the other holding her as she fought and writhed in agony, holding her until she passed out, until she died. They had chosen to kill because they were in a hurry. Simple as that. A matter of fact. A matter of business. Lena might have just as well been a plant, and they hadn't given a rat's toss about him or the police. They weren't worried at all.

Again Mark fought to keep the gun steady. He'd felt it jump in his hand once, and it wanted to again. How did it go? Guns were just tools, that it was people who killed? What bollocks. Guns killed. They controlled, seduced and conspired with anger, pain, the need for revenge. They tapped into weakness, rage, plain meanness, the inadequacies of challenged people. The inadequacies of strong people. The gun in his hand told him he should finish the job. Three not one. It made more sense. These two were the butchers, whoever Stellachi was. He'd killed the organ grinder, not the monkeys on the ground. Angelo was looking at him calmly, weighing up his own chances of survival.

'You are wrong,' Angelo said.

'What?'

'You think we killed the girl. We didn't. Agani told you the truth. It was a man called Stellachi. A Romanian, from Bucharest. Agani used him for stuff like that. Tony drove him over to the flat and waited outside. I give you the name because it will do you no good. Whether you kill us now or not you will be dead yourself soon. Run, hide, keep fighting, it's no matter. It's just a matter of time. Agani was only big here, there are others much bigger and they will never let this go.'

'Who the fuck do you think you are? You talk like you are supreme fucking beings, but you're just animals.'

77

Angelo shrugged.

'We are different,' he continued, 'we come from a different world, one where life is cheap. Very cheap. You can understand this. You also come from the outside. I know this, that's why you pulled the trigger. You had to, but what happened with the woman was business. It was nothing personal.'

'Bullshit. You talk like some idiot in a film. I could phone the police right now. Get them up here. What have I got to lose?'

Angelo's third shrug almost got him a bullet.

'But you won't. They can't help you, and you will be the only one in jail. You'll have a lifetime to think about your mistake. Lena doesn't exist any more. The only killing they can prove is the one on the floor here. Men like us don't need police.'

The big man said something to Angelo. They were more confident now that Mark would not fire again.

'Agani is not worth being locked up for,' Angelo said, with sudden vehemence. 'He slept with boys.'

He turned to the other and muttered a few words, and the big man smiled and answered. By Christ, Mark thought, these men have ice in their veins. Agani might as well be a piece of meat. Blood from his head was seeping into the floorboards, and slowly making its way towards the white rug that matched the leather suite. Like a dark red sea on the move.

'Stellachi is in Amsterdam,' Angelo said, 'most of us are there. It is a good base.'

'Why should I believe any of this?'

'Because this information will not help you.'

Amsterdam. One of the few places abroad Mark knew. No wonder Lena had gone there so often. Yes, these boys would be active there, burrowing like bugs in the red light shit, controlling drugs, the sprawl of suck-and-fuck clubs and the women who worked in them, encouraging the flow of money from the pockets of the curious, stupid and lonely to their own. Lords of a thousand scams.

'Better to go down fighting, for men like us,' Angelo said softly. 'Kill us now or try to kill us another time, it doesn't much matter, does it?'

'What about the deal?'

Angelo laughed.

'The deal? That was just words. Agani was talking to stay alive. He'd have killed you the first chance he got. Unless, of course …'

'Unless what?'

'Unless *you* had our goods. There were twelve, in a small black leather bag. The one Lena always used. Have you ever held stones like them? No, of course you haven't. Each one cut by a master. They seem to hold all the light of the world, and it sparkles just for you. People have always thought them worth dying for, but we know you don't have them, just as Stellachi knew Lena would never have hidden them in the flat. That would be as stupid as saying she'd lost them. No, his guess that they were inside her was a good one, but wrong. We underestimated Lena, like we underestimated you. We searched the flat afterwards, but you wouldn't know it, eh? We found nothing, but then we didn't expect to. Lena was foolish, not stupid. The diamonds are somewhere else.'

'Why did you kill Tony?'

'That you are here is the answer. I thought I'd got you also. That was my mistake. Who knows, maybe my future is the same as yours now. Our people will not like Agani dead.'

'Where did you take Lena?'

Angelo sighed. 'Does it matter, my friend? Does it really matter? You saw her, you know her fate. In my country we say the body is just a shell that the soul leaves. I envy her.'

Mark re-aimed the gun and Angelo closed his eyes momentarily.

'One thing I will tell you, Stellachi would have put her out before he looked for our goods. Not because he has mercy, Stellachi has none, but it is professional, no? Easier. That man works alone, always, and he would not want her fighting him. Only fools and amateurs do things the hard way. Lena would not have known what was going to happen to her. I doubt if she knew he was in the flat before his hand was over her face. Only Stellachi got it wrong. She hadn't swallowed them. Believe me if you want, or not. If you have the diamonds, or can find them, maybe we can do a deal. It's not up to me.'

'I still want to know what you've done with her,' Mark shouted, 'and don't shit me. Your brains will join Agani's if you do. I swear it.'

'In the sea,' Angelo said.

'What?'

'She's in the sea, or at the bottom of it. She swims with the fishes, no? Somewhere off Dungeness. It was how Agani wanted it. Stellachi left, and Agani sent us in. He always used us for stuff like that, cleaning up, fixing someone else's mess. But you got there first. Look, isn't this way better for everyone? If the police found a body you wouldn't be here now. You'd be in the frame, we could have easily done it like that, but it's not our way. As I said, the body is just a shell.'

Angelo was talking hard for his life as Mark fired again. *Men like us*, Angelo said. But he wasn't like them, even in his bleakest moments Mark could never be like these ghouls. Not even now. Let them think he was though, it might give him an edge.

This time he jerked the gun up at the last fraction of a second and the round ploughed into the wall. Once more the sound was monstrous. It made the nerve leap, and increase its grip on his head, but this time he hadn't obeyed it. He was looking beyond Angelo at Lena, at her lustrous, healthy face, and he felt an echo of the way he'd felt each time she came back from a trip. Protective, glad she was back, glad she was *home,* that word he'd dared to begin to use. He wanted to kill Stellachi but these men should also die. Something sweeter than the bitter iron taste of fear was salivating on his tongue, a taste that meant retribution, and a sudden end to the pain, if only for minutes. His mouth was no longer dry, and the nerve told him to finish it. *Go on, pull the trigger, get this over.* But he'd had enough. Every sense Mark possessed had been through the shredder in the last three days and he managed to stay his hand. He was allowing these two to fight another day, to maybe kill him another day. So be it. He had to get out, get away and weigh everything up. Stay alive.

'Lie on the floor,' Mark shouted, 'gut down, hands stretched out. Do it.'

The big man had a lot of gut to stretch out but he still looked dangerous so Mark kicked him heavily in the head as he got down. It did not seem to affect him much but it kept him still. He'd put his mark on both of them now. He searched for weapons with his left hand, but only Angelo was carrying – a 9mm automatic Mark didn't recognise. It became a new addition to his arsenal.

Mark took a last look at the hell he'd created. Agani was in a foetus-like position, his dark eyes were almost black now, fixed on the sky beyond the window, but seeing nothing. He looked like he wanted to go back to the womb from which life had ripped him. Agani might have been born in the crumbling back streets of a town, or maybe out in the sticks, another unwanted mouth to feed, one of a family too poor to do anything other than survive. Now it had ended on the floor of a million-pound penthouse in another world. Every foul act the man had committed to get here had finally cost.

'See you soon,' Angelo murmured, sure of his life.

Mark knelt by his head and Angelo was not so sure. Mark was breathing heavily now, his hay fever kicking in with the nerve, the bastards working in tandem.

'Stellachi,' Mark said, 'what does he look like?'

'You'll find out soon enough.'

Mark pressed the gun against his neck like he had with Tony. Angelo nodded his head towards Agani's desk.

'He's there, with Agani, in Rome. They share the same tastes.'

Carefully, Mark got up and went to the gold-framed photo. Agani was standing in St. Peter's Square with another man, amongst the pigeons and the families.

'He has blond hair now,' Angelo muttered, 'or at least he did have the other day. Stellachi does not stay the same for long.'

Mark fixed the man's face in his mind. It would be in there for ever. He was maybe six three, finely muscle-toned, no excess weight whatsoever, a lean, hard, face, tanned and high-cheekboned, with cropped hair. Stellachi had dead eyes. His eyes looked like Agani's did now. This man was another ghoul who was dead but didn't know it. The smile on the man's face was a lie and Mark felt he knew Stellachi already. Stellachi's eyes hated, he hated the world and the people in it, and would pay it back, for as long as he could, pay it back for being born. Mark had a small piece of this in himself, and thanked God it was one small piece.

He could see no way of locking the two men in so he just turned and ran. They were not the type who could get up that easily, let alone move quickly, and he was the man with the guns. He didn't trust the lift so he took the stairs, two at a time, almost crashing into each turn in the staircase, his nose streaming, eyes watering and head thumping. Not very heroic at all. If they came down in the lift and were waiting

82

for him at the bottom, it would all end quickly.

They weren't. There was no one around. He was out on the street, with barely time to conceal the weapons before he ran. It's hard to run and not look conspicuous but he tried it anyway, without glancing back. The air-conditioning of the penthouse was quickly blown away by the heat, and his clothes began to stick to him again. He could go back to the flat, wait for Stellachi to come to him, but it was a place where his future had ended. Kelly's place was out so he didn't know where the fuck to go. Three people had died, he was a killer on the run and he wasn't even sure what day it was any more. Maybe Saturday. The last few days had been a lifetime. He'd killed a man, but it seemed outside of him, a necessary action on his road to retribution. Even so, he was not a natural, and Mark knew he never would be.

A black cab was passing and Mark instinctively struck out a hand. It was empty and it stopped. Mark told the driver to take him to Kelly's pub, it was all he could think of, and sank into the back seat. The guns felt heavy, one in the jacket, the 9mm in his waistband.

Mark knew Dungeness a little, a job had taken him there once. A strange, flat, windswept place, with lots of sky and light, existing in its own space, as if it belonged to another time. Wooden chalets everywhere, holiday homes for the odd, but a power station as well, the old and the new bumping up against each other. He'd been watching some actor guy, a dick who'd made the job easy, and had thought that Lena would like it there. Maybe they could take a spin down and he'd show her around. Well, she was there for good now. With the fishes, as Angelo said. Feeding them. She'd never surface. Those bastards would have made sure of that.

Mark wasn't sure if he was talking to himself. He caught the glance of the driver as the man checked him over. For a moment he thought this might not even be a taxi and felt for the automatic. The nerve was stretching him to breaking point, he was jumping at shadows, but no, the guy was thinking nothing at all, except maybe if Mark was a good tipper. They hit traffic. It would take more than a few minutes to get to the pub. Mark stretched out and tried to control his breathing. There were specks of blood on his shoes, like dark freckles. Man-made uppers with man-made blood.

Chapter Seven

Angelo talked about souls. Something Mark hadn't thought much about since Shane disappeared because he didn't think he could afford to. What you were here for, where you came from, if you went anywhere when it was over, such thoughts had rattled around his head once, but he'd crushed them out, because there could never be any answers, not for him. His mother Julie had startled him a few months after Shane's disappearance, by banging on about religion, she went from saying there couldn't be a God, not after Shane, to talking about how the good were taken young. He'd worried about her, about the way her head was going, but then she stopped mentioning it. At least to him. As far as he could tell, God-squadders seemed to be making up for some loss, something that had been taken from them or that they didn't have in the first place. Lonely people, crazy people, people looking to fill an emptiness. People like Julie.

Lena had always worn a small silver cross, only taking it off when photo shoots demanded it, but they hadn't talked about it much. She told him once she wanted to believe in an afterlife that would be better, a heaven, but shared his cynicism. That was when he thought he knew her, knew who she was, and thought that they had a long future stretching before them.

'Nine-fifty, mate.'

They were outside the pub. In this condition Stellachi could pick him off without ruffling his bottle-blond hair.

'I said that's nine-fifty,' the driver said.

He probably thinks I'm an afternoon drunk, Mark thought. A moneyman on a liquid lunch. He gave the guy a ten and went into the Queen's Head. Kelly was coming out of the toilet and walked straight into Mark.

'Mr Richards. I wondered where you got to. There was an accident outside your place. Hit and run. I was comin' out the bookies down the street, and seen the crowd. If you don' know wha's happened I got some bad news for you.'

Mark let him tell it. About his shock at seeing it was Tony. About how sorry he was, and how awful it must be for Lena. Then Mark told him he already knew. They sat down at the usual corner table and Kelly got some drinks. While Kelly got served Mark rubbed his shoes along the side of a chair but the freckles wouldn't go away. They needed to be washed off. Kelly returned, and downed half his Guinness in one draught.

'I'm glad you know about it, Mr Richards. I knocked the flat, got no answer. Does your woman know?'

'Yes. The police got in touch with her. With us. She's gone away, to be with the family.'

'Oh, that's good. You ain't going, like?'

'I got things to do.'

Mark wished he hadn't said *us*. The word sounded so lost now. Kelly stared at Mark over the top of the glass.

'Wha's going on, Mr Richards?'

'Hmm?'

'You're miles away. First you wanted that car, then I had to go into the flat for Christ knows why and now Lena's brother is not long dead. You in deep shit or somein'?'

Deep shit is right, Mark thought. And I've just sunk further into it.

'You're asking questions again,' Mark said.

'I know, but, well, I don' wanna be dragged into nothing messy. Been on my mind all weekend.'

So it *was* the weekend.

'Spent all that money yet?'

'No, not yet. Look, I'm grateful for that, like, you always

been good to me, but I can' handle nothing heavy mind.'

Mark smiled at the thought, and was amazed that he could. And it was a smile, even if it had to force itself onto his lips, not like that cold slit he'd seen on Stellachi's face.

'An' there was something going on outside my place too,' Kelly continued. Charlie McKee told me earlier. Blokes fighting, he said. Hard-looking bastards. Said one of them looked like you, but he couldn't be sure.'

'Best to be sure,' Mark murmured. 'Relax, Kelly, there's nothing for you to worry about. I'll be going away soon.'

'What, for good, like?'

'Maybe.'

Kelly was relieved but also disappointed. Mark had been a major source of beer money in the last two years, and maybe the closest thing on the street Kelly had for a friend. The Irishman took out his tobacco tin and shakily managed to make a roll-up. Like the tin this man was a relic of another age, Mark thought. Like the old men who'd littered the valley when he was a kid. Bench-ridden, or standing on the steps of their front doors, all smoking the same hand-made fags, trying to relieve the tedium of retirement without money. Chests wheezing, coughing up the phlegm of their working lives, their eyes always on the lookout for someone else's action, something they could tie into and share, if only for a minute of two. Wistful watchers of the young. Other kids on the estate had always derided them, and worse, but Mark often stopped to talk, even on the way back from a job. They had no edge, no rivalry, ten minutes chat with the aged was like taking a warm bath. A tiny slice of security in his mean life.

'How old are you, Kelly?'

'Uh?'

'How old?'

'Oh, I dunno, 'bout fifty-four, five, I reckon.'

He looked at least ten years older. Mark had never given

Kelly's life any thought, past or present, but now he wondered. He knew so little about anyone apart from Julie.

How did it feel now that he was a killer? Not much different, but when he pulled the trigger to blow Agani away he did feel another emotion, not fear, guilt, or remorse – he'd long since conquered them – but a king size stab of fucking desolation that told him that this was the extreme act of a man on his own. Someone who no longer had anything to lose. Something akin to self pity welled up in him, and he had to crush it out quickly, kill it with more action, or it would paralyse him.

'What was it like, where you came from, originally?' Mark asked.

Kelly was pleased with the attention, but also suspicious. No one asked him questions like this.

'Donegal. Nice place, if you like space and not many people, and if you're not piss-poor, like. My lot were. Most of them got out in the old days, when the spuds rotted. I came over when I was a kid, working on the motorways. Loads of us done it. Lived in caravans, followed the work. Lived like gypsies we did. That's when the drink really started. I had the money, see, and there was not much else to do. Not when you looked like me, anyway.'

'Haven't you ever gone back? Gone home?'

'Nah. Been too long now. 'Sides, there's nothing for me there. The Kellys are strung out all over. I'm not in touch.'

'Would you say your life's been normal?'

It was Kelly's turn to smile. He gulped the rest of his beer quickly and rubbed the back of his hand over his face.

'There ain't no normal life, Mr Richards. Ain't you worked that one out? There's just life. Look, what's wrong, Mr Richards? You've never talked to me like this before.'

'Make me a fag.'

'You what?'

'A roll -up.'

Kelly's hands were trembling even more than usual. Mark knew he was making him nervous. Kelly was more used to caustic abuse, he could cope with that, it established his place in the world. He thought he was being set up for something, that Mark was drawing him into something dangerous. Maybe I am, Mark thought, just by being with him, but he needed the company, someone to hang onto while he came to terms with what had happened in the last few hours. And in the last few minutes he'd seen something different in Kelly, the hopeless derelict was still there, the life waster, but he sensed a spark of something else. Maybe even intelligence. Lots of stuff lay hidden under Kelly's rancid surface, Mark could see that now. Finding your woman slaughtered and blowing someone away did wonders for perception.

Mark drew on the smoke. It was like coming back to an old friend. He sucked it in like a kid experimenting, letting it fill his lungs, sear his chest, and make his eyes water. His body recognised the old habit but did not welcome it. It was all he could do not to splutter out a cough. Not very impressive for a hardened killer. All the old habits were coming back. His time in London was being blown away fast. Perhaps Lena was a dream, his steady life here a dream, his new found non-violence and lack of vices just a thin veneer on the skin of the real man. The one inside who was talking to him now. *Psycho Eyes*. He took another drag and drew out a speck of tobacco onto his tongue and this time he didn't splutter. The nerve liked it. It had another thing to work on and tapped out its approval. Kelly was still smiling.

'Not used to it no more, Mr Richards?'

'Can I come back to your place?' Mark asked.

'What, now like? Wa' for?'

'I need to get some rest. Don't want to go back to the flat.'

'This accident's really got to you, haven't it? I didn't

89

realise you was so close to the guy.'

Mark shrugged. He put a twenty into Kelly's moving hand.

'Give me your key and you stay here. Have a few more drinks.'

Kelly did what he was told.

Mark leant over Kelly as he got up.

'There might be people asking for me, but you know how to keep your mouth shut.'

Kelly's mood changed instantly, and he became a weasel again.

'What, the old bill?'

'I doubt it. No, you'll know these if you see them.'

'You can count on me, Mr Richards.'

Mark doubted that he could, not if Kelly really knew what was going on. He walked out of the dense atmosphere of the pub into a similar one in the street. The dregs of a long day were settling into the last of the heat. Cities at this time always felt coated with dust, and the collective tiredness of a few million souls. He knew he should be more vigilant, they knew about Kelly, they knew about the flat, but there was nothing he could do about it. He was too fucking tired and at least he'd taken them by surprise. Angelo had to report back to Amsterdam, that would be tricky, telling them their boss had been blown away in front of their eyes, by someone they had never heard of. At least they'd take him seriously from now on.

Kelly's bed-sit stank, of him mainly, body odours laced with old booze, old tobacco, unwashed clothes, a going-nowhere-never-been-anywhere kind of smell that rang bells for Mark. He pushed the door to the shower room open; the place wasn't big enough for a bath. The toilet was right next to it. He thought of trying to freshen up but thought again when he saw the lank shower curtain and the once white wall tiles, now multi-coloured with assorted stains. There was a cheap metal cross over the washbasin, rusting at its edges, and a cracked mirror seamed with dirt.

Mark sat down on the same chair he'd used before, looked out through the same jammed window and saw the same nothing in the street. They were probably cleaning the penthouse now. Putting Agani into something that would pass as a body bag. No one would have heard the gunshots, places that pricey had good soundproofing and incurious neighbours. It might be Dungeness for Agani too, sinking down to the bottom in his girlie gown. He might lie close to Lena, Mark hated the thought of that, but there was a kind of justice in it.

Mark was asleep in minutes, thinking of lost baby brothers, thinking of Lena that first time they met, when he went back to his grotty flat like an excited kid.

'Wake up, Mr Richards.'

Something was tugging at his shoulder. Mark pushed himself up quickly, catching Kelly by the throat and smashing him against the wall.

'Mr Richards, for fucksake! It's me, Kelly.'

For a moment Mark didn't know where he was. He could have been back in the valley, being woken up after a drinking session by Daniels, the one snotty mate he'd had back on the estate. Mark's face was inches from Kelly's and he saw the terror in the man's eyes. Kelly carried around the smells of the bed-sit with him, only more concentrated. They didn't mix well with Mark's pounding head. He slackened his grip, then released him, smoothing down his winter overcoat as an afterthought, which frightened Kelly even more.

'Jesus Christ,' Kelly said, 'jumpy or what? You frightened the crap outta me. Like I said down the pub, you're not right, Mr Richards. Not right at all.'

'What's the time?'

''Bout half 'leven. You been asleep all this time?'

'Must have been.'

If Angelo had come for him it would have been like killing a baby. Maybe this was what he wanted, maybe he didn't care any more.

It was raining heavily. A summer storm had emptied the street as Mark watched water make rivulets in the gutters, washing down assorted crap to the drains, where most of it gathered in pyramids of paper and plastic. A couple of kids hurried past, the boy trying vainly to protect his girl against the sudden rain. He had his arm around her and a hand raised against the sky.

'Why don't you go home Mr Richards? You don' wanna be staying in a dump like mine, specially at a time like this. If you take my advice you'd go and find that woman of ...'

Mark stopped him with a raised hand. Kelly lurched away from him as sharply as he could manage.

'Don't worry, Kelly, you're not going to get a slap. I'm not a monster, you know. I just don't want to hear that right now.'

Kelly looked unconvinced and Mark was lying anyway. What he really wanted was to tell Kelly everything. He wanted to badly. It was crazy, but the need to unload was great. The confession thing that Lena had talked about. He understood it a little now.

'Was anyone sniffing round for me,' Mark asked, 'in the pub?'

'Nah, just the usual Saturday night traffic.'

Mark made a decision. He'd go back to Wales for a few days. Try to take stock, get his head into some sort of shape. Let them come for him there, if they wanted. Despite his years away he still knew it better than anywhere else, and it might give him an edge.

'Can I stay here the rest of the night, Kelly? I'll be off first thing.'

Kelly scratched his head.

'Yeah, all right, I s'pose. You *are* in some kind of bother, ain't you?'

'Aye, some kind.'

'You're not gonna bring nothing down on me?'

'It's nothing for you to worry about.'

No, you're just harbouring someone who's involved in a murder feud with the Albanian mafia. Nothing to worry about at all, Kelly.

As long as Mark was gone early there wouldn't be any comeback for Kelly – he wasn't worth anyone bothering about, let alone killing. After Agani they would have to be careful. The sea off Dungeness might get crowded.

'I'll crash out then,' Kelly said. 'Had a few drinks, like.'

Kelly took off his heavy coat, letting free another wave of smells. He had a thin, multi-coloured sweater on, and it was threatening to come apart. Kelly slumped down onto his bed, without removing anything else, for which Mark was thankful. He was asleep in seconds and snoring shortly afterwards. Kelly looked like a baby wrapped in tatty clothes but for one crazy moment Mark envied him. His own rest came in small bursts, dropping into sleep for ten or fifteen minutes, then waking with a start and instantly checking the street, which was invariably deserted. He heard a siren one time, but it wasn't close, it was someone else's drama. As he watched the street lights make orange patterns on the wet tarmac he knew the hopelessness of his position. The need for revenge still burned strongly in him, and he would try to kill Stellachi if he could, but what then?

Mark dozed again and when he woke this time the glow outside was not so strong, as the sky lightened, and dawn was half an hour away. Grey streaks were already seeping into the edge of the sky, and the rain had stopped.

Making sure that Kelly was still dead to the world Mark checked his guns. Two empty chambers in the Smith and Wesson, a full magazine in the 9mm. Thinking of his mother and all that he had surrounded her with in the past, he knew it wasn't a good idea to go down there. Yet he felt the need to see her, to reunite for maybe the last time the remnants of the Richards family. He was surprised how strongly he felt this.

Mark put both weapons into his holdall, stepped quietly past Kelly and went into his shower room where he dashed some water in his face. He didn't use Kelly's towel. Stubble was sprouting up everywhere but he couldn't be bothered to shave. He began to wake up and wanted to clean his teeth but he'd forgotten to pack any toothpaste. No point looking for any in Kelly's fetid empire. So he just pushed a wet brush around a few times. It was better than nothing. He needed to put every sense on full alert now, or he'd be out of this game very quickly. Surprise had been on his side, but it was gone now.

Mark checked his money. What he'd paid out to Kelly had already made a hole in it. There was some in the bank and he had a credit card he rarely used. That had always been Lena's territory. He'd never even taken money from bank machines, there was too much native distrust for leaving a trail in him.

Kelly was catching flies, his open mouth revealing graveyard teeth in various shades of brown, and a tongue that was like a small pink snake moving amongst them. He'd probably wake up mid-morning, and get up midday. First thought would be a drink and a smoke, first action would be a drink and a smoke, and the same day would start up again. It had started up again for the last twenty years of this man's life. Mark put another twenty under the Irishman's chin and let himself out.

It had freshened up outside, mugginess had been replaced by a cooling breeze and the sun was getting up, early morning yellow bright, but not yet too hot. Like Kelly, this time of day had been almost unknown to Mark when he was growing up, but he'd come to like it. Even if fresh starts had usually been lying bastards for him, he was not so far gone he couldn't appreciate a sense of renewal. It was good to know that losing Lena, and killing Agani, had not taken this away completely. Even here, in the midst of eight million souls, he could think this, though Mark also knew this time of day was also a sham, for it hid all the punters, their mess, frustrations and rage. Nature had given the street a wash and brush up before people could get at it again.

Mark went out the back of Kelly's place, where he could cut across several blocks for the next tube station. He took the first train that came in, and crossed the city to Paddington, where a just-on-duty and already pissed-off man sold him a ticket for Cardiff. One way.

He had almost an hour to wait. It was Sunday. If anyone was watching him he wasn't aware of it. He hadn't been to Paddington for a while. A lot of money had been spent on it. New metal was everywhere, the station's guts had been replaced with aluminium structures, industrial style, he thought it was called, in an attempt to rid it of its old grimy look, though the roof was still the same. There was a sushi bar, not yet open, which made him think how times were changing. Times changed but not people. There were the usual weekend lost around, dossers, drunkards, people who had no reason to be here other than to shelter, and kill time.

Mark bought coffee and a roll, and a Sunday paper, the type that splashed tits and rubbish on its front. Lena would have been splashed here also if she'd been found. He imagined her cover shot, one of the best the agency could provide, good enough to interest the most jaded palette, men would eagerly turn to the additional pages inside, which would attempt to spin out her mysterious life in a few paragraphs. Shock, horror, and sex for wankers.

Mark sat in a corner that gave him the widest viewpoint while protecting his back. Gunslinger mentality. He thought about his killing of Agani. In his wild years he'd often thought what it would be like to take a life, and what it would do to the inside of his head. The answer was very little. There was just a sense of calm, of the inevitability of his action, even that it had been a natural thing to do. For Lena. He still couldn't control himself, not when pushed past a certain point. He'd worked on his anger since being banged up, and when Lena came along he'd thought he'd got the better of it, but background will out. Mark knew it now, and was glad, for background would be needed. These bastards had killed Lena and made him a murderer. Nice work for one weekend, but they'd already paid a price. What did he have to lose now, maybe all his life he'd been heading towards this point.

Mark was jerked out of his thoughts. Kelly was approaching him, at least he thought it was Kelly, for a moment. No, just a look-alike. Another man who'd lived inside a bottle for years. Same wasted face, same stink of old booze, same shuffling gait. Running on empty.

'Got a bit of change, mate?' the man asked.

Mark looked at him suspiciously and checked everything in his vision.

'Just for a cuppa tea, like.'

Mark felt for change and threw a pound coin towards him. His other hand was in his holdall, closing on the automatic. The man made a seal-like attempt to catch the pound, flailing his hands uselessly, but managed to put his foot on it to stop it rolling away. He had rivals in the station. Mark expected them to gather round him like pigeons as his train was announced.

'Cheers, guv.'

Mark made his way towards the train. He wondered if he would ever see Kelly again. Suddenly there was a sense of loss. It would have been laughable a few days ago, but Lena had changed everything.

Mark looked through the paper. It was full of sex and death, he wondered if there was anything else in the world. It told of tragic, violent and hopeless lives, but Lena's wasn't there, nor Agani's. He wondered how many others went unreported. All the underground tales of hoodlums buried in motorway concrete, in the sea, in the ground, seemed relevant now. This weekend told him it must be true. The country must be laced with its illicit dead.

Mark got on the train. There was no one sitting within ten seats of him. A few kids were down the other end, a woman with a baby, but that was it. Not many people wanted to head west this early today. He thought it safe to sleep, and did so fitfully, but alert to any movement or stop of the train, catching the odd patch of country in the corner of his eye. He wouldn't stay with his mother for more than a few hours, it was too dangerous. With the network these people had, Julie might already be in danger anyway. Blowing Agani away had seen to that. The more Mark thought of this, of the problems of protecting her, of even telling her about this mess, the more the nerve tapped. He was about to bring down another incredible load of shit on her, no more his fault than the last, but it still flowed through him. The nerve flexed against the side of his head, he rubbed along it with his hand and it felt like a skipping rope. The pain it caused followed the rhythm of the train, flexing every few seconds. The baby of the woman a few seats down started to cry, as if in sympathy. The mother tried to comfort it but it was determined to wail. I know how you feel, kid, Mark thought.

*

It was always hard for Kelly to come back to the land of the living. Each morning, or afternoon, his body found it more of a struggle. It knew that it didn't make sense any more, for living had become a grey line he crawled along, like a slug. Nothing too sharp, nothing too dull. Nothing too kind, nothing too human. Often nothing at all. Sometimes he wished life would let him go, before his organs packed up and a lifetime's abuse started to really punish. At his lowest ebb he thought of doing it himself but still had too much of the old faith in him, and too much cowardice. He hadn't been truly sober for twenty-five years but in rare moments of lucidity it amazed him how much his body had taken, and how tough his bony frame was. He was quite proud of his record in a way. Whenever he saw something in the papers about famous drunks he always related to them, feeling a kind of solidarity. When he could keep out the black dog of his depression Kelly became quite comfortable with his state, and shame and guilt vanished. Sometimes, when he came round, he'd think he was back in Donegal, under the big sky, where life was green and fresh, even hopeful, as he dreamed of crossing the water and making his fortune in the building trade. Coming home to buy a pub, his own watering hole, his badge of success in the community. *Kelly's Place.* Maybe even meeting a girl. These half-sleep, half-waking thoughts of Donegal brought on a calm within. They made him feel like another drink.

Kelly was going through this routine, thinking that it was Sunday and that every day was Sunday for him, when Angelo appeared over him. One moment Kelly was blinking in the clear light of his homeland, next it was being blocked out and he was yanked up by a powerful hand.

'Jesus and Mary, what's goin' on?'

'You are Kelly. You know Mark Richards. Where is he now?'

Kelly instantly felt sick. Bile tasted of sour whisky as it rose from his gut and fear ran all over him like ants as his eyes focused on the big man leaning against the door. This one spat on his hands and smiled. Angelo pulled him from the bed and pushed him down on the chair. *Play for time and act stupid.* It had been his one defence in times like this, and there had been a few dangerous moments on the street over the years. Fuck it, he knew getting Mr Richards that car would mean trouble. Something hadn't been right all weekend, but these guys weren't the police. Never in a million years.

Angelo slapped him across the face, his hand hardly moved but it was enough to jerk his head back and make it reel. He felt like he'd been kicked by a horse, and a rotten tooth crumbled.

'I can't hear you, my friend,' Angelo said, his voice barely above the level of a whisper.

'Richards?' Kelly answered, wiping the blood from his face with the back of his hand. Angelo had caught his nose, making his eyes water, and two thin streams of blood run down his face.

'Kelly, Kelly, we are not going to be stupid, are we? You do things for him, we know. This weekend you done bigger things. Let him stay here. That's okay, I understand. He's your friend, eh? Friendship is good, no?'

Angelo nodded to the big man and turned Kelly's head towards him.

'He is *my* friend, but not nice like me. Not nice at all. He likes to hurt people, he'd like to hurt you right now.'

Angelo pressed close to Kelly. They were almost cheek to cheek.

'Think of the pain. You are a small man, a thin man. He'll break you up, piece by piece. He'll start here.'

Angelo held Kelly's scrawny arm in his hand, displaying it to the big man.

'Yes, I know, you are frightened. I would also be frightened of him.'

No you wouldn't, Kelly thought, you fucking wap bastard. You've never been frightened like I am now. He felt his bladder getting ready to empty and tried to stay as motionless as he could, but couldn't keep the shake out of his body. His eyes continued to water, and he kept muttering *oh Jesus*. Like a prayer.

'I'm gonna be sick,' he muttered.

Angelo stepped away from him for a moment. Kelly was in a bad situation. He really didn't know anything but they didn't want to hear this. If he made something up they might know it was bullshit. These bastards were pros, like Mr Richards. He hated the Welshman now, for getting him into this, and he didn't even know what the fuck *this* was. He couldn't think, there was a ringing in his ears and by Christ he needed a drink. There was a half bottle of cheap whisky on table and some still left in a glass from last night. Kelly looked at it as if it was the Holy Grail. If he was a lizard he could snake out a tongue, just to get a taste.

'Ah,' Angelo sighed, 'you'd like a drink, eh? Maybe later.'

Angelo beckoned to the big man, who spat on his hands and smiled. He stepped closer.

Mark woke as the train entered the Severn Tunnel. For a moment he thought it was night. He felt inside his holdall for the guns. His hand closed around the automatic, which fitted snugly into it, unlike the Smith and Wesson, which was not quite so well balanced. A good enough tool of destruction though, powerful, and to the point. He'd found that out in Agani's flat. There'd be no trace of Agani now. They'd have taken him for a quick trip down to the Kent coast in the boot of a car, probably his own, then a short boat ride and an insignificant splash. Sinking down, his money and power over in the pull of a trigger. Mark wished now that he'd shot him in both knees and left him alive, that would have been more lasting.

He scanned his face in the train's window. It was getting to be a habit. Did he look like a hunted man? Tick. A haunted man? Tick. A murderer? What did one of those look like? The smudges under his eyes were getting bigger, like dabs of dark blue face paint, and he could smell himself. He was in a great state to see his mother. That time with Lena had been his only trip back in five years. They hadn't even managed a Christmas. Doubt crept in. Maybe it was better not to go there, just take off for the hills. Buy a few supplies and let them come to him. They would come.

Mark still missed the open places a stone's throw from the house of his childhood. The hillsides were the closest things he had to security when growing up. They hid him, when things were tough, and were quiet and calm when he was boiling inside; they replaced people. If you are running, it was best to run in a land you knew. It would not be long before they were on his trail, but Angelo, Stellachi and anyone else they sent were city boys, they preferred concrete and cars. There was a flash of light as the train exited the tunnel. Wales, Mark thought, whatever that meant.

He slept again until the train pulled into Cardiff. Half-hour naps might be the norm from now on, but at least he was used to this. It had often been necessary on the agency jobs, watching people like a thief in the night, and cat-napping in between. Mark trod cautiously around the station, it wasn't possible anyone would be here yet, but thinking the impossible might keep him alive. All was quiet. Tail end of summer traffic and not much else. He got another coffee and a sandwich and was filling up with caffeine and bread. It was a pity it was a Sunday. He needed to buy stuff, hillside stuff, clothes, food, maybe a tent. What he was wearing would have to do.

Mark delayed going to his mother's place for a while. She'd always had the ability to see right into him and he wasn't quite ready. Two young coppers walked past. It was true about the shaving, Mark thought, and I'm now old enough to think it. They walked just feet away from the guns. For a moment he wanted them to ask what was in the holdall. It would be the spot check of their lives and his problems would be over for the next twenty years. Nah, he'd rather go out with his boots on rather than be banged up, that would be a slow death of thousands of weeks. He'd learnt that as a young offender. The policemen walked away from him without another glance and Mark exited the station. He went to the nearest taxi.

His mother was five miles away, on the edge of Cardiff, and the sea. Mark walked around a bit before he relocated her flat, one of a block of ten. It had a good view of the channel. Even on a sunny day it looked like grey sludge, but the sky was high and free. He ran a hand through his hair as he rang the bell and stood back with the most upbeat look he could conjure up. A man answered.

It was not what Mark had expected. It hadn't occurred to him that Julie would ever meet anyone again, but at least this chap was in a different class from his many runtish uncles of the old days. They eyed each other suspiciously. The guy was in his early fifties, about the same height as Mark and had kept himself fit. Mark saw the edge of a tattoo on his T-shirted right arm. Three feathers. Probably ex-army.

'We're not interested in religion,' the man said.

'I'm not selling God, mate. I'm Mark, Julie's ...'

'Good God, what are you doing here?'

Julie appeared, pushing the man to one side.

'Thought I'd come down.'

Julie gave him that age-old look that told him she knew everything, even if she didn't. There was more than a moment's silence.

'You better come in then. Why didn't you phone?'

'Wanted to surprise you.'

'Well, you done that. Oh, Carl, this is Mark, my son.'

Mark stuck out a reluctant hand and it was taken by one equally reluctant.

'How do,' Carl said.

'All right.'

'Give your mother a hug, then.'

They held each other briefly. He'd forgotten how light Julie was, like a young girl in his arms.

He knew his mother would be seething inside, he'd intruded on her new life, without any warning, and on a Sunday, which would mean something was up. He wondered how much Carl knew of the Richards past. Not much if Julie been sensible. She had a new life, so why not a new man. He'd hated the endless succession of hopeless wasters when he was a lad, none of them interested in him, and some too handy with their fists. Until he got too big. This Carl was nothing like any them, he looked more a doer than a taker. Perhaps he came with the new territory.

'How have you come down?' Julie asked.

'Train. I had a taxi here.'

'Just you?'

'Looks like.'

Carl didn't like this. He'd be the type to say don't talk to your mother like that, if Mark had been fifteen years younger.

'Do you want something to eat?' Julie said.

Now that the shock was wearing off, his mother was glad to see him. She fussed with her hair, and pushed him towards the sofa. They'd obviously been in bed when he'd knocked.

'Sit there, I'll get you a coffee to start.'

Great. He was turning into caffeine city. From the sofa Mark could see through the window to the coastline and the town that curved away from it. Terraced roofs were catching the sun and flashing the sea a silver salute. His mother had found a nice spot. Mark put the holdall between his feet and could feel the guns through the canvas.

'Sorry just to barge in like this,' Mark said, 'spur of the

moment type of thing.'

Whatever he'd planned to tell Julie was now knocked off course, but after the last few days, this came as no surprise. His whole life had been knocked off course.

Carl picked up a Sunday paper and pretended to ignore him but Mark knew he was watching him over the top of the paper, checking him out and wondering if his presence would change things. He got up and went into the kitchen. Carl thought of saying something but kept the paper in front of his face.

'Why didn't you tell me you were coming down?' Julie whispered, pushing the kitchen door shut.

'How long's this guy been around?'

'Not too long. You're not going to stick your oar in, are you?'

'No, why should I? We've moved on from stuff like that now, Mam – haven't we?'

'I bloody hope so. What's wrong, Mark?'

'What?'

'What's going on? I know something is. As soon as I saw you at the door.'

The thought of telling her, with her new bloke yards away, was not on. Carl had made up his mind for him.

'Nah, everything's cool. Just fancied a short break, that's all.'

'It's awkward now. Carl is stopping.'

'Oh, I didn't mean here. I thought I'd hire a car, have a drive around, that type of stuff.'

'There is something up. You've finished with that Lena, haven't you?'

'Nothing ever gets past you, Mam. Okay, yes, I have. Just the other day. It's over.'

'I never thought that was meant to be.'

'What, after seeing her just the once?'

Julie shrugged, 'Just a feeling. It's difficult when a

woman is that good-looking. Most men would be always looking over their shoulder.'

She was about to spoon sugar into his coffee.

'Don't take that no more. Just as it comes.'

'God, you *have* changed. Well, I'd like to say you're looking good but you look like you've been clubbing all weekend.'

In the past it was Julie who'd always looked like she'd been out on the tiles, though it was usually just life taking its toll on her face. Their long grind on little money and even less opportunity. Julie looked good today, better than Mark could ever remember. She must be close to fifty now but her face had lost some of its tiredness and her blue eyes had regained a little sparkle. Maybe she was dealing with Shane at last, maybe this Carl fella was good for her.

'Where did you meet him?' Mark jerked a thumb towards the door.

'In a pub in town a few months ago. I was going to tell you, next time you phoned. Carl's all right. He's a builder, got a small business. He's on his own now, like me, so I thought, why not? And no, he doesn't know nothing about the wonderful Richards family.'

'Well, you're looking good on it.'

'Thanks.'

'I don' think you'll ever do anything normal,' Julie muttered. 'You turn up, disappear, turn up again, like you always did. The Richards family is good at disappearances. It's okay, I'm not going to start. And I don' want Carl to know neither. It doesn't help, talking about it.'

'Good at disappearances, Mam, not very good at normal. That could be our family motto.'

'Aye, you got that right.'

'So, you met Carl in a pub, eh?'

'I thought I might try returning to the land of the living, 'specially now that I'm working. I went with some of the girls from the factory. They *were* girls too, I was old enough to be their mother.'

'Moved in a bit quick, hasn't he?'

'Ah, now that sounds like the old Mark. Carl's had a messy divorce and needed to get away from his old place for a while. Besides, I've decided life is all about speed. For people like us, anyway. I'll make you a breakfast. I got plenty of stuff in. Carl eats like you used to. Go back in the lounge, we shouldn't be whispering in here.'

Mark went in and stood by the window. The sky was taking on a deeper blue, with just a few clouds scudding away over the Somerset coast. Carl rustled his paper. He'll start to check me out any second, Mark thought, but maybe it's better that he's here. I can't tell Julie anything now.

'Living in London?' Carl said.

'Aye. For a few years now.'

'Like it?'

'It's all right. It's where the work is.'

'What work's that then?'

'Bits and pieces. Bit of investigation work, bodyguard stuff.'

'Well, you got the frame for it. I used to be pretty fit myself.'

It's all right, mate, you don't have to fight me for my mother. Mark might have said this out loud a few years back. Before Lena. It would always be before Lena and after Lena from now on. BL and AL.

Mark sat in the chair opposite Carl. He wanted to shut his eyes but Lena lay behind them. On that bloody bed, in the boot of the Lexus, dropping into the black sea. He knew what would be happening to her body now and detested the knowledge.

'You look done in, mate,' Carl said.

'Been doing a lot of work. That's why I'm down. To have a few days off.'

'Oh.'

Carl studied his paper again and they sat in silence until Julie called them into the kitchen and the small table there.

'Two breakfasts ready.'

Mark ate everything in front of him. It amazed him how he could. How instinct took over when the brain had been fried as well as the crispy bacon on his plate. He didn't want it to be Sunday. He wouldn't be able to get a car and couldn't stay here now. Perhaps it would be better to take a train up to the valleys and find a B & B, if there were any left up there.

'I got a good idea,' Julie said. 'Since you've turned up like this, why don't we all go for a run in Carl's car, get a spot of lunch.'

Both men glared at their plates.

'We could have a few drinks. You an' Carl can get to know each other.'

She nudged Carl in the ribs. 'You can't drink much, mind, you're driving. I'm going to have a shower and get ready.'

'You're ex-army, aren't you,' Mark said. He nodded at Carl's arm.

'Yip, career soldier me. Made sergeant.'

'Mam said you were a builder.'

'Went into it after. Done all right, too.'

He's been in Ireland, in the Falklands, he's the right age, Mark thought. Pity he was getting on a bit, he might have been useful if Angelo showed up. Christ, get a grip, Mark. What you thinking of, shooting it out with deputy Carl from your mother's flat, the last act of a proven madman.

'You working now?' Mark asked.

'Got a new job starting next week. Don't worry, I'm not sponging off Julie.'

Carl's face reddened as he said this, and he jabbed hard at his bacon.

Time rushed back twenty years, when Mark had hidden upstairs in their two-bedroomed shoebox of a house while some new uncle played tricks with Julie's head, trying to close his ears to the wild drunken shouting that cut through thin walls like a knife. Sometimes they played tricks with her body - *don' you dare hit me you bastard* - then that dull, vicious sound of blows that he could still hear in his mind. As Carl waited for his response Mark saw himself sticking his head under a pillow to deaden the noise, wanting to be older, a man who would come rushing downstairs to protect his mother, not a ten-year-old kid who sometimes ran out the back of the house in fear and desperation, over the busted fence and onto the hillside, where he'd hide out on a dark night. Coming back hours later to Julie's marked-up face.

'No problem. Didn't think you were,' Mark said.

'All right, then. I wouldn't want us to get off on the wrong foot. I like your mother, she's got a bit about her. I know she's had a hard life. She hasn't said much but I'm not stupid.'

'I wouldn't want her life to be hard any more,' Mark said quietly.

'Point taken. How'd you get so big, anyway? Julie's only a little dot.'

'Old man maybe.'

'No contact?'

'Person unknown.'

'We got that in common then. That's why I went in the army. As soon as I could. All my mates were into that sixties stuff, but I shaved my head and got into guns. It helped a bit because I used to get bloody frustrated 'bout everything. Would have got into trouble if I'd I hung around the estate.'

You're singing my song, mate, Mark thought. I did hang around, and made my own trouble. Strange that Julie should take up with someone not unlike himself. Or maybe not so strange.

'You two having a nice chat,' Julie said.

'Can I use the shower, Mam?' Mark asked. 'It was a bit of a rush, catching the first train down.'

'I can see that. I didn't like to say. You could do with a shave too.'

Mark took the holdall with him. He showered, then shaved, looking at the face of a murderer. He'd finally got there. It was the eyes that were different, they'd always been hard, inward-looking, brooking no interference, but there was another quality there now. He didn't have the words to explain it, but he knew that they had changed, even as he stared at himself they seemed to be looking elsewhere. Looking at too much knowledge. It had taken him a long time to learn not to think back too much, Lena had helped him with this, but now all that forward movement was lost. Lena, then Agani, had told him the truth about his life, and its past. Maybe her loss was an overdue punishment for losing Shane.

Mark started to think about Stellachi. The man's image was fixed in his mind now, and he wondered if Stellachi would be doing the same with him. His face in that Rome photograph was gaunt, the smile a joke, the eyes button-dead. There was no excess weight on him, his body would be bone hard, heart and brain the same, and he would have enjoyed his work with Lena. Why else do it? But it had got Agani killed, other people in the organisation wouldn't like that. Stellachi would be under pressure, as much as a man like that ever could be. Mark would be hunted down, and Stellachi would have others to call on besides Angelo and the big man. Let them come, Mark thought, as he shaved off the last of his dark bristles. Let them all come, for I'm also hunting them. He knew that, in the end, it would come down to him and Stellachi. A matter of need for each of them. Maybe Stellachi would have another look round the flat, he'd have lots of images to study. Mark was glad he'd taken the one of him and Lena.

'Have you gone to sleep in there?' Julie rapped on the door. 'Come on, the day's half over already.'

She was excited, Mark realised. This was the first time he'd been anywhere with her and another man. At the age of thirty. The thought of Carl as another *uncle* brought the hint of a smile to his lips, though his face was dark, tired, and set in determination. Tight lines stretched from his eyes, and he'd managed to cut his chin. Killers might already be on their way from London, and he was about to go for a trip with his mother and her boyfriend. To the seaside.

Julie led the way and Mark blinked in the sunlight. There were plenty of people about, and he tried to check everyone out without Julie noticing it. Carl glanced at him a few times. His car was parked at the back of the flats. It was an old Merc, a geriatric version of the one Tony had. It was even the same colour, if you looked closely through the dirt.

'Bought this off an hairdresser,' Carl said. 'It's like me, old, but goes well.'

'Plenty of room in it,' Julie said, 'where do you want to go, Mark? Carl don't mind, do you, Carl?'

You poor bastard, Carl, feet under the table with Julie, a nice Sunday, and I show up. And he knows something is going on. Something more than the end of a relationship. I'm looking around like he did on the streets of Belfast.

'Wherever,' Mark said.

'How about down to the Gower, we went there last weekend, didn' we, Carl? I'd never been before. Can you believe it?'

Course I can, Mam. We never went anywhere, remember. I didn't make one school trip. Being banged up in Portland was my first real trip, in the back of a police van, looking through the bars at my first close-up view of the sea.

Mark had glimpsed the sea from the tops of the local

hills, like some peasant from another time who never left the village. That grey sliver of channel that looked like molten lead in the sun had been part of his landscape, a vital but unknown part.

Julie was living a little, grabbing at a tiny slice of life that had mostly been denied her – and he was putting it in danger. This was one reason to be glad Carl was with her, that she might gain a little happiness was another. Mark told himself that Angelo and the others would not want any trouble here. Carl would make it awkward for them, and they had nothing to gain from it. He kept telling himself this.

As Mark sat in the back of the car like a kid, the image of Stellachi knocking on Julie's door was a powerful one. The bogeyman calling, if ever there was one. He ran his hand over the worn leather of the seat and let himself drift into an uneasy sleep. Before he shut his eyes he caught Julie's, looking at him in the vanity mirror, and, for once, they weren't full of questions, or pain.

She gave him a shy smile, and thought she had a family back.

Chapter Eight

For Mark, the day became increasingly dreamlike. As Julie became more attentive, and Carl quite friendly, Lena, Stellachi and death lay somewhere else, on another road that he'd left behind. His head tried to repair itself and in one brief moment of relaxation he saw how life might have been for the Richards, in another time, another place, and with Shane.

They drove down to the beaches of the Gower, Carl's old Merc smooth and reliable. Julie chatted away about not much, clearly relieved that there was no problem between her two men. This was another major change in her life. Mark thought she might have been glad that, in her eyes, he was single again. She'd been overawed that time he'd shown up with Lena. Her looks, accent, work, told Julie he was moving away big time, the estate just a bad memory from an increasingly distant past. Deep down, with all the crap cut away, he was still *her little Mark.*

They stopped near a virtually deserted beach, marked by cliffs divided into three rocky points. Julie had already been here with Carl. As they walked down from the nearest parking place she nudged Mark in the back.

'Never imagined places like this when you were little, eh?'

'Oh, I *imagined* them, Mam.'

As Carl walked on ahead Julie lowered her voice.

'You know I always wanted to take you on trips, but it was hard to get off that estate with no money, no car. And all the other stuff.'

'That's all in the past, Mam. We're okay now, aren't

we?'

'We could have been here with Shane,' she murmured, 'he'd be about starting Comp now.'

He expected her voice to break and tears to come but Julie remained calm. She'd grown a lot since he'd been in London. Mark sensed a confidence in her that had not been present before and Julie was going to need it.

'Do you ever think about Daniels?' Julie asked quietly.

Daniels' short life ended with his face in a bag of glue. Mark was just sixteen, and his friend's death had made sure his late teens were rough and wild. Or rougher and wilder. The passing of Daniels taught Mark that someone like him had to fight for everything in this world. Mark had never called Daniels by his first name, no one had, and he couldn't remember it now. He hadn't thought of him in years but would never forget that last image, Daniels' dead eyes the same colour of the sky above him as he sprawled in the dirt of their back lane. Lena's face joined Daniels', then Shane's, they swirled around in a vile mix and each one accused. Then he saw Stellachi knocking on Julie's door, introducing himself as Mark's friend, his hard face creased with that thin smile. Oozing charm and malice, as Julie invited him in.

'Mark?'

'No, not too much, Mam.'

'You all right? You're shaking a bit.'

'No problem. It's the shock of all this fresh air.'

Carl waited for them to catch up.

'Quite hot, innit? There's a pub up the top there if we walk over the beach and up the other side.'

'Okay, Carl, lead on,' Mark said.

Mark scanned the beach. It was too hard to get to for many people to be here. A few couples were dotted around, kids chased balls, a few dared the edge of the sea. He realised the headache had gone and the nerve had stopped throbbing.

They crossed a small river that fringed the beach, and fed into the sea, Carl helping Julie over a causeway of stepping stones.

Julie was enjoying the day, while Mark ran a few ideas for his survival through his head. He wouldn't hire a car, but he'd get up to the valley tomorrow on the train. First, he'd have to buy some gear. He wanted to be isolated, to find a place he knew well, where he could take stock of all that had happened, and which he could defend. He'd already taken the decision not to tell Julie anything. It was impossible to unload this now Carl was around, but he was taking a chance. A big one.

'Let's have Sunday lunch,' Julie said, 'my treat. I'm earning quite good money at that factory now, Mark, with my bonus an' all. The girls there are all right, too. They don't pry as much as the ones back home.'

'No, I'll pay,' Carl said,' since Mark came down special, like.'

Mark had waited thirty years for an *uncle* to offer him anything. It was strange to hear Julie refer to the estate as home. Life there had been a grind punctuated by short, illusory spells of hope, more like little stabs than spells, glimpses of lives others led, which he'd paid for with the proceeds of his crimes. Illicit money had been his collateral for happiness, what he'd thought was happiness. Yet it *had* been home, the only one they'd known, and he still felt just a touch of kinship with it. A pride in its roughness and the way it clung onto life without an even break from anyone. Now they'd both got away, even if his new life had been ripped apart. Losing Shane had been the spur they needed. Maybe it was true something good comes from the most desperate of acts, yet Mark found it hard to think this way about the killing of Lena – or Agani, for that matter.

'You're quiet,' Julie said.

'Was I ever anything else?'

'No, not really. Look, things *are* all right, aren't they? Was it that serious with Lena?'

'I don't know. Maybe not. It's over anyway.'

'Maybe you should stay down here. Plenty of nice girls around, 'specially for a boy as fit as you. There's a few in the factory that would …'

'Thanks, Mam, but no thanks. I like it up there, believe it or not. I like the fact that no one knows me. All right, everything is fast and cold, but you are left alone, if you want to be. Like we never were.'

He was talking in the present about feelings that were no longer there.

'Aye, I know what you mean. I'm only a few miles from that hilltop but it could be on the bloody dark side of the moon now. It's so different down here.'

Julie breathed in deeply, 'Look at it. Everything's so clean.'

'The air was just as fresh in the hills.'

'You and your hills. You were always on them.'

'Well, not always, Mam. I was in plenty of houses as well, wasn't I?'

Julie laughed, and dug him in the ribs.

'You were a right little rogue, but don' bring that up, 'specially in front of Carl. That's all over and done with - isn't it?'

'Aye, over and done with.'

Carl rejoined them. Mark knew he'd been pacing on ahead to give them a chance to talk. He appreciated that. There was something solid about Carl he liked; he'd seen stuff too and his eyes were the proof. They were a firm brown, set slightly back in his head, alert, but also a little lost, as if they were looking back on something that couldn't be forgotten. Mark wondered if he'd killed anyone when in the army, and the answer was probably yes. How quickly Julie's world might shatter if she knew each of her men had

115

pulled the trigger, but only one legally.

'Me and Julie had a nice Sunday lunch here the other week,' Carl said, pointing to the pub they were approaching. 'Good grub and not too pricey.'

The pub was trying to stay old, a hand painted wooden sign swung in the breeze outside, and the seabird on it was painted a bright blue. Suddenly Mark wanted tradition, all the stuff Lena had disapproved of, and he'd never had. He thought of beef and Yorkshire puddings like the condemned man he probably was. Julie had tried the odd Sunday lunch when they had been flush, but often they'd disintegrated into rows and incrimination. The Richards family rituals. Mark knew just enough about the Bible to be aware of the Last Supper. Maybe this would be his Last Dinner, at least with Julie.

The pub wasn't too busy. Summer had tailed off and kids were back in school, and what was left were mainly pensioners, people with time on their hands, and finding it harder and harder to spend. Julie was right. This world was so different to the one they'd lived in. It reminded him of the Cotswolds, that Christmas with Lena. Lena had used a word to describe that place, *genteel*. He'd looked it up when she was away. It meant cultivated, elegant, refined, words that had one thing in common, none of them had played a part in his life before she came along.

Mark insisted on buying the drinks.

'I'll only have the one pint,' Carl said,' I'd be knackered if I lost my licence.'

'Get me a pint of lager,' Julie said.

'It'll be almost as big as you, Mam.'

'Oi, don' be cheeky. Women drink pints now, or haven't you noticed? My boy's old-fashioned really, Carl.'

They took a corner table, shown there eagerly by a man with a Midlands accent. Mark sat with his back against the wall.

'Have you noticed they're always from over the border in places like this,' Carl muttered. 'Never our own.'

'Oh, don' start that again,' Julie said. 'Carl got this thing about the English, Mark. Bloody racist he is, sometimes.'

Mark smiled but didn't take sides. Not liking outsiders, afraid of losing driving licences – things like this sounded so tame now, so normal. That word 'normal' kept cropping up in his thoughts. What had Kelly said, that there was no such thing. Maybe the old scally was right, but there was such a thing as extreme life, and he was heading there.

*

Kelly heard his arm snap before he felt any pain. Shock protected him for a moment, then it came. It surged through him like some mighty fist and his bladder lost control. He would have passed out had not Angelo jerked him back.

'No, my friend don't go to sleep.'

The big man said something in a language Kelly had never heard before.

'*My* friend says you are not a man at all, you wet yourself like a child, and you stink like an animal. What use are you to a man like Richards?'

Kelly knew he was making noises, whimpering, then a high pitched keening as Angelo prodded his busted arm, but they didn't seem to be coming from him. They were coming from far away, as if they were outside his body. They sounded like his mother shouting at him, and his father coming in through the front door with his belt in his hand.

'I don' know nuttin, right,' Kelly managed to shout out. 'Nuttin about Mr Richards, nuttin about fuckin' nuttin.'

The big man stood behind Kelly's chair, his gorilla-like arm about to close around his neck. Angelo waved a finger.

'A drink, Kelly, that's what you need. That's what you do, isn't it. Drink?'

For the first time since he'd fallen from a scaffold and

smashed both ankles Kelly did not want one. Angelo picked up the bottle and pushed it towards his mouth. Kelly squirmed until the big man held his head. It would be so easy for this one to snap his scrawny twig of a neck.

Kelly thought his bowels might have joined the bladder. This had to be a fucking dream, he'd wake up at any moment. If he did, he'd swear he'd lay off the booze. This was a warning, maybe from the Almighty himself.

Angelo began to pour. Some of it went down Kelly's throat, forcing him to swallow, some onto his chest. He was wet top and bottom now. The drink hit home immediately. It recognised familiar territory and mixed with last night's load. The pain in Kelly's arm turned from white-hot to dull fire.

'That's right,' Angelo said, 'good, Kelly, good.'

Angelo stopped pouring, as Kelly coughed and spluttered, his eyes trying to focus. Angelo held his head, and turned it towards the window.

'Look, the sun is out. Another fine day. See how soft and white the clouds are, how blue the sky. Life is always worth living, even for you. Where's Richards? What is his name, Mark? Where's Mark, Kelly? You know you want to tell me.'

'I never call him Mark,' Kelly murmured. 'I dunno where he is. I never know. Look, I just done a few jobs for him, now and then. He's a private dick.'

'*You* done jobs?'

'Yeah, me.'

'What could *you* possibly do?'

Despite the crippling fear, and the pain that pulsed through him, Kelly had a flash of defiance, an echo of old, pre-drink times.

'I'm not fuckin' useless. I'm good for getting stuff, and watching out for things.'

'Ah yes, like a rat in a sewer.'

'I got a car for him last Friday, that's all. He said he wanted a motor. He gimme a few quid.'

'What did he say when he stayed here? Why did he stay, Kelly?'

'Nothing, I dunno why he stayed. It didn't make sense. I thought he might have had a ruck with his girlfriend. Look, I said, he never told me nuttin. Look at me, for fucksake. Why should he? I didn't want to know. I only want to be left alone, an' he fuckin' should have.'

'But he has a nice apartment, a lovely woman. What was he doin' here, in this cess pit?'

'Jesus Christ, what you wan' me to say? I'll say anything. He's gone back to the flat, he's gone back to Wales. He's gone to fuckin' Buck House to see the queen.'

'Have another drink.'

Again the liquid poured down. A river to oblivion. Kelly had heard that somewhere, deep in his past. Maybe in church, when he'd gone as a kid, parents each side of him, like guards. When he'd stood in the cold, damp, musty atmosphere to hear all the frightening stuff about hell, damnation and burning in the fire. Their local priest was a throwback, with talk to match.

Most of the whisky was gone now. It had taken over him, he was hardly aware the men were there and the pain was in some distant place, but as Angelo tapped his head softly, and spoke in a soothing voice the terror came back. It was reaching a peak, and he was finding it hard to breathe.

'I believe you, Kelly,' Angelo said softly. 'I too think Richards has gone back to this Wales.'

'It's you he's running from,' Kelly said, 'isn't it, you fucking bastard. You and this other ape.'

'So, there is a little spirit somewhere still inside you,' Angelo said. 'We won't hurt you no more.' He nodded to the big man.

'Kelly, let's go the window, to look at the beautiful day.'

'No way.'

Kelly sprang up and tried to make it to the door but the big man caught him up and lifted him off his feet. I'm not going to get out of this, Kelly thought. No way. The thought cut through the whisky but it diminished his fear, rather than added to it. A decision was being taken for him. The big man tried the window while Angelo held him upright. He solved the problem of the paint-stuck frame with one kick. The sound of traffic, and Sunday people drifted up. It was a perfectly normal sound.

'This room needs air,' Angelo murmured in Kelly's ear, 'we need some air.' He gestured to the big man, who took Kelly by the scruff of the neck and threw him out.

Kelly might have been drowning. Donegal flashed up in millisecond scenes, the village dead before tourists could save it, his mother who did her best, the old man who beat the shite out of him, the torn black and white photo of his only girlfriend, the one who went away, taking his life with her. He heard a woman screaming, he'd never had that effect an any of them before. But maybe the scream is mine, Kelly thought, my final sound in this world, as the pain he'd felt in his arm exploded to all parts of his body. Time did not exist. and his eyes focused on nothing.

'Go and get the car and pick me up at the back,' Angelo said. 'His arm will just be one of many injuries now. They'll say this Kelly killed himself. He was down, now he's out. The police will not bother about him too much. Why should they?'

'But what if he did know something?'

'No, impossible. Go.'

Angelo stood in the bed-sit for another minute, lighting up an untipped cigarette. The room reminded him of his past. His first place in Tirana, shared with four others. He wished Stellachi hadn't killed the girl.

*

Mark tried to keep Lena from his mind as he cut into the beef. It was medium rare, how he'd always liked it, but as he put a piece into his mouth his mind rejected it. He saw the pink-red centre of the beef and dropped his fork onto his plate, splashing Julie with gravy.

'What's up with you?'

'Sorry, maybe it's the beer. I never drink at this time these days.'

'God, things *have* changed. Too much of that vegetarian nonsense from your ex, as well, I bet.'

'Leave the boy alone, Jool.'

'Ganging up on me already, are you?'

Julie pretended to be cross but Mark knew she was pleased. Carl was warming to him. *Hope springs eternal*, it had always been on the kitchen wall in the estate house, a cheap plaque made of plastic wood, with a flower motif at its edges. That saying had become a joke between them, and she'd taken it down after Shane's disappearance, but Mark could see that the words were still ingrained in her.

Mark ate what he could of the meal, feeling Julie's eyes on him the whole time. Carl also watched him, but in a different way. He was checking Mark out, knowing that he was here for other reasons and wondering what they were. Mark remembered talking to an ex-army guy who'd worked for the agency. He'd told him about Ireland, the feeling he had when he walked down dangerous streets, how the hairs on the back of his neck twitched in expectation of a bullet. Anytime. All the time. You never get rid of it, even when you're home from fucking leave, the man said. Maybe Carl still had it. Maybe Mark had given it back to him today.

'You want another pint, Mark? Carl asked.

'OK.'

They sat on the patio at the front of the pub's dining room, enjoying the best of the sun. To Mark, the sea looked strange, for it was not part of his land-locked world. It was

121

full of shifting movement, a sluggish turning of itself. Stretching away from all that the land held for him. It would be tempting to accept its invitation, but it would be useless to go abroad. He'd lose any edge being home might give him, and, even now, flying was still out. He saw himself a gibbering wreck in an airport lounge, disarmed by his phobia, a sitting duck for Stellachi, or anyone halfway good.

As they sat and drank a wind started to get up, whipping the tops of the waves into foam.

'White horses, they're called,' Julie said, 'Carl told me. She zipped up her jacket. 'The sun's going. Come on, let's get back, it's getting a bit parky.'

His mother was tipsy but not in the way Mark remembered, when she'd totter home from the local club full of booze and recrimination, let down by one man, used by another. Sometimes obeying the plaque by bringing home a punter, who'd disappear with the new day. His childhood and her prime time, or it should have been. Suddenly, Mark wished he could change it all, give Julie another chance, not continue to smash her life with what he had always brought to it. She thought she had a new start now. Perfect fucking timing. If he'd known Carl was on the scene he wouldn't have come here. Whatever was going to happen could at least have been kept away. But Mark didn't know about Carl, because they were crap at communicating. He'd been absorbed in Lena and where she might lead.

Julie ran her hand over Carl's shoulder as he drove. Mark watched as she toyed with the back of his neck. These two seemed to have something real, and if he hung around Julie would think her new world was complete. Telling her he was not staying would be difficult, Mark tried to think of something but his brain would not play ball. As the last of the sun came back out, Mark dozed, like a tired boy on his way home from the seaside. Like it might have been twenty-five years ago, if they lived a different life, in a different place.

Mark was alert when they got back to Julie's flat. It was hard to imagine any action here, but bad things happened anywhere. He knew Carl was watching him in the rear view mirror. He knows I'm on the lookout, Mark thought, he knows the signs, but there was no one around, no gold Lexus parked nearby.

'It's bin a lovely day,' Julie said, 'I'm going for a lie down. I think I drank a bit too much.'

'Want a brew?' Carl said, 'you look like you could do with a coffee.'

'Ta.'

Carl made the drinks and they sat down in the main room.

'Want the telly on?'

'Nah, don't use it.'

'That must make you some kind of freak in this day and age.'

'Probably.'

'I usually watch a bit of sport Sunday afternoons.'

'Don't let me stop you.'

'No, it's okay.'

They were silent for a while, each man drinking his coffee and weighing the situation up.

'So what you running from?' Carl said eventually. 'Police? Your girlfriend?'

'What makes you think I'm running from anything?'

'I know the signs. I learnt them well in the forces, apprentice in Ireland, graduated in the Falklands. You got twitchy written all over you. You haven't relaxed a second, not even when you nodded off in the car.'

'So, you were in the Falklands, as well.'

'Aye, but I haven't told your mother. Some of the guys like to bang on about it, I'd rather let it lie in the past, where it belongs. She don't ask much anyway. You haven't

123

answered, Mark.'

'The police aren't after me. I've kept my nose clean since I did a stretch in a young offenders' place.'

'Aye, Julie did tell me that, but something's up, something more than being dumped by a girlfriend.'

Mark shrugged.

'Maybe it's my natural state. I'm not much of a mixer. Look, I'll be gone soon. Going tonight, as it happens. Things to do, like.'

'Your mother's gonna be upset. She'd like you to stay.'

'How about you?'

It was Carl's turn to shrug. 'It's her place. And it's a big sofa.'

'Thanks, but I've got plans.'

'What, Sunday night, and no car?'

Mark realised this guy wasn't going to give up. 'I'm meeting up with a few guys I work with,' he said.

'What, you're on a job down here?'

'That's it, but don't tell Mam. It's nothing much anyway, routine surveillance stuff.'

'Sounds interesting.'

'No, not really. That's only in the films. I'm going to the bog,' Mark said.

When Mark went back into the living room Carl had the holdall by his side. It was open.

'My old sergeant used to have one of these,' Carl said. 'He took it off a Yank mercenary on a hillside near Goose Green. Shot him in the head with it. Bit of a museum piece now, I'd say. This other one is much more like it. German, I think, but the name and number's been scratched off.'

Carl picked up the automatic in his other hand.

'Two-gun kid, eh? Better tell me, Mark, and quickly.'

'Perhaps I'd just better go.'

'Like fuck you will. 'Carl jerked a thumb towards the bedroom. 'You can't think much of her, bringing these here.

And the S and W has been used recently. Blow a hole in a wall, that would, and other things.'

Carl put the guns on top of the holdall, carefully, neatly, they nestled there like a kid's toys.

'Julie will be waking up soon. Better start.'

Chapter Nine

Angelo sat behind Agani's ornate desk. He liked the view from the window, and the way the sun brought up the finish on the polished wood, like rich gold. London spread out all around him, so many stone and glass fingers pointed upwards, each one announcing its wealth. Sometimes in his village someone would have a tattered magazine and he'd see cities like this. All the big ones in all the big countries, dripping with money. Even on worn pages they shone and the people also seemed to glow. Angelo fingered one of the gold rings he wore on each little finger. Those fingers were not good for much and rings gave them a purpose. A ring like this could buy that village, and the people in it. He was ten years older than Agani, it had taken him longer to get where he was. He was not so clever, but he was steady, sure, and he learnt. There was an intricate design carved on Agani's table, two eagles flying. Agani had brought someone over specially to do it, to remind him of home, he said. Angelo did not want any reminders.

The big man came in and he stood before Angelo, like he'd stood before Agani. Angelo thought that maybe this Richards has done him a favour. Amsterdam would need a replacement, so why not him? Angelo would let the matter end now, if he had his way. An eye for an eye, and it was over. He doubted if this Richards would ever bother them again, and it would be better not to bother him. As Agani said, it was business. But those in Amsterdam clung to old ways. The Welshman had been a fool to let them live.

'What's happening with Kelly?' Angelo asked.

'They came, took him away. A policeman who looks like

he should be in school stands outside that pigsty. In that bar he drank in they say he jumped. They say they could see it coming.'

'Good. We have an address for this Richards from the girl's flat, somewhere near Cardiff. His mother lives there.'

'Where's Cardiff?'

'Near his birthplace. Less than two hundred miles west. Another country, they say, but not another country.'

'What are you talking about?'

'They even speak another language there, I think. It's the way this Britain is.'

'I have not got very far with English.'

'I've noticed, but we're a long way from the village.'

The big man smiled, his two gold teeth putting on their own display.

'Yes, we are, so was Agani, but he died in a girl's gown with his head on this wall.'

'It was his time. Get a car ready. We'll go down in the morning.'

'The Lexus is being fixed. Shall I take Agani's Mercedes?'

'You mean *our* Mercedes.'

The big man smiled again. 'How do you know he's gone there?' he said. 'He could be anywhere.'

'I know, but Lena told Tony that this man will not fly. He will never fly she said. In his position I would go to the place I know the best. My homeland.'

'Won't fly?' The big man's grin became wider. 'What about Stellachi?' he asked.

'He won't come unless we need him. Get my things ready. We'll go early.'

The big man is getting old, Angelo thought. Still as strong an ox, but also as slow-thinking as one. They were both getting old. He would not have been surprised by this Richards even five years ago. London had made them soft.

Richards was like Stellachi, he moved fast like Stellachi, had the same sharp eyes as the Romanian. But Angelo had seen him kill and he was not like Stellachi in that. He'd seen Richards' face when he pulled the trigger. This man was fighting himself, and he'd be fighting himself now. His woman was gone, and he had killed. Maybe this man was soft at the centre, but Stellachi had no soft, he was a man who hated every second of life. Angelo understood this, and feared it. He stretched out his hands so that his rings flashed, and he saw his reflection amongst the eagles. He hoped they weren't coming for him.

*

Mark began to talk. He told Carl everything, keeping his voice low, like one of Carl's old comrades reporting on a Falklands hillside. He couldn't believe how easily it all came out, and what a relief it was when it did. By the time he got to the end it seemed like he was describing a film he'd seen the other day.

Carl did not interrupt or say a word until he'd finished.

'By Christ, I knew it was something bad, when I found the guns,' Carl said, 'but nothing like this. This is the last place you should have come.'

'I know, but it's done now. Even if I hadn't come down, they'd know where Julie lives. They'll have found her address in our flat, or maybe Lena told them. You being here is a bonus, Carl. Julie might have been alone when they came, not knowing who the fuck they were or what was happening, and not being able to tell them anything. That doesn't bear thinking about. We have a chance to get her away now.'

'We?'

'OK, you'll have to do it, if you're up for it. They'll know nothing about you. You do have your own place?'

Carl was silent for a long moment, looking at the guns,

and moving them slowly around in his hands.

'Fucking hell,' he muttered. 'Only a few hours ago I was reading the Sunday paper, thinking I've met a good woman, and looking forward to a bit of quality time. Thanks a lot, Mark.'

'I wouldn't blame you if you just walked out that door.'

'No, but *I* would blame me. Yes, I have got a place. Swansea way. It's only an old council house. The divorce was messy, and it cost.'

'What about your kids?'

'Long gone. The boy's in Australia, and Megan is an au pair in Florida. They both wanted to get away when their mother and I fell apart.'

'Does anyone know you around here?'

'Nah. I've only been on the scene a few months and Julie keeps herself to herself.'

'Does your ex know about Julie?'

'There's no contact now. She's with her new fella, further west. He's minted, and she's still not bad looking. It's all right, I'm well out of it. At least I thought I was. Now you bring me this.'

'Bit different to 'Dad I got drunk and hit a copper,' eh?'

'Just a bit. Look, Mark, I'm sorry about this Lena. I don't know how you've held it together today. Your mother is oblivious to it.'

'Oh, she knows something is up all right, but she's used to thinking that's normal with me.

'Surely it would be better to go the police, for Christsake.'

'They'll think I'm barking. They'll never find any sign of Lena or Agani, and if they did take me seriously, with my form, they'd put me in the frame for Lena straight away. And I wouldn't trust that lot to protect Julie. No, people like Agani never really exist. They have false everything. You never know what their real names are, or where they're from. I'm not sure now that I knew Lena at all. That's the worst thing. Two years that might have been just a game, and me the stooge.'

'What *are* you going to do?'

'Go back to the valley, lie low. Let them come to me and see what happens. It's not much of a plan, but the only one I've got. I'll pick up some gear tomorrow morning.'

'I get it. Meet 'em on your own ground. Do you think they'll track you down?'

'If they don't, then I'll try to find this Stellachi. It won't be over for me until I do.'

'None of this is fair on your mother.'

Despite him saying this, Mark could sense the excitement in Carl. His worn eyes took on new life. He was running from fire in Bluff Cove, bending in the wind on the Falklands hillside, wishing he had eyes in the back of his head in the Falls Road. Carl was alive again, alert to each passing second, sucking in life with every breath and glad of it. Mark caught the mood, and knew why soldiers liked to work in teams. They had killing in common. Carl had witnessed a summary execution on the battlefield, he might have shot that Yank himself, murder in the eyes of some, but a just killing in his eyes. In his head his mates would still have been burning. Not many men experienced stuff like that.

'What about these?' Carl tapped one of the guns. 'It would be best to get rid.'

'No, things have gone too far. I'd be naked out there without them.'

'If anything goes down here the police are bound to get involved. You can't go shooting up the bloody hillsides, man. This isn't Texas.'

'Maybe they won't. If I go down, they'll make me disappear, like they did with Lena, and Agani.'

'They went public when they ran over that Tony.'

'Not really. It was hit and run. It happens every day on the roads and if they'd got me it would all be over. I've seen these people, Carl, they don't give a fuck about life or death.'

There were sounds of Julie stirring.

'How the hell am I going to fix this,' Carl muttered, 'what can I tell her?'

They looked at each other.

'Well, let me put the artillery away for a start.'

Mark pushed the guns to the bottom of the holdall. He was zipping it up as Julie came back in.

'You two look nice and cosy. Had a good chat, have you?'

'I'll be getting off soon, Mam,' Mark said.

'What? You only just got here.'

'I know, but I'm not meant to be here at all. I'm working. I've got to get over to Bristol tonight. There's a car waiting for me in Cardiff.'

'Oh. I see.'

Julie looked at him the same way she used to when he came home from a job, wondering if the police would be there minutes after him. Mark felt like shit, and he was dishing more of it out. Why didn't Lena tell him what was going on, just shown a little faith, just believed in him enough to include him? Now he was passing the buck to Carl.

Carl looked at him helplessly. He was Mark's one piece of luck. Anyone remotely normal would pick up the phone as soon as he was gone, but Mark didn't think Carl would. The man had only been on the scene a matter of weeks, looking for a bit of comfort after a bad domestic. He'd have every right to scarper, but there was something real about the man, something true. As a man who could hardly spell *trust,* Mark still thought this. He had to. He had to trust Carl, like he'd trusted Kelly. Two alien acts in one weekend, and it made him think how limiting it was to be always on your own. He'd needed an Irish bum and now he needed an ageing ex-army man. He was glad Carl had found the guns. If he'd said anything before he might have thought him just a nut spouting nonsense but guns were good for concentrating the mind, he'd learnt that in the last few days.

'Stay and have a bit of tea, at least,' Julie said.

'I'm still stuffed after that pub, Mam.'

'You hardly ate anything,' Julie muttered. 'I'll make you a cup of coffee, you *have* got time for that?'

'Course I have.'

'Do you want one, love?' she asked Carl.

'Okay.'

'Get her down to that house of yours in the morning,' Mark whispered, as soon as Julie was in the kitchen. 'If they find me they won't be interested in anyone else.'

'How am I going to do that? She's got her job and everything.'

'The job's no problem. Just phone her in sick. As for getting her down there, you'll have to think of something. Do this, please, Carl, for both of you.'

'Both of us?'

'You can be good for her. Good for each other. Listen, when I was growing up it was one long line of wankers. It wasn't her fault, it was just our situation. I thought it would never change, but it has. Even if I've fucked up again it doesn't have to change that. Keep her down your place as long as it takes. Gimme your mobile number and I'll stay in touch. If you don't hear within a week, expect the worst. Oh, you better keep a check on the news too.'

'Expect the worst, by Christ. What do I say then? You're her only son.'

I am now, mate. Shane's baby face loomed large in his head. If he lost out with Stellachi how *would* Julie cope with it? Another Richards disappearance, as final as the first. And if he got lucky, what then? Banged up for life? That would really bring some cheer into her life. Mark began to notice the unintentional movement of his hands, the way his fingers made shapes that his brain had no part in.

'I've made one for all of us,' Julie said, 'and there's some biscuits too.'

Perhaps he should have also told Carl about Shane but there was only so much the guy could be expected to take at one time. Mark tried to pick up a biscuit but it crumbled in his hands, pieces of it falling into his drink.

'That's what I call a dunk,' his mother said.

Julie sat close to him on the sofa. He could feel her warmth on his leg, and for a moment was back twenty-five years, waiting for her to smother him after she'd slammed the door on another loser.

'That girl hurt you, didn't she?' Julie said quietly.

'What?'

'That Lena. It's obvious, been obvious all day. Was there someone else?'

'Sort of. It's over, Mam, best let it alone.'

'You sure?'

'Oh aye, I'm sure about that.'

'And you *have* to go?'

'Yip.'

'I'm going to the loo,' Carl said.

'You got Carl now,' Mark said. 'Seems all right to me.'

'God, I never thought you'd say that about one of my boyfriends. Remember all those fights we had over them.'

'Well, you certainly could pick 'em, Mam.'

'But I couldn't though, could I?'

'We've moved on a lot since then. Maybe this Carl will be good for you. You deserve it.'

'It's early days yet, but I think he might. Thanks, love … listen to us, we're almost doing a normal family routine.'

'Had to happen sometime.'

'When will I see you again?'

'Not sure. I've lots of work on.'

'I can't believe you live in London. I never thought you'd leave the valley, 'specially the hillsides. Don' you never want to come back?'

'We didn't exactly leave nothing behind, did we?'

'Except Shane.'

'Aye, except him.'

'Do you think it'll ever be solved?'

'Been a long time now. He'd be a teenager.'

Julie sniffed and pushed even closer as Carl came back in.

'Right, time to go, Mam,' Mark said.

'All right.'

'I'll give you a lift,' Carl said.

'No need for that, mate.'

'No trouble. Come on, then.'

Julie hugged him at the doorway. He was once again reminded of how small she was. It was like picking up a twelve-year-old.

'Still a size ten,' she whispered in his ear. 'Take care of yourself.'

'Don't I always?'

They drove off in the Merc. Mark saw the diminishing figure of Julie in the wing mirror. She was smiling, and waving vigorously. He fixed this image in his mind, just in case it was the last time he saw her.

'Drop me off in the centre of Cardiff,' Mark said. 'I'll get a hotel tonight. Make sure you're gone in the morning, I don't think those guys will hang around too long.'

'I still haven't a clue what I'm going to tell her,' Carl said. 'Any ideas?'

'How much are you into Julie?'

'We clicked straight away. And I'm not on the rebound, if that's what you're thinking. My marriage died a slow death for years. It was a relief for both of us when it finished, even if she did take up with that slimy ponce. Come on, gimme a reason why I should suddenly want to take her from here.'

'Say that you've booked something as a surprise,' Mark said. 'You were going to tell her then I showed up. I know, take her to Ireland, she's always wanted to go there. Try Donegal, I've heard that's nice. You'll be safe there, just in case they managed to connect you to Julie.'

Kelly came into Mark's head. If he got through this, he'd take him a case of Irish whiskey and says thanks. He doubted it was a word Kelly had heard much in his life.

Carl pulled up outside a large hotel, built since last time Mark was here. He thought it would be better to be anonymous in a multi-roomed chain than in a small B & B.

'I don't know whether to shake hands or not,' Carl murmured. 'Before you appeared I was thinking that maybe my life's getting straight, that I've met someone who might be right. I haven't thought like that since that fucking war, and that was twenty years ago.'

Mark stuck out a hand anyway.

'Sorry, Carl, I thought the same just a few days back. I'd change it if I could, believe me.'

Carl took his hand.

'Aye, I know. The thought of anything happening to Julie like what happened to that Lena ...'

'It won't. You'll be there. Anyway, these people don't kill for no reason. It's not professional.'

'Oh aye? The code of fucking killers, is it?'

'Something like that. Look, you all right for money? I could let you have a few hundred.'

'No thanks. I've got enough for Ireland.'

'All right, let's have your mobile number then.'

Mark logged it on his own phone. He'd charge it up in the hotel, for there'd be no electricity where he'd be sleeping for the next week. They shook hands firmly.

'See you, then,' Mark said.

'I hope so, son.'

Mark watched him drive away quickly, anxious to be back with Julie. Apart from himself, Mark had never known her have a defender.

The weather was changing. What was left of the day had turned dark, and it was starting to rain. Small drops as he stood on the steps of the hotel, then harder as he pushed open its doors. I'll bet it will be wet all next week, Mark thought, summer ending just for me.

The young man at reception didn't like the look of him, and he was bored. He fingered his dark red tie with the hotel's logo on it as he scanned Mark's battered holdall, and was suspicious when he paid the deposit with cash. Mark half expected the git to put the notes up against the light.

It was a room like a thousand others in a thousand towns. Identikit furniture, decoration, a modern cell for modern man. It didn't care if you liked it or not, but it was on the fifth floor, which gave Mark some kind of view over the city. He stood looking out at it with his hands in his pockets, watching the last of the light slip away. In the years he'd travelled around chasing people it had struck him how alike everything was becoming, same city centres, same brand names, same places to sleep. It was like he was on an endless journey that never stopped and never got anywhere.

He was running the water for a bath when his mobile rang, *if you're looking for trouble* echoed around the room. He thought it would be Julie, she always wanted a last word. It would be another query into his state, or maybe Carl had come out with something. He answered.

'Hullo, my friend. You are well? I have a message from Stellachi. He's impressed, and says he will see you soon. Why don't you meet with him, man to man? Get this over with? You are only delaying things.'

Of course, why wouldn't they know his mobile number as well?

'Won't you answer?' Angelo continued. 'We know where you are. We know where you're going. Shame you can't fly, isn't it? You'd have more choice then.'

Mark cut Angelo off. There was no point in responding. Lena must have told Tony his life history, in case they needed it for any future use. They did, and the future was now. Lena stabbed at him again, and the thought that these bastards might know about Shane made him burn. Maybe he *should* have killed Angelo, and his big friend. Stellachi would see this as a flaw, a weakness he could exploit. Let him try. Mark's heart was hardening, taking on its old granite texture, and his resolve would have to match it. He turned off the phone.

Mark ran the bath deep and sank into it. Although he was safe for the moment his senses were on permanent alert, practising for what lay ahead. He imagined the door quietly opening, whispers in a strange language, then a knife or gun. Probably a knife. Whenever he heard footsteps in the corridor, he tensed. Once someone paused near his door and he was almost out of the bath and searching in the holdall.

The bed was welcoming but his sleep was troubled. Lena was with him throughout. His brain picked over her memory, their times together arranged in order, each piece of happiness paraded until his brain tried to salve itself by telling him it was all a bad dream, and that he would wake with Lena by his side. Then reality would be back, and her drained, stone-like face, that fixed the horror she'd endured. Each snatch of sleep ended like this.

He was up very early, showered, dressed and back at reception with maroon-tie man by eight. The night clerk was just knocking off his shift, his female replacement waiting bright-eyed by his side. She smiled at Mark and he tried to arrange his lips into something similar. Mark could see now that Maroon Tie wasn't much more than a kid, realising he was on the slow grind of work, going over all the things he could be doing as his long night dripped away and wondering how long he could hack this. Dreaming of running the place. A sprinkle of dandruff was on each shoulder of his padded black jacket, like epaulettes. He made a point of carefully checking Mark's bill and said *thank you sir* the way that snotty hotel clerks did the world over, when they thought you were beneath them. Mark hadn't bothered to shave, it would be better for the hills. The girl was interested. A scruffy guy checking into a place like this might be someone, a rock star maybe, an event to push her day forward, to mock Maroon Tie for not recognising him.

Mark spotted a twenty-four hour convenience store on a corner. He put tinned stuff, cheese, bread, water and some tired fruit into a basket. From a rack near the counter he added a half bottle of unknown whisky. The guy smirked at him knowingly but packed the stuff quickly when he saw Mark's glare. He was charged at convenience prices.

Next door was an army surplus place which wasn't yet open. Mark went into the adjacent cafe and ordered another plate of grease. His good eating of the last two years had been crushed in four days.

Day four was starting. Two coppers passed outside. About the same age as Maroon tie, but happier. They had the jobs they wanted. Mark could go out to them now, hand them the holdall and tell them to look in it, let them rush him to the station, excitement reddening their baby faces as they showed off their trophy to their sergeant, who'd listen dumbfounded to Mark's story before getting his inspector.

As he pushed undercooked bacon around his plate Mark began to doubt his shaky plan. He was bringing pain back to his homeland, where it had always thrived, writ large with his chaotic upbringing, his crime and the vanishing of

Shane. Maybe this was the inevitable final chapter, and already he'd managed to involve Julie; his family. It was starting to rain outside, solid stuff that came down quickly, rain that would go straight through him on the hills. He needed to buy wisely.

The man in the surplus shop looked surplus himself. The shop smelt of musty canvas, a dead-end kind of smell that matched Mark's mood. The man behind the counter had a grey face as creased as one of his tents, but it might have been healthy once, and in the army a long time ago. Mark bought a small rucksack, sleeping bag and a camouflage jacket, the type kids wore when they wanted to strut. The shopkeeper perked up, these were good sales for first thing Monday.

'Going on a trip, are you?' he asked.

'Not really. I'll have a pair of them too. Thirty-four waist, long leg.'

Mark pointed to a pair of waterproof trousers, a match for the jacket, and picked up a pair of boots. And these in a ten.'

The guy was almost in ecstasy at the unexpected sales. Mark thought about a small tent, which would really have pumped the man up, but decided against it. He needed to see around him at all times, and made do with a waterproof sheet. He could rig this up to keep the rain off, if he had to.

The man rang up his till.

'That's £160, dead on. Anything else?'

Mark saw a small pair of binoculars and a Swiss army knife, and added them to his bill.

'You in the army?'

'No, why?'

'Only asking. Just that you look pretty fit and I've had a few of those boys in since Iraq kicked off. Army don't give 'em enough stuff, see. Pathetic.'

Mark's money had decreased quite a bit. Mark wondered if Kelly had drunk his way through his share of it by now.

Probably. There was a national paper open on the counter. As the man bagged up his stuff Mark turned it towards him. It was full of the usual nonsense he never bothered with but a smaller paragraph halfway down the page caught his eye. *Man jumps to his death in London on Sunday morning. Shoppers were shocked as ...* The man was handing him change and Mark almost turned away until he saw the name. *Patrick Michael Kelly, a well-known character in the area ... police are not treating the death as suspicious ...*

'Your change, mate.'

'What?'

'Change.'

Mark took the money and picked up his purchases.

'Have a nice day now.'

Mark needed the rain on his face. There was a tightness in his chest and he found it hard to get his breath. Too many people were dying. He stood in the rain in the middle of the pavement, making people walk around him. It was several minutes before he could move. The shopkeeper was watching him from his doorway. He'd go back inside and scrutinise the bank notes, then be relieved that this nutter hadn't stiffed him.

Mark went to the nearest newsagents and bought the same daily. There were public toilets across the road, so he locked himself in a cubicle there and read about Kelly. He hadn't told Kelly where he was going, that was his first thought. The second was that Kelly hadn't jumped anywhere. Poor bastard. He shouldn't have involved him, but this thought was too late now. He imagined the terror the man must have felt. It didn't take much to frighten him at the best of times. He wouldn't have known what the fuck was happening, he'd have snivelled and pissed his pants with his night's booze but his last thought would have been clear – that it was all Mark's fault.

A well-known local character. Kelly's fifteen minutes of

fame, or was that fifteen seconds. They'd come for him, and the poor bastard couldn't have told them anything useful. Mark shut his eyes and saw the big man picking up the skin and bones that was Kelly and tossing him out the window. Fuck it. His brain couldn't take many more images like this. Tony smashed on the road, Kelly airborne, Agani's head saying bye bye, and Lena. Always Lena. Someone old shuffled into the cubicle next to him, he heard the man cough, splutter and sigh to himself. A sigh that was only Monday old. Out early on the streets because he was bored shitless, Mark thought, nothing to do, no place to go, and another long day beginning, but right now he'd swap places with him.

Mark loaded the holdall's contents into the rucksack, and left the holdall in the cubicle. The guns went in pockets either side with an apple over each of them. The man in the shop had said the sack was waterproof, Mark hoped it was, else the guns might prove useless. He hoisted the sack onto his back and made his way to the train station, trying to walk steadily, breathe easily. Kelly was a signal they were sending him. Thank Christ Carl was around and Julie was out of that flat, at least he hoped she was.

Mark caught a train to the top of his old valley with Kelly jostling with Lena for first place in his waking nightmare. Julie was bringing up an honourable third. He was the only one in his carriage. The train was almost empty. Everyone was going the other way, to work or to shop. A few miles out of Cardiff, as the train began to climb, it stopped raining. As it passed into the gap in the hills that led to the valley, the sun struggled out, enough to make a faint rainbow on the hillside. Mark hadn't been back here since they'd sent him to the Shetlands. While he'd broken his heart over dead whales, his mother had moved from the estate. It had been better for her to leave everything behind while he wasn't around. She'd swapped a windswept hilltop house full of the wrong memories with an anonymous flat at the seaside. The council had made it easy for her.

Mark was close to his old stamping ground now. He got off at the last stop, went across the street to the nearest store and bought a small amount of extra supplies, then he shouldered his load and started to walk. There were quite a few people about, and one man gave him a long stare from the other side of the road. He might have been someone from the estate but Mark didn't recognise him. His one friend was long dead, and he'd blanked everyone else out in the last ten years.

Despite his time in the city he was still good a good walker. Long, even strides that soaked up distance quickly. He was on the hillside in minutes. He'd almost forgotten how close it was, the way open country took over so quickly here, the built-up areas nestled on the valley floor, terracing hanging onto the lower slopes, as if gnawing at nature, then throwing it back out. In all his years of ducking and diving on the hillside he'd met very few people, and those he did were always old, out with their dogs. No one his age. Legs for the young had gone out of fashion.

Mark was on the edge of forestry now, regulation conifers planted twenty years ago. They were well grown and offered plenty of cover, and he knew from the old days they would be quite dry at their heart. Like a natural tent. The valley was showing its two faces at once. On the far hillside sunlight picked out the trees and bracken already starting to brown, on his side the wind drove fine rain into his face.

Mark had kept to the hill road so far, but now cut across country. Another twenty minutes' walk and he could see his old estate. You could hardly miss it, it was a modern day hill fort, rows of housing trying to blend in with the contours of the hilltop. Multiple roofs caught the light and flashed him a salute but there was something missing. It took him a while to realise that some of the houses were gone, rows of them had been removed. They must have tried to sort the place out, Mark thought, cut out the bad bits, like rot from an apple. The old Richards house was still there, and Mark wasn't sure if he was glad or sorry.

He'd camp near here, close by old nightmares, and let them merge with the new. They'd find out about this place if they didn't know already. Stellachi might be piecing it all together right now, but Mark knew nothing about him, or Romania for that matter. What he did know was that their backgrounds would be similar, at least in terms of the shit doled out to them. He'd robbed a teacher's house once, a history guy, and had taken some of his books home to keep. A first. Lots of pictures of the old days in the valley and one about famous generals. He was into war then, and even tried to read some of the words, something he'd avoided in school. He read about the way different leaders kept photographs of their opponents, trying to see into their minds, guess their moves. He hadn't got it at the time but did now. Keeping that one Italian image of Stellachi clear in his thoughts would keep his own mind focused. Mark had hate on his side, killing Agani didn't take it away, it just stirred the pot. Stellachi was the enemy general and Angelo and the big man his foot soldiers, cannon fodder that Stellachi might use to draw him out.

Mark looked around for a likely spot to camp, just far enough inside the forestry for cover, but not so his field of vision would be obscured. As he entered the forest everything came back to him. The smell first. He'd loved September, the heady smells of decay as the land prepared for the cold, the crisp air of darkening evenings ready to welcome him to a new season of crime. Large chunks of his early life had been lived here, away from the stone-clad pain that lay below. Mark's childhood memories were laced with it. He'd built up an intimate knowledge of each changing month, becoming a homespun weatherman, botanist and birdman. He could name very few birds, but he knew them all and how they went about things. When his life boiled down on the estate, here all had been calm, life had an order it kept to and he'd felt he was part of it. There were no people.

The smoke of garden fires was drifting up the hillside from the terraces. Thoughts of Lena mixed with this earliest of all childhood smells. If he lived through this Mark wondered if he would always look back with such clarity as he did now. His light mood when he turned the key in the flat door that last time, eager to see her, more so than usual. Thinking he had a future at last, that his feelings which had twisted all ways in his life, had a focus now. It had always been just him, lying to himself that this was the best course, all that he needed. Letting his early life rule him, keeping him hopeless, lost and arrogant in his despair. Lena gave him a new life, or he thought she had. Then it was gone. Mark's eyes welled up for the third time since Friday. It would be the last time, he determined, until all this was over.

It was right that he was here, where it all began for him. If they came for him, it was the best place to succeed, or go down. If it was the latter, they'd probably bury him up here somewhere, and that was right too.

Mark realised he was close to the spot where he used to hide some of the loot from the houses. It had been safer here than in his own house. He'd let it build up until the man came up from Cardiff in his fancy car. Then the money he received would go under the floorboards of his bedroom, where it stayed most of the winter, like some hibernating animal, growing all the time. He'd been the richest kid on the estate.

Mark walked a little further into the trees. His footfall was muffled by layers of old leaves and pine needles. He was treading on a soft and lifeless carpet. Mark remembered there were the remains of a farmhouse close by, long since abandoned to the forestry. He found it. Its walls were still a few feet high, but part of nature now, moss and lichen covered, so that they seemed to be growing from the earth. A stone plant. He put his sack at the right angle of two walls, and stretched the waterproof sheet over a few sticks to make a narrow, makeshift shelter, room enough to slide in his sleeping bag and not much else. He cut down some of the last green bracken and pushed it inside to soften the ground. His hideout was quite well camouflaged, and would be hard to spot, unless someone entered the trees at this precise spot.

Mark was ten metres inside the forestry, it was a good vantage point. He swept the valley with the binoculars, and all the old haunts jumped out at him. He noted the scattering of new buildings, small developments that had sprung up where the old industries used to be. The valley looked cleaner, but less lively.

It was still only midday, yet it felt like much later. Mark turned his mobile on. He'd always hated them, much to Lena's amusement. He hated the way they wrested control from the user, the way he was at the beck and call of voices and messages, wherever he was. He hated the way people couldn't live without them, when they always had before, and most of all, he hated the fact that he was one of those people. The agency had insisted he had one. Lena too.

There was a message. Julie on the voice mail. He listened to her message, expecting anything. It was the voice he'd grown up with: tense, a little shrill, panic and anger shaping it in equal doses.

Mark, Carl's told me everything. I can hardly believe it, even with you. I knew something was up as soon as I saw you, I bloody knew it. But nothing like this.

I wanna go to the police but Carl says no. My head's going round. Can't think. Carl's made me phone in sick. I'm going down his place. Phone me. Please, Mark, please.

Well done, Carl, for getting her away. Top man. Mark was surprised he'd told her though, maybe Carl wasn't any good at lying. He texted Julie. It wouldn't be a good idea to talk to her. Angelo could wait.

Mam, try not to get in a state. You're in safe hands with Carl. He's sound, like I said. No problems with me, either. I'm OK, and I plan to stay OK. Sorry for this mess.

It was pathetic, and wouldn't reassure her for more than a few seconds, but it was the best he could do for now. At least he didn't say *it's not my fault.*

Mark leaned against a tree trunk and let the sun strike his face. It had warmed to modest autumn heat now, hot enough to soothe. He'd got to first base with his plan, he was here, and as ready as he'd ever be. Even Angelo and his friends would have to work hard to find him and they'd have to spend a lot of time. Maybe they'd think he wasn't worth it, and give up. Maybe pigs could fly to the moon.

He must have dozed for twenty minutes, and woke with his face burning. At first he didn't know where he was, he almost expected to find Daniels next to him, out of it on a flagon of cheap cider. The phone was still on. He rubbed his eyes, stepped back into the shadows, and read Angelo's text. It reminded him of his spelling at school, and the class they put him in.

We are cumin. We now where you are. Why don we meet? Finish this like men.

Ah, you mean you only have a rough idea, pal, Mark thought, and when Julie isn't where you expect her to be you'll be well fucked. He didn't answer it, but he might later.

*

Why did things turn upside down whenever Mark was involved? It was the first thing Julie asked herself. She prayed he hadn't done anything to that Lena; he'd never been violent to girls before. Carl had been unsettled all night. He couldn't keep still, and got up for a smoke several times. Maybe Mark had upset him. Her son usually had that effect on people, sometimes without even trying, but the two men had seemed to get on. She'd been so happy to see him, standing tall and healthy in the doorway, even if he did look really tired. She was proud too. Glad to show her fit son off to Carl, two big, capable men together. Big, capable, they were new words to her, runt and waster were the old ones. Men who flitted from nest to nest, pouring all their money down their throats and sometimes into their arms. The good old days.

It was almost seven in the morning when Carl came back into the bedroom.

'You all right, love?' Julie murmured. 'You're awful restless. Mark hasn't said nothing, has he?'

'No. Well, yes, in a way.'

'I bloody knew it. You've had a row, haven't you? What's happened?'

'Nothing. No, it's all right between us.'

'What's the problem then?'

Carl had been thinking of something to say for the last ten hours, ridiculous things that would never wash with Julie, but was the truth any less ridiculous? Mark had breezed in and brought a horror film with him. If it was true. That had also crossed Carl's mind. Maybe Mark was some kind of freak who lived in a fantasy world. His mother hadn't said much about the past, but enough for him to know that things had been difficult, very difficult. No, Carl believed what Mark had said. He'd learnt enough about men in the army to be sure of that. A part of him wanted to get out now. After a divorce that had spluttered and sparked in his head for the last three years he didn't need this. He could tell himself it wasn't his business. Tell Julie to phone the police and clear off, but that wasn't his style, and she was worth more than that. Even after a short time Carl was sure of this. They had connected. Julie was rough around the edges all right but there was something real about her he liked. He hadn't trusted his ex for years, but this one he felt he could, and, if he was honest, what Mark had told him had been as exciting as it was shocking. He felt a bit like he had when he'd fixed his pack before walking over the Falklands hillsides. The metal of his rifle so cold in his hand it almost took the skin off, wind and rain whipping down off the heights to batter his unit. Frightened, but every sense on full alert, stretched and alive, making him feel so necessary, and that everything in his life was coming together for this moment. That was more than twenty years ago. He was still quite fit, but far from young.

'I'm waiting,' Julie said.

'I want you to phone in sick today. I want you to come down to my place for a while.'

'Jesus, he *has* done something, hasn't he?'

'Well, it's complicated.'

'Aye, it always is.'

Carl sat on the edge of the bed and reached out for Julie. She was sitting up now, wide awake and she knocked his hand away.

'Tell me, Carl, for God's sake.'

Carl did tell her. It was an instant decision. Anything other than the truth would have been impossible, and he knew he would have to tell her sometime. Better now, than in the wake of Mark's death. He was interrupted every other sentence by Julie's disbelief, anger, then fear. Fear turned to resignation as tears blocked her words. Carl felt so sorry for her. She was small anyway, but now Julie seemed to diminish further. She hugged the bedsheets like a child and moaned to herself.

'This can't be happening to me,' she murmured, 'not

again.'

'What?'

'We must have done something awful bad to be punished like this,' Julie said, her voice cracked now. 'I thought Shane was it, I thought we'd reached the bottom then, but we haven't.'

'Shane?'

'I don' want to talk about it. Something long ago.'

Carl knew better than to push this. Shane was obviously a guy from her past, Maybe Mark's father.

'We'll be all right, Jool,' Carl said. 'You'll be safe with me.'

'Will I? And what about Mark? What chance does he have? I'm gonna phone him on his mobile. Tell him to turn himself in. You should have done that yourself. It's the only way he can keep alive.'

'I did think of it, but Mark isn't built that way. And I think he was trying to protect you, Jool, not just from those bastards, but from the media, all that shit. The police don't know anything yet, and Mark wants to keep it that way.'

'So wha's he going to bloody do? Shoot it out on the hillside, like kids playing fucking cowboys?'

Just about right, Carl thought to himself. Men *are* kids. Especially when at their most destructive. And life is always a game, he'd learnt that much, though Mark's games didn't take place in any playground.

Julie was sobbing now, her body wracked. She punched the bed with little fists, then punched Carl's chest in a rapid staccato attack which he barely felt. She punched herself out, then she let him hold her, crushing her in his arms like he had with his children. His two were grown and doing well now, but Carl could identify with what Julie was feeling. Desperate for Mark to be okay, and hating him for getting himself into something like this. For getting them all into it.

'Come on, love. Get washed and dressed. I'll help you pack. We want to be out of here asap.'

Carl checked outside. All was quiet, though he wasn't sure what he was looking for anyway. Two large wops, Mark said, in a gold Lexus, that was all he had to go on. There was a framed photograph of Mark and Lena on Julie's mantelpiece. Mark had given it to Julie the one time he'd brought the girl down. Carl picked it up. She was a looker all right. Had been. He saw that they were in Paris. Mark must have thought he was quids in then, working in London, exotic girlfriend. Now he was hiding out on a hillside somewhere, with rain pissing down. All he could do was make sure Julie was all right, and would stay all right.

Julie put down the phone.

'Told Ann the secretary it was the menopause,' she said. 'I'm bloody old enough, even if it hasn't happened yet. Mark will probably gimme a heart attack before then. 'Julie looked out of the window. 'Look at the bloody weather. Knowing Mark, he'll already be up there by now. He swore he'd never go back.'

'No one could have expected anything like this to happen,' Carl said.

'I could. I know him. He shouldn't have been doing work like that, or taken up with a girl like her. It's always gotta be different with him, but he's always ends up on the outside - in deep shit.'

'Come on, love. Best get going.'

Carl paced around the flat while Julie got ready. His knee hurt, it usually did at this time of the year, then other parts joined it when winter set in. His body was a map of his time in the army. He put Julie's stuff in the boot of the Mercedes, checked around again, then brought her from the flat.

'That's not him,' the big man said.

'No, not unless he's aged twenty years,' Angelo

answered.

The black Mercedes eased out of the side road, its engine practically noiseless.

'Don't get too close now,' Angelo said. 'Don't want to alarm this man, whoever he is.'

'Why should we? Why should they know anything?'

'They know. Richards has been here. They are running. We are chasing.'

Chapter Ten

There was a pub Mark knew on the other side of the hill, and securing his camp as much as possible, he decided to walk there. It might be the last chance he would get, and a lot of early memories were in that place. He took the Smith and Wesson in an inside pocket. It seemed more suitable to the terrain than the automatic. That was a city piece. Clouds raced overhead, fat and black-edged, the sun cutting through them in shafts of pale light. As a kid, in weather like this, he always thought they were guiding him. Searchlights to show him the best tracks through the forest. His forest. His sun.

Mark wished he had the eyes of a hawk, or an insect that could see behind itself. Stellachi wouldn't be the first one looking for him. He'd be the final solution man, coming only if and when needed.

The bar was almost empty. It had a valley equivalent of the elderly man in the Cardiff toilet. Old, worn, slumped over a pint that had long gone flat. There was also a middle-aged couple with London accents. Visitors, maybe even tourists. It amazed Mark that any came here, but they did, in dribs and drabs, now that the valley had been cleansed. Perhaps they were here to look at the churchyard next to the pub. It was unusual. With its crazily listing headstones clinging to twisting turf, it seemed to surf the hilly ground it was built on, its dead moved around by the mine workings underneath. Many of the graves were broken up now, some with black holes that dared you to look in. Mark had loved it there when he was a kid.

He ordered a pint from a kid barman, much too young to be stuck in this place.

'Out for a walk, are you?' the boy asked brightly.

'Something like that.'

'Dried up nice, hasn't it?'

'Yip.'

The kid wanted to talk. The English were leaving and Mark was a better bet than the old man, but Mark cut off the chat and sat in the corner. He'd always sat in the corner. The place hadn't changed much, if at all. Old-fashioned wallpaper was so faded it was hard to tell the original colour, and it was stained dark brown by generations of smoke. He'd drunk here a lot in his late teens, walking over from the estate, usually on his own, sometimes with any girl who'd dared to go out with him.

This might be his last drink and it was tinged by bitter memories, old and new, but Mark was glad he was here. It was a small comfort. There was another message on the mobile but he didn't read it. Let it wait. There was nothing he could say to Julie at the moment and he had plenty of time now. Carl would have got her away, that part had to be a success, it might be his only one.

Two thirds into the glass he read the text. *Mark, I'm worried stupid. Where are u? Get in touch - now.*

He finished the pint, got another, and answered. *I'm all right. Stay with Carl at all times.*

Mark drank the strong local brew and was feeling a little tipsy. He ate the only hot food on offer, a micro-waved meat pie that tasted of hot plastic. It would have revolted Lena, and almost had that effect on him. Mark felt the clash of old and new ways, but he ate it anyway. Hot food would be hard to come by now, unless he risked a fire, another thing he'd loved back then. Hunched over them in all weathers, acting out whatever fantasy was uppermost in his head at the time, always thinking of the better times that lay ahead. Sometimes Daniels was with him, sniffing and whining about the cold, anxious to be home, even if home was an

153

even colder place.

The old geezer hobbled out, and Mark was alone in the pub. He heard a car start up, as old and as wheezy as its owner. Playing out time, Mark thought, waiting. Suddenly the thought of going out at thirty didn't seem so bad.

The kid made a fuss of wiping tables, not sure whether to approach Mark too closely. He was bored, and finally dared to engage Mark again.

'You local? Don't think I've seen you in here before.'

'I've been here. Not for years though.'

'Oh. I'm not here for long. Going to college next week.'

He wanted Mark to ask where but had to supply the answer himself.

'Only Cardiff, I'm sharing a house down there, with the boys from school.'

Mark finished the last of his pint, and licked away the slight moustache from his lips.

'You pull a good pint,' he said, 'for someone going to college.'

He let the kid puzzle that one out and left, walking out into the September afternoon. For him, this time of year had meant nights drawing in and more cover for his stealing. Not many of his generation had managed to get off the estate, not of their own free will anyway. Maybe it was different now. He hoped so. Even if it wasn't, Mark realised he'd rather be hunted on the mountainside than trapped back there.

This day seemed never ending. Despite being out in the open, *his* open, Mark hadn't felt like this since he had been banged up in Portland, in that young offenders place. When he'd looked out on the Dorset shoreline from his multi-bunked dorm, saw the windblown freshness of the coast outside, ached for it, and cursed himself for a fool. Like he was cursing himself now.

As Mark walked a little unsteadily along the track that

fringed the mountain road, he saw the main arteries of the valley floor start to choke up. It was that time of day. Cars chased each other home up and down the valley, most of them coming up from Cardiff and the coast. Some already had their lights on, forming a flashing, linked chain he could sweep from his vantage point. He wondered if the Lexus was one of them.

He'd picked a good spot for his camp. Nothing could come at him without making a lot of noise. The undergrowth at the edge of the forestry was a mess of old stumps, and tangled, decaying wood and front-on from the edge of the trees he could see a hundred yards each way, and anything driving up the mountain road could be heard a mile off.

Mark found a log to sit on and thought again about a fire, just for this night. It would be dangerous, but he felt the need. All the old feelings were coming back. He'd never felt a kinship with people, but he did with this place. If he lost out and they buried him here, he'd be feeding it, nourishing it, becoming a permanent part of it, like the people buried in the lop-sided graveyard. Mark liked this idea, he liked it more than he was afraid of death.

Mark built the fire further into the forest and banked it all around with logs. Its glow would only be visible for a very short distance, even in the dark. The light was going and by the time the wood had caught it was well into dusk. Mark realised he didn't have a torch, so got his stuff together quickly. He opened one of the tins and spooned beans into his mouth. At least the rain had kept off, for he doubted if his makeshift shelter would be too waterproof. He'd be stinking in a few days, a larger version of Kelly. They were two peasants who'd ended up in the big city. Maybe Kelly would achieve a kind of fame amongst his own. His drinking buddies might talk about him for a while, and his star would rise with one brief glimmer. Mark raised an imaginary glass to Kelly now, but it didn't take the guilt

155

away.

He sat close to the fire, on the stump of a tree. The evening had some nip to it. Maybe a hard winter was on the way, but it wouldn't concern him. Mark could not allow himself to see beyond the next few days. There was plenty of dead wood to keep a good flame, and it was summer-dry. It sparked and spat at him as sap bubbled from the ends of logs. Mark was entranced by the red flames, he always had been. When Julie had taken up with someone worse than usual, he'd get away like this, and, if it wasn't pissing down, he'd start a fire and sit out all night. There was a kind of comfort in it. He'd feel cleansed, and in control, and would allow small pieces of self belief to crawl into his thoughts as he watched the fire battle against the frost. When he got home, the new man was usually gone.

Mark took the Smith and Wesson from his jacket and examined it in the firelight. He knew its power now, the way it turned life in an instant, and hated it, but he was still glad it was in his hands. Its snub-nosed barrel glowed in the flames, and it felt right in his grasp. It was easy to think the gun was becoming part of him.

Mark hadn't expected Carl to tell Julie the truth. It hadn't even crossed his mind that he would. As he lay back and watched the sky turn black, he relaxed with the idea. Carl had done right. Maybe Julie would tell him about Shane now and everything would be out in the open. That would test Carl, shake him even further, but if the man was still around tonight, he always would be.

Mark watched the first stars appear. There was not much man-made light here to lessen them, just a hint of orange glow from life below. One of his earliest memories was of his mother telling him that stars were fairies lighting up the sky, as she tucked him up in bed and went back downstairs to whoever. There was also a new moon starting, just a small slice of yellow coming up over the far hillside, but enough to cast the lower slopes in the palest of light. He saw the outline of the valley he knew so well, its contours only hinted at now, but filled in by his memory.

All my old friends are coming out, Mark thought. The moon and the stars and the black night. He'd got to read his patch of sky well in his thieving years. He couldn't name anything apart from The Plough but he knew which stars winked white, yellow or red, and where the brightest ones lay in the map above his head. He'd missed this in the city. Everything was over-lit there, as if they wanted to banish night altogether.

Mark let the fire die down, had a leisurely piss at the edge of the trees, making something scuttle away in the darkness, then pushed his way into his narrow shelter. He used his jacket for a pillow but kept the rest of his clothes on. Despite the weather it was still dank on the ground, and the smell of crumbling wood was all around him. He wasn't the only animal that had watered the ground here either, he smelt the heavy mustiness of a fox that had been past recently. It might be watching the dying fire now, intrigued by this interloper and wondering if food was around. Mark needed to sleep but Lena competed with it, and he saw Julie at bay, until all images faded.

Carl's place reminded Julie of her old estate house, a good view from the window, if you looked far enough away, but crap nearby. It was about the same age too. Sixties stuff that had fallen apart all too easily.

'I bought it off the council when I come out of the army,' Carl said. 'Not much to look at, is it, but it's quiet enough round here. Most of the kids live on the other side. Haven't spent much time here anyway, since the missus left. I had to buy her out.'

'You shouldn't have bothered.'

Carl wrapped himself around Julie's shoulders, as she

stood in his living room, scanning the road outside.

'If you stand on the roof you can see the sea,' Carl murmured.

'Carl, what the hell am I going to do?'

'What are *we* going to do, you mean.'

'Mark's on his own out there.'

'I'd say he's more than capable.'

'Don't give me that man-talk rubbish, I bin hearing it all my life, and it usually ends up as an excuse for something stupid, or dangerous. Oh, he's hard all right, whatever that means, but not for stuff like this. He's not a killer, for Godsake, people shooting each other, girls getting cut up. We're ordinary people, Carl.'

Carl thought he was going to have another pummelling but Julie let him hold her. She sobbed without making any noise, her body shaking in his arms.

'Mark had a good idea,' Carl said,' about going to Ireland. We could drive over in the morning on the ferry. There'll be plenty of space this time of year. We could lose ourselves over on that west coast for a while. No one would ever look there, Jool.'

'Aye, but what about him, though? It's Mark they want, not us. He'll be on his own.'

'Jool, he's on his own now, girl. We can't help him. Going to the police won't stop this - even if they did believe us, which I very much doubt.'

'I dunno. I just dunno.'

'Look, it's the best way to help him. He'll have one less thing to worry about. If he can keep away from these guys long enough perhaps that will end it.'

Julie turned to face him. 'Do you really think that, Carl?'

'Course I do. They won't be hunting for him for ever. Maybe he can skip the country then. A boy like him will always find work.'

Lying wasn't Carl's style, but it seemed to calm Julie.

'Have you got any food here?' she murmured. 'We might as well eat something.'

'Aye, in the fridge.'

'These people are poor,' Angelo said.

They were parked a few hundred yards from Carl's house. The big man had followed well, never too close, but always keeping them in sight. A skill that had taken years to perfect.

'This is poor?' the big man answered, sweeping a hand around the estate.

'For here, yes.'

'We could have done with some of this poverty back home.'

'Tony said the mother was on her own. This man complicates things.'

'Not much.'

'We must finish this cleanly. If the police here get involved in any way, Amsterdam will not be pleased.'

'When are they ever? We are still ruled, just like back home.'

Angelo slapped the big man's shoulder.

'Look at your clothes, the rings on your fingers, this car you drive. This is not like back home!'

Angelo took an untipped cigarette from a gold case and handed it to his friend.

'That was Agani's, wasn't it?' the big man asked.

'Twenty-two carat, made in Istanbul.'

'Turks! Not worth pissing on.'

'Their cigarettes are. Black Sobranie. Agani knew about fine things. Calm down, put some music on.'

The big man clumsily inserted a CD into the player. A strident Albanian band played, lots of tight strings and lamenting voices. Both men sucked on their smokes and tapped large fingers on knees. A woman passing with a pram paused and glanced at them.

'Turn it down,' Angelo said.

Lights came on in Carl's house. Angelo could see him pass across a window. As with most of his life, Angelo was unsure what was going to happen next. They knew where this Richards had lived, about his crimes, and the baby brother he had probably killed. Tony had been good for stories. Maybe Richards had told the mother where he was going now, maybe he'd told them about Lena and Agani, maybe not, but Angelo could not afford to take any chances. It would not be enough to kill Richards if others knew.

'Are we going to kill them?' the big man asked.

'Be quiet, I'm thinking.'

Angelo did not like thinking. It never got any easier. Far better to let others like Agani do it, but Agani was gone, and Stellachi was not here, not yet. These two people would not be so easy to get rid of as that Kelly. He went through options in his mind. It could be an accident, maybe a fire, or a car crash, or the man could kill this Julie and then kill himself. Maybe they could just disappear. Yes, that would be best.

Angelo pushed the seat back, and inhaled the opulence of the car along with his smoke. He ran his hands along its leather seats and noted the brushed chrome fittings. He closed his eyes and let the music take him. It was from the hills of his birth, they used to play it in the small café in the village. He'd grubbed in the dirt outside with the big man and others long dead. The big man was the big boy then, always ready to protect him, hurting other boys with increasing pleasure. He'd never changed.

Two kids were watching the car from the opposite pavement. One stuck up a solitary finger to Angelo. Angelo smiled and made a gun shape with his hand and pointed it at the boys. They smiled back, then got scared and ran off into an adjoining lane. Angelo had the real thing in the inside pocket of his jacket. He nudged the big man.

'Put your cigarette out. It's almost down to your fingers. Come on, we'll leave the car here. I've decided what to do.'

They were both getting old but the big man was still eager. He plodded behind Angelo towards the house, smiling and flexing his fists. Age had not dulled his malice one bit.

'Are these eggs all right?' Julie asked. 'they look a bit old.'

Carl was surprised she could think about eating. He thought she'd be in bits about this.

'It will have to be egg and chips then,' Julie said, 'you're not exactly stocked up.'

'Fine. Look, what do you think about this Ireland idea?'

'We'd be abandoning him. Maybe Mark should be with us. Stick together, like.'

'What, you want to be a cowboy too?'

'Don' be stupid, Carl.'

'Sorry. No, he'd never have it, Jool. I'd never have it. Like I said before, he needs to know you're safe.'

'He'll be up there by now. On them hills. He used to know them like the back of his hand.'

'Probably still does. That's a big advantage.'

'This is all so bloody unreal. Mark used to always go an about films when he was a kid, video mad, he was. Sometimes I thought he got them mixed up with real life. And I feel like that now. That we're all in a bloody horror show. Talking about Mark shooting it out with thugs, trying to stay alive. It's ridiculous.'

'Maybe. But it's real all right. Come to Ireland with me, Jool. You can keep in touch with him on your mobile.'

Julie put the food on two plates but pushed hers away.

'I can't eat mine. Don' really see the point.'

'What's the good in thinking like that?'

'Whatever happens it's a nightmare. After Shane went I

didn't think life could get any worse. And it didn't. It calmed down, became something that never changed, always grey, but I got used to that. Until you come along.'

'Was Shane Mark's father? Look, you don't have to tell me anything if you don't want to.'

'His father? Hardly.' Julie stared at Carl and made her decision. 'Shane was Mark's baby brother. I was stupid then, and got pregnant with some waster off the estate. He wasn't interested and neither was I after I got to know him. He left me with a little boy - Shane. Nothing like that sod, thank God, nothing like Mark either. He was lovely, Carl. Blond hair, blue eyes, Christ knows where he come from. A little scamp, mind. He adored Mark, hung around him all the time. I thought Mark would bugger off when Shane was born but he didn't. It was hard for us at first, but we pulled together. What do they say now? Bonded.'

'Did Shane pass away?'

'Maybe. Passed away from us, anyway.'

'What do you mean?'

'He disappeared. From the garden out the back.'

'I don't get it.'

'No, no one did. I'd left him with Mark and had gone shopping. It was a beautiful day, so Mark had him out the back. He answered the phone and when he came back out Shane was gone. Don' you remember about it? It was in all the papers for days, telly, everything. They were around the estate like a cloud of flies.'

'No, I don't. When was it?'

'Bout twelve years ago, now.'

'I was still in the army then. Away somewhere, probably.'

'There was never no trace of him, Carl. Never. Everyone thought Mark had done something. They always thought he was nuts on the estate anyway. Used to call him Psycho Eyes.'

'What about you?'

'I wasn't sure for a while. It was just the way Shane went. They never found nothing, no clothing, no trace of Shane at all. But I know now Mark didn't harm him, that's the one thing I am sure of. Every other thought has gone through my mind though, it's always there, some days worse than others.'

'Jesus,' Carl whispered, as he pushed his own food away. 'I had no idea. No one deserves that.'

It was getting harder for Julie to talk.

'Some of the women up there thought we were in it together. Oh, they give me a social worker, all that stuff. She was all right, too, but all she could offer was words in the end. She said kids had disappeared like that before but it was very rare. No one saw nothing, that was the thing. They were a nosy bunch around me at the best of times but everyone was deaf, dumb and blind that day. We'll never know what happened now. Sometimes I think he might be alive somewhere, with a new life. Maybe living with rich people. Sometimes I think other things.'

Julie was crying freely now. Carl took her to the sofa and held her. A few weeks ago he'd thought he'd met someone for a bit of fun. Someone like him, who'd been around the block a few times and wanted no complications. He'd need to think about this. It put a new slant on Mark. For a black moment Carl wondered if Mark might have turned it all around, that he'd killed Lena and that Agani fella, because she was having it off with him. No, it wouldn't do to go there. He'd have no future with Julie if he did. Future! What the fuck was he thinking off? This was a mess. He'd been better off in the Falklands. At least there you knew who was shooting at you.

Carl kept Julie in his arms for a while, hoping she'd drop off to sleep. He felt her tiny fists pull at his shirt like a baby, as she cried softly and mumbled the occasional word. He was almost falling asleep himself when he heard someone moving around outside.

*

Mark was cold when he woke up. Cold and damp. It had rained in the night. Soft stuff, but enough to gather on his sheet and drip into his bracken shelter. Lying on his back he listened to a dawn chorus of crows, and the nerve locked into their harsh, raw-throated, communal call. They were in the trees at the edge of the forest, gearing up for their day. He'd never liked them, or any other noisy birds. Crows, jays, magpies, gulls, they were all a waste of space. He preferred birds that went quietly about their business, like the hawk that moved above him now. Moving effortlessly, wings trying to catch the weak sun that had struggled out, looking for any nocturnal straggler that was late getting home. The crows saw it and made off with loud warning cries. They made a living down below, and had allied themselves to mankind long ago.

Mark got up and stretched the stiffness out of his neck and the lumps from his back. He was glad it had turned fine again, it would give him a chance to dry out. Sitting on his already shapeless rucksack Mark surveyed his new kingdom. Most foliage around him was browning up and dying, some stuff still grew, but in the last flush of growth. As a kid he'd noticed how thick and green grass was at this time of the year, now it was slicked with dew and shining at the verge of the hill road, lush in the first light. He liked this sense of life turning. It matched his own.

Reluctantly, Mark turned his phone on. He had several voicemails. They would be pleas from Julie. She would have had a night to think over things. She'd want him to turn himself in. He'd blown it. Angelo and the big man should have gone the same way as Agani. Then maybe he'd be running all over the world, but never coming back to Wales.

Never bringing trouble home. He'd reverted to type, bolting for the burrow, like all hunted animals. He put the phone to his ear.

It was Angelo's voice. *Mark, your mother wants to talk to you.*

Mark froze. Julie's voice was distorted. It had the scalding quality he'd last heard when Shane disappeared, like she was shouting from the bottom of a pit, with all hope shaken out of it.

Mark, listen to me, for Christsake. They come in here. They hurt Carl. He's bad. Get away Mark, don' meet with them ...

The phone went dead, but there was another message.

Your mother is upset. We understand. We want to see you, Mark. We'll bring your mother. You say where. Your mother will be our guide. Our helper. We need to hear from you by ten in the morning. It would be best that you phone.

Mark sat down heavily. The time on his phone said eight thirty and Angelo had phoned at two in the morning. He should have checked it again in the night, he'd woken up often enough. This was worse than his worst nightmare. He had to think. If they came up here with Julie, they'd never let them leave alive. She knew too much now.

Mark got the guns out of the rucksack, and checked them. They had his mother, and Carl was probably already dead. They'd killed a man who had nothing to do with this, whose only crime was to walk in on the world of the Richards family.

Mark moved around for a few minutes, trying to get the circulation coursing through his stiff body. He wasn't sure if he was talking to himself, and he jumped whenever he heard a noise. The hawk was still gliding around but Mark didn't look so kindly on it now. He was jealous of the bird's freedom, and its control over its short, uncomplicated life. He phoned Julie's number. It rang ten times before Angelo answered.

'Ah, Mark, it is you. So you are well?'

Mark wanted to scream and shout down the phone but no words came.

'Do you want to speak to your mother?'

'Yes.'

'Mark! Are you there? They just appeared. Carl's unconscious. Oh God, I can' handle this.'

Angelo was saying something to her.

'Mark, they want to meet. Want me to take them up to the valley.'

'All right.'

They wanted an empty space and no people, then it would be a bullet in each of their brains and maybe a trip in the boot of their car to Dungeness. It would be too much fuss to bury two bodies. Carl might already be in the boot. The Lexus was big enough for three. At least he had some time, if they were still down on the coast, but Mark couldn't even be sure of that.

'Pick a place, my friend. Your mother will guide us.'

'The churchyard by the pub. She'll know which one, she'll know where.'

'At ten then,' Angelo said. 'Don't disappoint. And Mark, please, no tricks. For your mother's sake.'

The phone went dead. Maybe the church wasn't the best spot, he did think of the shrine near the estate, a stone statue on the hillside that had marked his early life, but that would have been crazy, even by his standards. Within minutes the whole estate would have turned out, then the police force. It would have been the Richards' finale, a very public one. No, the church was practically unused now, the people in its ground long dead and unvisited.

The light was a soft yellow, haze rising from the valley floor as the sun gathered strength. Cars on the road again. Maybe this would be the last warm day of the year. His anyway.

Mark forced himself to eat, trying to think of a plan that wasn't pathetic. Trying to think of any plan. Events had been one step ahead of him throughout all of this. He hadn't expected Kelly to get killed, he hadn't expected to kill Agani, and he hadn't expected Angelo to get to Julie and Carl. Carl *must* be dead, they'd never leave him otherwise.

Mark checked the guns again, making sure he knew how to use the automatic. It was easy enough, there was nothing hard about guns. Point, press and shoot. One long steady pull on the trigger and it would shoot its load. Nine slugs that could go anywhere because he had no idea what his aim was like. Agani had been close, can't-miss material.

He packed both guns back in the sack. He packed everything, in fact, like some old warrior going on the final journey, taking his essentials into the next world, but there was no time to think about what came after death, if anything. It was ten minutes to the churchyard, so Mark would have an hour before they came, an hour to come up with something.

Chapter Eleven

'What was that?' Carl said.

'I didn't hear nothing.'

'I did, there's someone outside. Maybe it's just kids.'

Carl checked the window, looking for a gold car. There was the usual assortment of bangers up and down the road, and a black Mercedes farther up, its nose just sticking out from a side road. It was a new version of his car, someone here must be doing OK, Carl thought, as the back door burst open. The big man slammed into him before he managed to turn. Carl saw something blur in his hand, heard Julie scream, then nothing else.

Angelo followed and he slapped Julie hard.

'You must stop that noise,' he said.

Angelo raised his hand again but Julie stuck hers in her mouth and managed to control herself, despite tasting her blood. Carl had crumpled to the floor, with a huge man standing over him. She tried to go to him but Angelo held her.

'Leave him. His worries are over.'

'You haven't killed him?'

Angelo shrugged and half carried her to a chair. He forced her down on it with his hand.

'Where is your son?'

He asked for Mark but Julie saw Shane. Her last image of him, as she left him in the garden with a reluctant Mark, to go shopping. He was playing on a mound of sand the council had left. His own private beach. The only one he'd ever seen. This was her final punishment for losing him and it came through Mark. Again.

Carl didn't seem to be moving. He was curled up on the floor like a large baby. Like Shane. A brute in an expensive suit stood over him, and winked at her. The suit didn't fit, his body wanted to escape from it, muscles and hard flesh pushed against its seams. There was something in his hand, that thing they used to change car wheels, and she saw a thin trickle of blood seeping from Carl's skull.

'I see your son has told you about us,' Angelo said. 'You are frightened, but not surprised.'

'He hasn't told me nothing.'

'Maybe this man then. No matter. It's a pity though, a pity for you. Where's Mark?'

'He's gone away. To Spain.'

'Really? But he doesn't fly. He *can't* fly.'

Julie just about stopped herself asking how this bastard knew that but she could answer it herself. That bitch Lena. She must have told them everything she knew about Mark. Angelo put his hand over her face. It enveloped her and she thought she was going to choke. She tried to kick out at him, but the man was like a tree. He let her breathe again.

'Where's Mark?'

'Look, you can fuckin' kill me but I still won't know. I've never known where he is, not for years I haven't.'

'He's close. Let's phone him. I think he'd like to know we are here, with you.'

Angelo changed languages and told the big man to get the car and bring it to the front door. He dialled a number and handed Julie the phone. The bastards even knew Marks mobile number, she realised. Angelo's ear pressed close to her mouth as she spoke and she felt his breath on her face. It was sweet, and smelt of mints, and behind that, old garlic. Julie was not sure what words came out. She wanted to tell Mark to get away. She wanted to curse and blame him; she wanted him to live. That came to her as clear as Angelo's lousy breath. Despite all the shit, blind alleys and despair, she wanted Mark to live. She wanted Carl to live and she wanted to live herself.

Julie glanced down at Carl. He'd had no chance and might be dead already. The other man, even bigger than the one that held her, stood over him like a hunter showing off his kill. How could Mark have got mixed up with people like these?

'Tell him we'll meet with him,' Angelo said.

Julie did what she was told. The numbness she felt was the same as when Shane vanished, but that had come without any warning. She'd had time to think about this. She wished that they'd all kept together. Maybe they would have had a chance then; she knew Mark's capabilities. But he didn't tell her, he couldn't tell her, that had always been their problem. Just the two of them for so long, but their thoughts miles apart, and their tongues locked with the distance. Maybe if Carl hadn't been there Mark might have blurted it all out. Maybe.

The men were talking in another language again. The big one prodded Carl with his foot but got no response.

'My friend wants to take your man with us,' Angelo said, but we'll come back for him later. He's not going anywhere.'

'You bastard!' As she shouted, Julie tried to strike up at Angelo's face but he caught her hand and twisted it.

'So, a little spirit. Like your son. What is your name?'

He twisted harder when she didn't answer. Another millimetre and her wrist would snap.

'Didn't that slut tell you? I thought you knew everything.'

'You mean Lena? She just called you the mother. Don't make me ask again.'

'Julie.'

'So.'

Angelo repeated it to himself, but had trouble with the

'J'.

'You will be our guide. You will be a good guide, then we can talk to your son, work things out.'

'Like you worked things out with Carl.'

'That was necessary, he would have caused a fuss. He's not important.'

Julie wanted to launch herself at Angelo again, to try to give back a little pain, but she controlled herself. She felt sick to the pit of her stomach. Carl lay a few feet away from her and looked dead, but she had to choke this down – concentrate on staying alive herself.

'Get what you need,' Angelo said, 'but don't shut any doors.'

'I need the toilet.'

'If I don't see you, even for a second, I'll break one of those pretty wrists.'

Angelo looked at Carl's body.

'He must have had a thin skull,' he muttered, and, to the big man, 'I could hit you all day like that and nothing much would happen. When we kill this Richards we'll come back for the one here. We'll take them with us.'

'And the woman?'

'Her too, what choice do we have? Then it will be over, and we can get back to business. There'll be no need for Stellachi and Amsterdam will like that.'

'Let me kill this Mark,' the big man said.

'Hah, you still feel his boot on your face, eh? Sure, if you want.'

Julie came back into the living room. Angelo's eyes hadn't left her, and she felt dirty, and helpless.

'You should have a coat,' Angelo said. 'The sun is out but the wind is quite cold. Summer is over here, what summer you have. We will walk calmly to the car. If anyone sees us, you will also look calm. This makes sense, doesn't it, Shulie?'

They went out the back way, through the flimsy door the big man had demolished. As Julie glanced back at Carl, tears came again to her eyes, despite her best efforts to keep them out.

Carl waited until the footsteps outside faded. Everything he'd learnt in the army had kept him still when he'd come around. That big bugger hit hard, and it had knocked him out before he knew what was happening. All he'd seen was a blur of metal in the man's hand. He hadn't been much help to Julie and he cursed himself for it now, but at least he was alive. Those two bastards thought he was dead, that was a mistake and he had to make it count.

Carl got up unsteadily, his head crushing him with pain. He got to the bathroom, threw up what he'd eaten then doused himself with cold water. He washed the blood from his short hair and felt better. He'd always taken a good shot, and that bastard had connected with the thickest part of his skull. It was not easy to focus, and he felt weak, but thought he could function.

Carl had been conscious for the last few minutes. He didn't know where that church was but he knew how to get to Julie's old estate; he'd worked up that valley, on and off. The church must be on the mountain road on the hillside above.

Carl took the largest kitchen knife he had, not much good against guns, but it was better than nothing. His old assault rifle would be useful now. He'd pick those two off on that hillside no trouble, they'd be dead before they knew what was happening. It would be a pleasure, but it was wishful thinking. If any of them got out of this it would be a miracle. There was always the police, but it was too late for them now. This was hardly a usual occurrence down here. Ex-local now London private eye shooting it out with Albanian gangsters on a Welsh hillside. They'd just think he was barking and would faff around until it was too late.

Carl drank some water, found his car keys and went out the front door of the house. Getting to his car was harder than he thought and his left arm seemed to be stiffening up. These guys were not so clever. They should have done more than just prod him with a foot, even the greenest kids in the army knew that. They were too cocky by half and perhaps he could make them pay. They were only a few miles in front, and this time it would be their turn to be surprised.

The sun was well up now and Mark was hot and sweaty by the time he reached the church. He sat on a fallen headstone and drank from his bottle of water. There was no one about, and the pub further down the road was not open yet. That kid would be cleaning out the bar, and counting down the days. If there was shooting it would carry for miles here, but it was not uncommon on the hillside. He doubted if anyone around these parts could tell the difference between a shotgun and a hand-gun.

The hawk was still out, wheeling above him, checking out this figure in the churchyard. It was looking for food and Mark knew how prey felt now. Creatures always on the look out for danger, and death the penalty for missing it. He'd always been the strong one, the hunter, now he too had become furtive, seeing danger everywhere. The hawk's outspread wings caught the light, and looked like a gold fan for a moment. Mark raised a hand to it and it veered away.

Carl was out of the picture, and they had Julie. Angelo and his big friend would think they were home and dry, but that might make them over-confident. They'll want to get me into their car, Mark thought, try to avoid any action out in the open. They'll try to make me think they'll let Julie go, give me a snippet of hope, but that's something I abandoned four days ago.

Mark looked around for the best place to stash the

automatic. He placed it in a gap of the grave of a woman who'd died before she was forty. He read her headstone. A teacher. Watch over that for me, he murmured. Then he went to the middle of the graveyard. Let them come out here for me, he thought, let them disarm me, and search the bag. It was a gamble. He might not be able to get at the other gun, they might shoot him and Julie out of hand. If the kid came running up from the pub he might get it too, they weren't particular. But at least a plan had formed, such as it was.

Mark opened his sack and found an apple. He was surprisingly calm. It was very quiet here, just the faintest of road noises from down below, and the hawk above calling a few times, a thin-pitched cry, wanting him to be gone from its domain. It was very still, as if nature knew what was about to unfold, and had stopped to watch. He thought of Lena and Paris, when it had came upon him that he was happy, for the first time in his life. Such a strange sensation that he didn't know what it was at first. Something seemed to grow inside, that put a cloak over all the bad times, and drew him out into a world he'd glimpsed before, but had never thought his.

Mark ate the apple and threw the stump over the church wall, attracting the attention of a pair of magpies. As he watched their display of blue-black and white he saw a car climbing the hill road, just for a second before it was out of sight again. Something large and black, not a gold Lexus, but he knew it was them. He felt inside his coat for the Smith and Wesson. Julie was alive, but he had just minutes to keep her that way.

The car was getting nearer now, then it was out in the open, a few hundred yards from the church. Mark had positioned himself so that the church blocked out any view from the pub. If anyone else appeared, maybe someone deciding to visit the long dead, it would be too bad.

174

The first thing Carl did was drive into the kerb. His vision was not too good. He reached the motorway, and sped along it, flashed by more than one speed camera. I'll lose my licence, he thought, ha ha. He'd almost lost his life, and was about to gamble it again. He did drop his speed to seventy though, it wouldn't do to be chased by the police now.

He was on the road to the valley in thirty minutes, but there was no sign of the black Merc. The back of his head pulsated with pain and each beat clouded his eyes. His vision was clear for a few moments then blurred again, as if the car's wipers were working on his eyes, and his arm was getting worse. A few cars beeped him as he swung too far to their side of the road, and he was bleeding again. He felt it drip onto his neck, then down his shirt.

Carl was climbing into forestry. The sun was out but the landscape was still bleak, every tree mimicked the next, in dull, dark green. He'd never been a man for the great outdoors, there'd been enough fresh air in the Falklands to last him a lifetime. More than once down there he'd felt stuff whizz past his head and wondered if the next round had his name on it. He'd been glad to get away from that bloody cove, to feel a fresh wind in his face rather than the smell of diesel burning that settled into his guts. Better to be shot clean than burnt to a crisp, like some of the boys, he'd thought. Until he was actually shot at. He'd got through that but here he was again, in another crazy situation not of his own making. Julie said that Mark attracted trouble like shit-flies and maybe that was true about him too. It was usually his patrol that had been in the thick of it in Belfast, but he'd been protected by his age then. Not quite twenty and thinking he'd live for ever, and playing at soldiers was still exciting, a natural progression from the games on the estate he played with his mates. Some of them had got into serious troubles over the years, some had sorted themselves and escaped, some, like him, went into the army. A sort of halfway house towards respectability. So he wasn't that different to Mark, just a bit luckier.

After a few minutes Carl skirted Mark's estate and headed for the hill road. He slowed down, taking the old Merc down to third and just gliding it to the edge of the trees which fringed each side of the road. Ahead was a few hundred yards of open road, and the church. The Mercedes was parked outside, but he couldn't see into the churchyard. From this angle its surrounding wall blocked any view. Carl stopped the car and let it idle. He was barely conscious and there was a numbing sensation spreading up through his arm to his face. It was in his cheek now, which felt like he'd had a shot off the dentist. He tried to flex his arm but it wouldn't obey him.

Carl waited. Surely nothing would happen in such an open place, Christ, there was a pub not far down the road. This was all so unreal, but then everything had been, since Julie's son knocked on the bloody door.

The Mercedes had the sun behind it when it came into the open. It stopped on the brow of the hill above the church, then left the cover of the trees and came on slowly towards the church.

Mark wanted to scream, to let everything out, as if it might give him a solution. It was a ridiculous thought but the need came on him strongly. He'd seen a film with Lena once. He remembered it because it was the first time he'd ever gone to the cinema, as an adult. It had always been video crap in the house when he was a kid. Julie took him to see *Snow White* once, but even at the age of seven that was something from another world, and it had bored him rigid. Lena liked old stuff, classics, she called them. With her, he'd sat through something about Germany before the war, lots of dancing, singing, and poofs prancing about in

176

nightclubs. There was a woman in that, who liked to scream under railway bridges when a train passed overhead. He hadn't understood that scene then, but he did now. All that woman's rage and frustration was being pumped out. She felt better afterwards. Something bad was gone from her. That was just a film, but this sudden urge was shaping up his jaw as the black car stopped outside the church.

Angelo and the big man got out of the car. They were dressed in city overcoats, which meant they couldn't move very fast. Not that they had to. They had Julie. They'd killed Carl. All the power was theirs. The big man had his arm around his mother, it was almost an affectionate hold, but Julie squirmed like a kid. She looked tiny and ashen-faced. Mark had done it to her again. Perhaps they'd both been slowly dying since that day Shane vanished. Perhaps that was what the need to scream was all about. All that lay within exposed to the world in one, long, desperate shout.

Angelo pushed open the iron gate of the churchyard. It creaked, emphasising the still quiet that was around them. Mark saw the hawk head swiftly away down the valley. You're not dull, mate, he thought. Mark stood up by the tall headstone of the dead teacher and Angelo saw him. He approached Mark, the big man staying back with Julie.

'So, Mr Mark Richards. Here we are again.'

Mark didn't answer at first. Each man studied the other. Mark saw Kelly, hurtling through space, a lifetime's booze washed out of him in a second. Hitting concrete. His hand tightened on the Smith and Wesson in his right-hand pocket. Angelo glanced towards it.

'That would be stupid.'

'Let my mother go.'

'Can I come closer? We can talk.'

Angelo shouted something to the big man.

'I tell him to keep your mother safe, not to harm her. Unless, of course, you *are* stupid.'

'That's close enough,' Mark said.

'Okay, I'll sit here.'

Angelo brushed leaves from an elaborate marble gravestone, long since fallen to the ground.

'What is this language?' he murmured. 'Not English.'

'What have you done to Carl?' Mark said.

'It was unfortunate. Sometimes people get in the way. If he hadn't tried to take your mother away it might have been different.'

'No, it wouldn't have.'

Angelo smiled. The same thin smile Agani had used, one which didn't reveal any teeth.

'Maybe not. It's business, no? I've said this to you before. Such a pity you shot Agani. You should have accepted things. Got on with your life.'

Mark nodded towards Julie. 'Let her go.'

'Maybe, maybe.' Angelo patted his pocket. 'Can I get a cigarette?'

Mark nodded. Better for Angelo to occupy his hands this way.

'There was no need for that bastard to kill Lena. He didn't gain anything from it. That's not *business*.'

'You have me there, Mark. I agree. But Stellachi is Stellachi. How do you say it in English - a law to himself.' Angelo sighed. 'My English is good now. My mother would be so proud. She's still alive, you know. Eighty-three. I send her things.'

'Let her go and I'll come with you. Let her walk down to that pub.'

'Mark, Mark. How can I? What I say to you is, give me your weapon and get into the car with us. We can talk there, not out in the open like this, in this place of the dead.'

'I thought it was the perfect spot.'

'I like your style, man. We could use someone like you. You'd fit in well. Agani was annoying too many people, his

178

death might be forgiven. You have balls, Mark.'

He was being fed a crock of shit but Mark decided to go with it. Angelo was used to dealing with stupid people, with stupid values and stupid lives.

'Come on, Mark. Give me your gun. Give me both your guns.'

'I only have one. I gave the other to Carl.'

Angelo pulled hard on his smoke.

'Oh, I am forgetting my manners. Do you want one?'

Mark shook his head.

'Which gun do you have, you say?'

'The 38.'

'Put it down then - there.'

Angelo pointed to a spot between them. 'That gun behaves, it is from the old days. Automatics are unpredictable.'

Angelo shouted something else to the big man, who put a pistol to the back of Julie's head. It was dull black but the sun still caught it, and displayed it to Mark. Anyone out for a walk on the old hill road would get the sight of their life. And the fright.

'No tricks now, Mark. Just place it on the ground.'

The gun did not want to leave Mark's hand. He felt it declaring an ownership. If this was Hollywood he'd drill the big man between the eyes before he could react then down Angelo as he struggled to free his own gun from his coat. Then wrap up Julie in his arms and get her away. Carl wouldn't be dead, and Shane would come back, a clean-cut teenager who'd escaped to a better life. If this was Hollywood. Mark wasn't sure if he could even hit Angelo and he was just feet away from him.

Mark put the gun down.

'Now kick it away.'

Mark did. It slid into the long grass like a snake.

'Good, good.'

The big man put his own gun away but kept a brawny arm around Julie's neck. Anyone passing would think it was an awkward embrace.

'Lean against that headstone,' Angelo said. 'Come on, Mark, we're almost there. You are still alive, and so is Shulie. Angelo kicked Mark's legs further apart, police style, and searched him for the other gun. Mark sensed his wariness. Angelo knows Carl never had that automatic, but he can't find it on me, he thought. He's worried about that.

'So,' Angelo said, 'you are clean. If your friend did have the other gun it didn't help him much, did it? Guns are overrated. They cause too much trouble, you know that now, eh?'

'I always knew it.'

Angelo looked around quickly, then hit Mark hard into his rib cage. He didn't see it coming and was badly winded, dropping onto one knee for a moment.

'You take a pretty good shot,' Angelo said. 'That's for what happened in London.'

Mark heard Julie shout out something but her voice was smothered by the big man's hand.

'Come on,' Angelo said, 'let's go to the car.'

The big man moved farther back with Julie, they were just outside the church gates now, by the side of the car. Mark knew he had to walk as close to the other gun as possible, grab it, stick it in Angelo's ear without him resisting, and pray he could get the big man to swap Julie for Angelo. Easy, Mark. A piece of piss. The big man might snap Julie's neck in a second and let Angelo sink or swim, but it was the only plan he had.

'Don' come, Mark,' Julie shouted, her voice thin, and almost lost in the wind, but loud enough to startle a few birds. They replied to her nervously, chattering from the trees that fringed the churchyard. They'd been quiet up until now, sensing that something very strange was going down, even by human standards.

'Save yourself,' Julie added, rather forlornly.

'Too late, Mam.'

As Mark said this he pushed Angelo over as hard as he could, dropped to the floor and fished for the automatic. He got it at the second attempt, but was still too quick for Angelo. His size was no advantage here. Mark had the gun against the man's temple as Angelo was trying to scrabble up with his own gun. Angelo shouted something short to the big man that Mark knew must be *kill her* in their language. The big man's fingers tensed on the trigger but nothing happened. He shouted something back but did not increase his grip on Julie's neck.

'Stupid,' Angelo shouted, 'stupid, Claudan.'

'Tell him to let her go,' Mark said, 'tell him to get in the car, then you can join him.'

'I told him to kill her,' Angelo murmured.

'I know you did, you bastard. Why hasn't he?'

'Because we are brothers and Claudan is a fool. He still thinks he looks after me. He still believes in family, and blood, and he doesn't think the woman is worth it. Any woman.'

'Are any of us? Do you really want to die that much?'

'No more than you, but if we let you go, we are dead anyway. That's how it works. Is it not a lovely world, my friend?'

Mark stood behind Angelo, and it was the Albanian's turn to be searched. He took back his Smith and Wesson, and another automatic, the twin of the one he held, and a small notebook. He was now the three-gun kid but Angelo seemed more concerned about the notebook.

'You are only stretching things out,' Angelo said. 'Even if you get away now, where will you go? What will you do?'

'Why can't it be over? No one has to know about this. Agani's dead but you've killed Lena, Tony, Kelly and Carl.

Four for one. Four eyes for one.'

'Maybe it would be, if it was up to me. I agree, Agani was not worth all this fuss, but if you take an eye from us, and if it is an important eye, we demand both yours, and the eyes of your loved ones and anyone else who gets in the way. That is how it is. Everyone will know about Agani, in all the countries we operate in. How do you say it - the grapevine. They are not interested in why he died, but they are interested in you now, and how *you* die, and how soon you die. And who kills you. A lot of them will like this. It's like the old days, before we were rich, and behaved like whores.'

'Yeah, I know - it's business.'

'More tradition, but you are learning.'

'Why my mother?'

'As I said, because she's part of you, and she knows too much now. This is your fault, if you wanted to protect her you should not have come back. You should have put a gun to your head.'

Angelo's words sunk home. Mark changed guns. He did not trust the trigger of the automatic, the Smith and Wesson felt more solid, a gun for outdoors, and he could see the barrel start to revolve as it prepared to go to work.

'Don't say anything else that isn't English,' Mark said.

'Or what? You think Claudan won't snap your mother's neck like a twig if you shoot me?'

Mark stuck his head close to Angelo's, and pushed the gun's barrel hard against the back of his neck. He smelt peppermint.

'I think I'm past caring. We'll all go together, you and your brother, me and Mam.'

He wasn't past caring, but this had an effect on Angelo. Mark pushed him forward until they were close to Julie and the big man. He talked to Angelo's brother himself.

'Let her go, if you want Angelo to live. Then get in your

car. Keep your hands on the wheel and Angelo can join you. Then you go.'

The big man nodded and pushed Julie forward.

'Get behind me, Mam,' Mark said, 'but keep to the side.'

He was aware of Julie passing him, heard her racked sobs as she stumbled over the cracked-up ground of the graveyard but he did not look around. He didn't take his eyes off the big man, or relax his grip on his brother. The big man did what he was told, and held the Mercedes wheel with his bear-like hands, heavy gold glinting from his fingers. Mark dared a glance around to check on Julie.

'Get behind that large headstone, and stay there.'

'I'm not leaving you.'

'Mam, for Christsake, just go. I'll be with you now.'

Mark pushed Angelo through the church gate to the car. He realised he could probably shoot the pair of them. For the second time.

'Get in the car and go,' Mark shouted. 'Just fuck off.'

Why couldn't he shoot? He had before, but he was not like these men, not by a long chalk. Ripping up women, throwing old men out of windows, it was all far removed from anything he'd done. These were creatures from his darkest fantasies, but they were real, they were here and they put his petty felonies into perspective. Mark doubted if either man had a heart any more; what ticked within was just a machine, any humanity had been brutalised out of it a long time ago, like it had almost been with him. Almost. Mark knew now, at this most extreme moment, that *almost* was a very important word and it gave him strength. He had to take this chance to get Julie away. Extra time was the only prize on offer here, Mark knew it, and so did the brothers.

Angelo got into the car, shut the door, and pointed a two fingered gun at him. His thin smile came back as he leant forward in the car and came up with the real thing, a short-barrelled shotgun. Angelo pushed the door back open and levelled up the gun. At this range it would take anything out. The man was calm, sure of his actions and did not rush, making his movements look like a slow-motion replay. Mark had plenty of time to shoot but his finger locked on the trigger and did not press. In his mind Agani's head was separating again.

The shotgun fired but it did not hit him. It did not hit anything, apart from sky. The Mercedes spun out on to the road, as an older one smashed into it.

Chapter Twelve

The old Merc was travelling fast. It slammed into the new one, pushing it down the road, until both cars crashed into the wall at the end of the churchyard. Carl's blew up. A fireball that engulfed both cars. Two smashed lumps of metal locked together like lovers started to burn. Mark saw the big man desperately try to smash the front screen before his face was lost in flame, and there were further explosions as ammunition went off. Angelo's side of the car was badly mashed and there was no movement at all there. Mark couldn't see Carl but he heard someone call out. He turned to see Carl fifty yards up the road, crawling along the grass verge, his head like a red rag. Mark ran to him, stuffing his gun back into a pocket. Other people were also running, from the pub further down; even at this range he could see the excitement in the face of the kid-barman, and he was followed by several others.

Mark pulled Carl into the trees, hoping that no one had seen them, and hoped that Julie would have the sense to keep out of sight. If she had any sense left at all, if he hadn't stripped the last of it from her.

Smoke from the cars plumed into the air. No one got too close but Mark saw the barman using his mobile, shouting into it desperately.

'Are you all right?' Mark asked Carl. 'Where the fuck did you come from, anyway? Christ, I thought you were dead.'

'Never mind about me. Where's Julie? I could see she wasn't in the car, that's why I crashed the Merc into it. I just pointed it, revved it up and threw myself out the door.

Couldn't think of nothing else to do.'

'Nothing else was needed, mate. Julie's OK. She's in the graveyard.'

Carl sank further onto the ground.

'Thank Christ,' he muttered, 'thank Christ for that. We done it, Mark, we beat the bastards.'

'Stay here, out of sight,' Mark said, 'I'll go and get Julie.'

Carl looked bad, and didn't answer. Mark skirted the rear of the church, away from the burning cars and the action around them. Julie was still crouching by the grave of the teacher, shaking and moaning to herself. She seemed unable to move, but at least she was out of sight.

Mark shook her gently.

'Mam, come on, we gotta get out of here, before we're seen.'

It took a few moments for Julie to recognise him, as her mind struggled to free itself from her waking nightmare.

'Just leave me, Mark, I've had enough.'

'Carl's here.'

'Carl? He's dead.'

'No, he's not, and he's just saved our lives. Come on, I'll carry you.'

It was easier this way. Mark bundled her into his arms, and made sure he kept the church between him and the action. He doubted if anyone had eyes for anything other than the burning cars. He trekked back to the wall and dropped Julie over the other side. They were in the trees with Carl in less than a minute, and as far as Mark could tell, no one had seen them. He looked back on the scene. The kid-barman had gone back to the pub for a small extinguisher, but it was useless. It was hard to distinguish two cars now, let alone anyone in them. Smoke had almost obliterated the church and the pub below, Mark looked down on a war zone. His war.

Maybe the fire would be bad enough to confuse the authorities for a while. They had no reason to expect anything, other than a terrible crash. Two cars, two bodies. The problems would start when they traced the Merc back to Carl, maybe they'd find the remains of a shotgun. There would be no information on the brothers or record of their car which would make the police suspicious, especially as all this had taken place on a quiet valley hillside, but it would all take time, time for all this to be over, as far as Mark was concerned. Creative thinking was not a police strongpoint, he'd learnt that in years of dealing with them, and they had no leads at all on this. He had to keep Carl and Julie out of it, now that they'd survived. Kill or be killed by Stellachi, that was Mark's aim now. Angelo had talked about the grapevine. It would be shaking itself apart in the next few days.

There was a mixture of old and new blood all over Carl. Old from the original head wound, new from the many cuts, bumps and bruises he'd taken when he'd hit the road. He's twenty years older than me, Mark thought, tough old sod.

'Can you walk, Carl?' Mark asked.

'Just let me get my breath for a bit,' Carl answered.

Julie was very quiet. She hugged the ground, shaking like the leaves around her. Mark thought it best to let her be for a while. He'd run out of any words that might help. He heard sirens coming up from the valley. A police car first, then a fire engine not far behind, and an ambulance behind that. The usual convoy of death. The hillside would be buzzing soon, not that anyone would be looking for an ex-con, his mother and her broken-up boyfriend.

'Come on, let's move away,' Mark said. 'I've got a sort of camp a bit further up.'

Carl was able to walk if Mark supported him, but life was draining from his face. It was the colour of a dirty cloud, speckled with dark red spots. An eye was closing and his shoulder looked busted. Mark held him up one side, Julie held on to the other.

They stood in the trees and watched the police pass. How many times had Mark ran from them in the old days, blue lights flashing in the night. Flashing for him. Dashing away from houses with his bag of goods, exhilarated, knowing that the black hillside would hide him, knowing that they never had a snowball's chance in hell of catching him. Until it all went sour and he let himself be taken. They reached the camp and Mark put Carl down as gently as he could.

'Just want to sleep for a bit,' Carl murmured.

'No, don't do that, mate. Try to stay awake.'

Julie knelt beside him, rocking back and forth on her heels.

'You all right, Mam?'

Her eyes just looked over his shoulder. The rain was holding off, but the sun was gone and it was turning cold. A few days ago Mark had sweltered in London. He wondered if he could chance a fire. He doubted that smoke would be noticed, not with what was going on down by the church. Black smoke was still spiralling up in a black funnel. They'd have to separate what was left of the brothers from the metal. Two charcoal lumps to make a pathologist's Monday.

'He's bad, Mark.'

Julie tidied Carl's hair with her hand.

'You got any water here?' she asked.

'There's a few bottles.'

Mark handed her one, and she took a tissue from her pocket, dampened it, and tried to clean Carl's face. Bits of it stuck to his bristles, and made him look worse than ever.

'I'll make a small fire,' Mark said, 'warm you and Carl up.'

'Make a fire! Jesus, you're right back there, aren't you? Back to when you were a kid, always messing about up here, dodging, thieving, breaking my heart. Why did you come back, Mark? Bring all this down on us.'

'I've been asking myself that, Mam. Because I know this place better than anywhere else, I s'pose, but you're right, I should have stayed away. Stayed away until it was all over.'

'We gotta get Carl to hospital.'

'I know, but we'll have to stay here for a while, until all the fuss dies down.'

'He might be dead by then. Why shouldn't I walk back down there right now, tell the police everything? We'll be safe then.'

Mark couldn't think of a good reason that didn't involve saving his skin, prolonging things, and giving himself the chance to have a crack at Stellachi. Maybe he *should* phone the police right now, Julie and Carl would be out of it then. It would be an act that didn't involve putting himself first, rare, but something he had found himself able to do with Lena. Hesitantly at first, like a dog learning a new trick, then it became easier, even enjoyable. He started to grieve for her again. Suddenly the forestry was very calm, the sky cleared of smoke, and the hawk was out again. What a view it must have had of everything that had just gone on. Maybe the explosions had freaked small animals out into the open. Something always gains.

Mark had the mobile in his hands. Just press three numbers, and all this could be over. The police were only a stone's throw away. His fingers locked as different needs clashed inside him. Even if he made himself scarce when the police came, he'd have no chance of getting at Stellachi. He'd never be able to leave the country when the full story came out, and Stellachi wouldn't come to him. Not now. Mark wanted this man. *Psycho Eyes* hadn't changed that much. Revenge was the only way out of this, revenge for Lena, Kelly, Julie and Carl. Angelo and his brother had died hard, but Mark didn't feel any sense of retribution, not yet.

'Carl's awful cold, Mark,' Julie said.

'Probably going into shock,' Mark muttered. 'He saved us, Mam. We were going down until he appeared. It's funny, but that's the first time any man has ever helped you, isn't it? Or me, for that matter.'

'It would have been better if he'd never met me. How can everything turn to shit so quickly? I thought I was getting somewhere, maybe twenty years too late, but he gave me a bit of hope. I thought you were getting somewhere too, Mark.'

'I was. We both thought we'd found something.'

'Aye, then you done a Richards on it. Blew everything apart. I can hardly take it all in.'

She doesn't even know about Kelly, Mark thought, or Tony. They would be the last straw. He put the phone away but made an instant decision.

'Phone the police, Mam, if you want. Get yourself out of this. You've done nothing, and no one going to blame Carl for doing what he did, not if it comes out straight. It'll be me they want.'

'I dunno. My head's shot, but we have to get help for Carl.'

Julie shook Carl gently by the shoulder. 'Don' go to sleep, babes.'

Carl moaned and roused himself. 'I'm bloody cold,' he murmured. His eyes focused on Mark. 'Not bad for an old man, eh?'

Mark knelt beside him and kept his voice to a whisper. Not that Julie was listening, she had drawn into herself again, hugging her small body tightly.

'No, not bad.'

'Are they dead?'

'Very.'

'Feels like I've busted a few ribs. That's okay, I've broken them before, and it takes the pain away from my head. And my fuckin' shoulder.'

'Do you think you can walk?'

'Maybe, but not far.'

'Do you want me to phone for help? Get you and Mam out of it? I've got you bad hurt, almost killed the pair of you.'

'It should have been all right. Those bastards got down here so quick.'

'Aye, but they're out of the frame now, and you and Julie, I think. I hope. They'll still want me, but I'll go to them now. Take it away from here. This Stellachi is in Amsterdam. I'll find him. He'll want me to.'

'What chance will you have then?'

'What chance did I have half an hour ago? I've got this notebook I took from Angelo. Looks like it's full of names, numbers, stuff in English, and mumbo-jumbo, Albanian probably. It might be useful.'

'Julie looks out of it,' Carl said. 'Poor kid.'

'You haven't answered my question.'

'Eh?'

''Bout phoning the police.'

'Nah. Unless your mother wants to. We've come this far. What I do want you to do is to get me to hospital. I'll tell them I fell down the stairs. Always useful for people who've had a good kicking.'

'I could call an ambulance.'

'Look, I've had a thump on the head but my brain's not addled. Not yet. How the fuck could we explain being up here with no bloody car? And it's too close to what's just gone down. No. Get a car from somewhere and drive us down to my local hospital. I'll take it from there.'

'I don't know if Mam will hack that. What about the Merc, anyway? They'll trace it to you.'

'I'll say it was nicked last night. Didn't know for a while because I've fallen down the stairs and knocked myself out, haven't I? It might work. I've got no record, why should the police ever know what's gone on? They might be suspicious, sure, but come on, gunfights, Albanians, none of it sounds real, does it? Julie will be all right, she'll have to be. We all need time for this to settle. It's been a hell of a fucking day, kid.'

'Amen to that. Stay here, then.'

'I wasn't about to take the scenic tour.'

Mark got some spare clothing from his shelter. 'Wrap up with these. You too, Mam.'

Mark turned to his mother. 'Look, Mam, I'm going to get a car. Stay here with Carl. You got to keep him awake. Don't let him drift off. He might not come back.'

Julie looked at him like Mark was a stranger. He could still see the young girl in her face, a glimpse of the past, but layered with the worry of the last twenty years. She was quite lined now, and he'd put most of them there. Mark pressed her shoulder gently with his hand.

'Mam, I'll keep my mobile on.'

She barely acknowledged him but Carl managed to clench his teeth into a smile.

'Mark, just like an outlaw bunch, ain' we?'

'Aye, just like.'

Mark cut through the forestry, keeping away from the mountain road. He saw more police and ambulances speeding up the hillside, it wouldn't be much longer before the news-boys got on the scene. They'd have the scoop of their lives if any of this came out. For a mad moment he wondered how much he'd get if he sold the story. Enough to set Julie up for a few years at least. It would be tabloid heaven. Then he thought of that Portland prison, looking through the bars in those poxy dormitories, trying to get a glimpse of the sea, trying to guess what the day was like by smelling the air. Dealing with his fellow inmates, beauts, one and all. No, he'd rather put a bullet in his brain, if it came down to it.

It took him twenty minutes to get clear of the trees. He was on the edge of the old place, but amongst new private housing. There were plenty of cars about, but he took a van. It might be better to put Carl in the back, out of sight. Taking cars had never been his thing, he hadn't learned to drive until well into his twenties, but Kelly had given him a crash course a few years ago. It was easy, just a quick rearrangement of wires, a child could do it. They did.

He was now a White Van Man for a while, nothing could be more anonymous than that. Any police that passed him on the way back to Julie and Carl wouldn't give him a second glance; they were far too busy.

It took him a minute to break in and another two to drive the van away. He was soon back on the hillside. Mark pulled the van off the road, as far into the trees as he could. Carl looked better. There was a little more colour in his face but none at all in Julie's. In the gloom of the trees she looked like a ghost.

'All right,' Carl murmured.

'I've got us some transport.'

'Just get us out of here, Mark.'

Mark carried Carl and propped him up on the seat of the van, covering him with most of the clothes he had. Julie got in on the other side and cradled Carl's head in her hands. Mark drove to the hospital, a few miles from Carl's house. Carl drifted in and out of consciousness but Mark thought he had a good chance of pulling through now. What worried him more was Julie, whether she could cope with the questions she might be asked at the hospital. Thank Christ they hadn't shot Carl. The hospital would be straight onto the police. No, Carl had the right type of injuries, the worst they'd think was that he'd been beaten up by somebody and wanted to keep it quiet. Maybe it wouldn't go any further. It all came down to Julie now, and who could blame her if she cracked?

'We're here,' Mark said. He drove up to the A & E entrance, parked the van outside and helped get Carl in.

'He fell down the stairs, remember that,' Mark said to his mother. 'Fell down the stairs.'

Seeing the state of Carl, a porter ran out to meet them. Mark let him take Carl from him.

'Stay with him, Mam. Look, can I have the key to your place? I need to go back there and get straightened up.'

'Others might come for you.'

'No, they won't, Mam. They won't even know about this, not today, at least.'

Julie fumbled in her pocket, as the porter put Carl in a wheelchair and pushed him into the building.

'Bloody stupid,' Carl was muttering. 'Missed my footing and went straight down 'em. An' my car's been bloody nicked an' all. What a morning.'

'Here,' Julie said, 'take it. Just leave us, Mark. Leave us alone.'

Her face was desperate, and the horror of this day was already being played back in her eyes, but they were still alive.

Mark turned to go, anxious to get the van away. Julie caught at his arm, reached up and hugged him briefly.

'You've topped everything with this,' she whispered, tears streaming down her face.

'I know. Look, Mam ...'

'No more words. I have to go in with Carl.'

'The worst is over now, Mam.'

'Is it?'

Mark pushed notes into Julie's hand. She stood at the entrance to casualty as Carl disappeared inside, torn between him and Mark. Ambulances were honking at his obstructing van, so Mark turned away quickly.

As he drove away Mark kept the look on his mother's face in his mind. He'd seen it many times in the past. In the early days it was able to renew itself with the false hope he'd offered time and again, until it changed, became harder, until it no longer believed anything Mark said. That was how it looked now.

It took Mark an hour to get back to Julie's place, driving carefully, feeling every roadside camera on him. He left the van half a mile away and walked the rest of the way along the sea front, still smelling of last night's fire and glad of the air. Quite a few people were about, mainly old. He passed an elderly couple who smiled hesitantly at him. He nodded back, and realised he probably looked quite menacing in his unkempt clothes with the sack slung over his shoulder.

Mark needed to get some sleep and it would have to be in Julie's flat. Dangerous, but it all depended how much Angelo had communicated with his people. Mark's hunch was that they had come after him on their own initiative. They wanted a result, good news to present to Amsterdam, and he was too tired to look for anywhere else.

He let himself into the flat, dumped the rucksack by the door, and slumped down on the sofa. There was no message from Julie on the mobile. He thought of checking how Carl was but let it go. Best not to bother her now. He took out Angelo's notebook and began to thumb through it.

The phone woke Mark up, the notebook falling to the floor as he jumped.

'I've been texting you for hours,' Julie said. 'Why haven't you answered?'

'Must have fallen asleep. What's the news on Carl?'

'He went unconscious as soon as he was inside. They're operating on him. His head. Something about relieving the pressure on his brain. They said it's serious but they haven't told me much. I'm just the girlfriend, aren't I? They've been in touch with his ex, but she hasn't showed up yet. Perhaps she won't bother.'

'Right.'

'What are we going to do, Mark?'

'Just sit tight, Mam. It's over, as far as you and Carl are concerned.'

'You've already said that, and I didn't believe it then.'

'Has anyone asked any awkward questions?'

'Not really. We kept to the story. It was the last thing Carl said before he passed out, 'bout falling down those bloody stairs. If he doesn't make it, the last thing he said will be a lie.'

'He will make it, Mam. Believe it.'

'You'll be saying you will, next.'

'I'll be doing my best.'

'If Carl hadn't done what he did, they'd have killed us, wouldn't they?'

Mark didn't answer.

'Wouldn't they, Mark?'

'Probably.'

'Probably!'

'Okay, yes.'

'You needed help, Mark, and you'll need it again. Didn't you make any good friends in London, anyone who could help. Hide you, even?'

'Not really. You know me. Anyway, I've always been good at hiding myself.'

'Aye, from a few idiots and half-arsed local cops. Not animals like these.'

'Maybe the worst is over anyway. They couldn't have expected anything like this to happen. Could be they'll let it go, now.'

'Mark, no more bullshit. My head's coming round now, I'm starting to go over what's happened today. Starting to really believe it happened.'

'Look, Mam, however it pans out, I'll keep it away from you and Carl. I swear to you, and I'll be off in the morning.'

Julie was silent, but he could hear her rapid breathing.

'I'll phone you before I go,' Mark said. 'Stay in a hotel near the hospital for a few days. Use some of that money. They won't know about Carl or his place, I'm sure. Those two must have followed you from the flat, they'd know about that from Lena. They were working on their own, it wasn't orders. Trust me, just this one time, Mam.'

Julie turned her phone off quickly. Mark felt like she was turning *him* off, off and out of her life for good, and there was nothing he could do about it. Except maybe survive.

Mark looked around the flat. There were no photographs of Shane around. He checked her bedroom. None there either, but there was one of him and Julie, when he was about ten. He had a hard glint in his eyes even then, but she still looked hopeful. She was glad she'd had him, no matter how tough it was, that was what she used to say. As he grew older, the more he felt under pressure to make up for her lack of a steady partner, and the more pressure he felt, the more he fucked up.

Mark ran a bath, put some of the contents of Julie's bottles into it and sank down under the foam. It was still only Monday afternoon. Four days post-Lena that had lasted for ever. He needed to go over it all now, to force himself to work out a position. He'd been lucky so far, even if he might have got Julie's new man killed and freaked her out for good, it was still luck that he was alive, and four of them were down. He couldn't stop his mind making it into a scorecard. Four-two to him, maybe four-three if Carl didn't make it.

Maybe his instinct had been right all along with Lena. He wondered about that night she came onto him. He'd had good-looking women before but no one like her. Now he couldn't be sure if he'd ever really meant anything to her. Maybe she'd picked someone who was hiding from the past because that made her own life easier. No questions. No explanations. Mark had opened up more and more to her, daring to feel things he'd thought had been crushed out of him long ago. Mark didn't want to think she'd been faking. If only he could have got Tony to talk to him in Coventry, he might have had the sense to step back, even let it go. No, even if those bastards had forced his hand, he *was* fooling himself. The hurt and loss was too great. There had been nothing to fight back against when Shane was taken, this time there was plenty. All that had been in his head when he opened Agani's door was the need and desire to kill, he knew it now, and had to deal with it. Everything had been lightning fast. A weekend of killing, and maybe an end to it within days, not the drawn-out hell of waiting for news, like Shane. Mark just prayed that he was right about Angelo and his brother being the only ones who knew about Carl.

Shane was in his usual place. Somewhere deep underground, maybe an old mine shaft. Calling to him, his voice faint, tear-stained, and echoing off dripping walls, asking why he'd been left, asking endlessly until his cries dwindled to nothing. Then Lena was there, but her world was light, full of movement, she was on the catwalk, taking his picture in front of the Eiffel Tower, pulling him onto her on that king-sized bed. Shane and Lena were together now, Shane was holding her hand and taking her down.

As he awoke Mark shivered and his eyes burned with the bath salts. The water was barely warm, he turned on the hot tap but he'd used it all. He got out of the bath quickly. Black dog was a good name for depression and it was snapping at him now. He was cold to the bone and the nerve started up again. So much had gone on this day it had been pushed away, but it was there again now. The headache wouldn't be far behind.

Mark found a towelling robe that must have been Carl's, for it fitted, and made himself coffee. He poured what was left of his cheap whisky into it. He should eat, but couldn't face it, so he sat in a chair by the window with the drink, and

Angelo's notebook. There was a trace of Julie's perfume on the robe, better quality than the stuff she used to use. It summed up her recent life, a stab at something better, which might have worked.

There was still some light in the sky, and the Bristol Channel was just visible from Julie's window, a sluggish grey-silver in the autumn light, an enlarged version of the smudge he'd seen from his hilltops.

Mark thumbed through the book. Agani's name was here, and Tony's, Lena's and many others that meant nothing to Mark. Their London address was next to Lena's name, and their phone numbers, including his mobile. There were lots of notes in Albanian and figures that were probably sums of money. He was surprised that this was Angelo's writing. It was very neat and small, almost girlish. There seemed to be a whole section on Amsterdam, names he couldn't pronounce, but he found what he was looking for. _Stellachi_. Angelo had even underlined the name for him. A few others were grouped with it, and the name of a club. _SexLand_. At least this was in English. International language, international activity. Underneath this were a list of addresses.

Mark had been abroad twice. Paris with Lena, Amsterdam on a job. He'd been asked to find a Brit hiding there. An accountant who'd gotten greedy and legged it with a fair bit of his company's cash. The agency was onto a good payout if Mark brought him back. He did, without too much trouble. That man had almost faded from his memory but Mark remembered where he'd been holed up. A squalid hotel overlooking the girls in windows, people pushing crack on corners, and as good an assortment of multi-racial lowlife as you could ever invent, milling around alongside dark canals, waterways that looked like they didn't want to be there. It hadn't seemed so bad in the night, when he'd first hit town, darkness was always good for covering up crap, but when he'd followed that man in daylight, it was different. Neon club lights looked pathetic in the grey November light, women his mother's age looking expectantly through the glass at would-be punters, like animals bored stiff in a zoo; middle-aged tourists checking out peep shows on pavements, Japs and fat Yanks gathered in excited groups, pointing fingers, and giggling like girls. Stuff Mark would have laughed at once, but at twenty-nine it made him feel pissed-off. Even as a kid, porn had bored him. He'd preferred to live it himself. The man he was after was middle aged and nervous, had a complexion like uncooked sausage, and most of his new life lay under his bed in fifty-quid notes. *Proctor*, Mark suddenly remembered the man's name. When Mark turned up, Proctor was docile and obedient, becoming once again the man he'd always been, before that one rush of blood, frightened at what he'd done, and the raw life on the street outside. Mark thought he might have even been glad he'd been found. It was the only attempt to break out the poor bastard had ever made in his life, but at least he had tried something. Mark almost let him go.

Julie had a chair that you could kick back and rest your feet on another section that sprang up. Mark took advantage of it as he made his plans to be on the ferry by tomorrow evening.

*

'Must have been a hell of a flight of stairs.'

'How do you mean?'

The doctor was tall, as tall as Mark, but much better groomed, and safe. That was the thing about hospitals, Julie realised. Even if they dealt with death and sometimes were a lie, they still *felt* safe. The world outside was somewhere else and always would be.

'Well, Mr Phillips has a serious head injury, a few broken

200

ribs and a dislocated shoulder. He's gone up for a scan to his head now. We'll have a better idea of the damage then. You just found him in the house, you say?'

'I've already told the nurse. At the bottom of the stairs. Got him here as soon as I could.'

'Why didn't you dial 999?'

'I wanted to get him in straight away.'

'I see. How did you manage him? He's a big man.'

'Carl managed to walk a bit. He didn't seem so bad, at first.'

'You're not Mrs Phillips though?'

'No. Carl's divorced, almost. Things are almost settled with that. I'm his girl … his partner.'

It had a more solid ring to it than girlfriend. Please don't even think how I got him here, Julie thought. I can't even fucking drive.

'Is he going to be all right, doctor?'

'As I said, he's had a very nasty blow to the head. He must have come down those stairs pretty fast.'

'Most people do, when they fall.'

'He'll probably need an operation, to remove pressure from his brain. We'll need to contact his next of kin. Would you have an address, phone number?'

'Can't help you there. There was no contact. Look, can I see him?'

'He's not conscious, but, yes, for a moment.'

Carl was all wired up. Things bleeped and whirred. Lots of activity going on around him. Just like on the telly, Julie thought bitterly. She'd never felt more alone when that doctor had talked about next of kin. What was she? Someone Carl had picked up in a bar, on grab-a-granny night. His ex had more rights than her. Julie had never been to hospital, apart from having Mark and Shane. Staying healthy had been the Richards' one success story. Healthy in body, at least.

Carl seemed to be breathing all right, but his face was grey. Julie touched his arm lightly, as if she was waking him up to go to work.

'Sorry, Carl,' she whispered.

If and when he came round, Julie wondered if he'd want to bother with her any more. Mark was still out there, capable of God knows what. This hadn't ended yet, not by a long chalk.

A nurse beckoned her to leave. As she did another woman was coming down the corridor, taller than her, and a bit younger. She knew instinctively that this was Carl's ex-wife. They exchanged glances but Julie stepped past quickly. She had to get out of this place, before she was asked any more awkward questions. Mark's money was heavy in her pocket. He'd given her a few hundred pounds, enough to stay somewhere near the hospital for a while. Julie thought of getting a taxi back to Carl's place to get her suitcase, the one she should have been taking to Ireland, but couldn't face it. Maybe Mark was right about them not knowing, but she didn't feel up to taking a chance. Perhaps she could pick up some essentials in the morning. She left her mobile number at reception and gave Carl's address. She told the pretty, bored receptionist that word *partner* again, more confidently this time. She liked the sound of it.

Julie couldn't do anything for Carl now, so her thoughts turned back to Mark. She didn't want them to but she couldn't help it; it was all true about blood and water. If Mark had told it straight, it wasn't his fault about the girl, yet the mess was still the same. As it had been with Shane. Never Mark's fault, but life still smashed to pieces. Perhaps her son was cursed. Julie trembled in the cold air and waved at a taxi that was dropping someone off.

'Where to, luv?'

'Do you know a decent B & B close by, nothing too expensive?'

'There's a few down the road, like.'

'OK. Take me to one of them, then.'

'Travelling light are we?'

Nosy git, Julie thought. People always wanted to know, and anything out of place got a question.

'Came down to the hospital, with my mother,' Julie murmured. 'It's an emergency, I didn't have time to pack a bag.'

'Oh, I see.'

The room at the B & B was all right, and the woman not too interested, not when Julie told her the same tale. Julie dialled Mark's number, but cancelled the call before it could ring. She didn't know what else to say. He was running again. Always to and from danger, it seemed he'd been the same since he'd fought his way out of her. That hadn't been easy either – she'd yelled herself hoarse for a long time before Mark appeared. The father wasn't around. He'd scarpered as soon as she was showing. No maintenance money from men in those days, not that any of her old boyfriends would have had anything to give anyway. At least that sod had kept away.

As Julie gazed out on a landscape of old industry scarring up the coastline, tall chimneys funnelling smoke into the air, she thought of phoning the police. It was the one way to save Mark's life, but a lifetime's training wouldn't let her. She couldn't go through it all again, the endless questions, all the stuff in the papers, television, swimming around like a helpless bloody fish in a bowl. Shane brought back in all his mysterious glory. Anyway, from what she'd seen of those men who tried to kill them, she doubted that Mark would be safe in prison. Better he took his chances. Maybe that made her a bad mother, but at this moment she was past caring.

Julie waited a few hours before she phoned the hospital. An older woman was on the desk. *Partner* got her put through to the right ward, then an agonising minute's wait while someone was fetched. 'Please, God, please,' she muttered to herself. Hardly aware she was saying it, such words hadn't passed her lips for more than ten years. A young man's voice answered in a foreign accent. *Yes, Mr Phillips has had an operation to remove pressure from the brain. He's stable, but very ill. No, he has not regained consciousness. His wife is with him.*

Julie turned the phone off. The doctor's last sentence was a gutter, but not enough to kill the relief that she felt. Stable-serious. She preferred to go with stable. Julie turned the room's comfy chair towards the window. It was threadbare and well past comfy, but still welcome. She lit up a cigarette and watched the sky darken. The steelworks a mile away was bringing out all its colours. Hot reds and oranges gaining strength in the night, necklace-like patterns of lights, and stacks releasing smoke of various densities. It looked like hell, perfect for the way she was feeling, but there was also a kind of beauty in it. It reminded her of those sci-fi and horror videos Mark used to knock off, for a brief time he'd been obsessed by nonsense like alien worlds, and space ships, and the steelworks looked like a giant one landing in the night. A few of the men from the estate had travelled here to work. They were like millionaires compared to the rest, and they got away as soon as they could.

If she could face it, she'd get over to Carl's place tomorrow, and ask the taxi driver to wait while she got her case. That would be long enough. Julie got up and took the thin duvet from the bed and wrapped it around her. It was a double bed, and she did not want to sleep in it.

*

Mark woke at first light. He'd transferred to Julie's bed in the middle of the night. For a moment he thought he was back in the flat in London, encouraged by the residue of

Julie's perfume in the room.

The blues ring tone on his phone sounded, breaking the silence in the flat in a very eerie way. He could almost hear Elvis's voice echoing around the room. It was Julie and Mark steeled himself for bad news. It must be, at this time in the morning.

'Mark, you awake?'

'I am now.'

'What's the time?'

'Before seven.'

'I didn't notice. Didn't sleep much.'

'Is Carl …?'

'He's alive. They had to operate on him. I just phoned now. He's stable, whatever that means. They wouldn't tell me too much. I'm not next of kin, see.'

'Operate on what?'

'His head, stupid. Something about relieving the pressure.'

'Where are you now, Mam?'

'In a B & B. Couldn't face going back to his place, but I will later. Just to get my stuff. I'm not staying. When the money runs out I'll go back to Penarth.'

'You can't do that. They know about the flat.'

'You got any better ideas?'

'Look, if you stop in Carl's house the money will last a lot longer. They don't know about his place, or him, for that matter. That knowledge died with those blokes up at the church. I'll try to send some more money when I can.'

'I dunno. It would be freaky going back there. We're not all made like you, Mark. Christ, I never thought I'd miss the estate, but at least you knew where you were up there. Maybe people like us don' deserve nothing better.'

'Don't talk like that, Mam. You were doing fine. New life, new place, new man. It's not all gone, Carl *will* get through this, and he'll stand by you. I know he will, he's sound.'

'What, stand by a woman who's going round the twist 'cos she's lost both her sons.'

'You haven't lost me.'

'Just a matter of time, innit?'

They had been here so many times before. Hopeless attempts at reassurance that led nowhere. All Mark could hope for was to keep any further chaos away from her.

As Mark stood looking out at the sea he thought of Angelo's last words, *you take an eye, we'll take many*. He was starting to focus on Stellachi now, that hard blond face. He wanted that bastard to suffer, and had nowhere else to go now. Mark felt he knew the man already, but Stellachi's early life probably made Mark's upbringing on the estate seem idyllic.

'Mark, you still there?'

'Aye. My battery's running low. I'll have to look for the charger.'

'Don' know what to say to me, do you?'

'Well, I'm not going to say something stupid like don't worry, but you *will* be all right, Mam. Stay close to Carl now.'

'Why don' you turn yourself in to the police, love?'

'You don't really want that, or you would have phoned them yourself. You must have thought about it. No, no more publicity for the Richards, Mam. I'll keep this as private as possible.'

As he said this, Mark saw Lena sinking down through black water. If he lost out over there, he'd go in a similar way. He'd never be found, he was sure of that. Each of Julie's sons will have vanished and she'd never know the truth about either. The rest of her life would be one of dark guesses.

'Time I made a move, Mam.'

'You're going after that man, aren't you?'

'Better you know nothing from here on in.'

'I wish you'd kept it that way from the start.'

'If I could change it, I would, but it's done now. At least we're all still here.'

'Go on then, go off and get your bloody self killed. What do I care any more?'

But care was shot through her racked voice, Mark heard the tears and felt like he was being kicked in the stomach. He'd always hated his mother crying, though it had saturated his early life. Mark tried to think of something positive to say before he hung up, but it was hopeless, Julie would have been waiting for ever. She ended the call.

The room was very quiet. She hadn't even said goodbye and Mark couldn't blame her. For a moment going to the police was attractive. He felt drained, like he had when the thieving had got too much in the old days. When he became increasingly careless in his house-breaking, careless enough to let himself be caught. It was all he could think to do to end it, after Shane went. To give his mother a break and put himself in the hands of others. The scraps of care and punishment offered by the state, though hated, became a way out and he'd taken it.

Mark turned his own phone off, went to the bathroom and showered. He stood under it for a long time, letting the water penetrate. He'd been grubby as a kid, but even one day on the hills had been enough to tell him how much he'd changed-outwardly. Skanky hair and three-day-old underwear were a thing of the past, and he never wanted to return to it.

Mark got dressed, using some of the clothes that had been on walkabout with him. He looked crumpled but clean. He took a look at himself in the mirror, and the stare back was even wilder than usual, but he hardly noticed this; his mind's eye was focused on Stellachi. That man must stay in central position now, his one image of him, framed by old

Rome, waiting for him like the gladiators of old. People forced to kill for money, need, and even pleasure a long time ago, but nothing had changed much in the world. It was a pity he couldn't go back to those times. Meet Stellachi in a bloody ring, winner takes all. Mark made sure the notebook was safe. There were numbers for Stellachi in it. He logged them in his mobile and put the notebook in the inside pocket of his coat. Its contents were mainly unfathomable to him, but his enemies didn't know that. The notebook had to stay next to him at all times, it might be a lifesaver.

Mark emptied the rucksack and borrowed one of Julie's small weekend cases. It wouldn't look so conspicuous. He left what he could, putting Lena's Amsterdam doll on the mantelpiece. It looked at home there, and Julie might not even notice it. A decision had to be made about the guns. Terrorism had made things tough for honest crooks and security at the ports would be too tight to get through. The guns would have to go.

There was milk, juice and cereal in Julie's kitchen. He made himself a large bowl of muesli which tasted of liquid cardboard and drank a glass of grapefruit juice, so sharp it almost cut his throat. When Julie phoned he'd been sleeping soundly. He felt guilty about that, in the wake of so much killing, but survival instinct was taking over. His brain, body, senses were adjusting to what had gone down over the weekend. It no longer seemed dreamlike. Everything had happened and he couldn't change any of it. It was Tuesday morning, day five, PL.

Mark stepped out into a fine, mild day. The weather was all over the place, but he remembered Julie saying how much better the climate was here, just twenty miles away from the valleys. It was still early, not many people about as he walked down to the seafront. There was an old pier here that had been tarted up, its boardwalk sanded and painted. He walked out on it, nodding to an old man getting his fishing stuff ready.

Mark had an automatic in each pocket and the S and W stuck in his belt. He stood at the end of the pier, looked around a few times and dropped them quietly into the sea, three splashes, three histories disappearing. The sea wasn't very deep here, but it was murky enough. The guns would be rusting sculpture in just days, encrusted with sea-life in weeks.

Mark walked up and down the seafront. He ought to be off, on the first train he could get to London, but something held him back. If Carl hadn't been so badly hurt he would have driven them to the ferry port for Ireland himself. One loose end could have been tidied up. He wished he could actually believe his confident words to Julie. They shouldn't know anything about Carl or where he lived but *shouldn't* wasn't *couldn't*.

Perhaps it was fear, and his guts were not as rock hard as people had always said. Perhaps, now that he was back in Wales, he felt something for the place. The language, history, and assorted bullshit had always passed the Richards by. He'd never seen the point of any of it, other than to divide people. But it was where he'd spent his first twenty years, and maybe Shane was still here somewhere, dead or alive. When he'd read the Welsh inscriptions on the headstones in that valley church, as he'd done so many times before in his youth, all his tortuous upbringing came back to him. Maybe it did mean something, even if belonging for the Richards family just meant clinging on. Valley people *were* different, he'd found that out when he'd been banged up in Portland, surrounded by English rogues, and in his early years in London.

Mark grinned, or rather grimaced to himself. His thoughts were getting soft. Time to put them away and get on with business. *Business,* that was what Agani and Angelo had called it. A neat eight-letter word which covered everything, cleansed it, made evil acts seem normal.

Mark stopped in a store and bought two papers, national and local. In the local, the brothers had made front page. They would have liked that. *Havoc on the Hillside*, the headline read. There was a picture of the two cars locked together and burnt out. Like one of those overpriced sculptures Lena had liked to look at. *Mystery surrounds the identity* ... good. The more mystery the better. There was no mention of anyone else being at the scene. Even better. They had got away with it. For now. There was a much smaller piece on the inside pages of the national paper. This was something that happened in that place west of England, just another accident. No mention anywhere of Kelly. He'd had his few inches of fame. Kelly was yesterday now, his sad life rubbed out in seconds. Mark saw his snivelling face, imagined its terror, what he must have gone through before they realised he really didn't know anything, and didn't care. The local council would have to pay to put him in the ground, and Mark doubted that there would be many mourners. Mark went back into the newsagents and bought a pen and pad much the same as Angelo's, stuffed the papers in a litter bin and made his way to the local station. In Cardiff he caught the first train to Paddington that came in, and for the next few hours copied out everything that was in Angelo's book.

Paddington again. Same new makeover, same sushi bar, but mid-morning Tuesday it was busier, more people chasing their lives through London, as he had, just a few days ago. Mark sat down at the sushi bar, an instant decision, and ordered something he could at least recognise. He thought it might be prawns and rice. A businessman in a pin-striped suit sat opposite him, waiting for his meal to come around. When it did, he tucked into something that looked like someone's nightmare. They exchanged glances, eyes from completely different worlds collided. Mark had sometimes wondered what it would be like to have a straight job, but not often. He seemed to be following Lena's diet, healthy breakfast, healthy snack. He tried to push rice into his mouth with chopsticks and wondered if anything could be more ironic, eating healthy at a time when people were trying to snuff him out. A large man who stank of garlic sat down next to him. He looked a bit like Angelo and Mark instinctively reached for the Smith and Wesson. He'd got used to the weight of it against his heart, and, for a moment, felt quite naked. How quickly those lethal tools became a habit. Angelo was right. They did take over, the user and the situation. Guns hadn't really helped him in the churchyard, it took a middle-aged ex-squaddie to do that.

Mark sat at the bar longer than he intended. It was as hard as ever to form a realistic plan. Instant action and reaction was what he was good at, or at least used to be good at. The Angelo look-alike left the bar and left his paper. Mark picked it up. It was opened on the travel page. Cheap flights to everywhere. *Amsterdam.* The name jumped up at him. Lots of companies offering to fly you there from London for peanuts.

He was shaking a little. First healthy food, now flying. He wasn't sure he could do it. Mark wasn't sure at all. But it would make sense. They would know about his flying phobia. Getting there that way might give him a slight edge. It might also turn him into a gibbering wreck, someone Stellachi could pick off with ease.

'Anything else, sir?' a friendly Eastern face inquired.

'I'll have a bottle of lager.'

It was early but Mark needed it. The bottle was well-chilled and he realised how hot his face was when he put it to his lips. He looked at the advert for a long while then phoned the number. Within minutes he'd bought a ticket on his card. Another first for him. He'd be in Amsterdam by evening, if he got over to Heathrow quickly and if he could keep his funk under control. Mark drank the lager from the bottle in two draughts, and went out of the station to the taxi rank. It would cost, but so what? His money only had to last a few days.

He sat in the back of the car as the driver mumbled on about traffic chaos. After what had happened in the last five days getting through one short flight should be OK. That's what he told himself, that's what he kept on telling himself. As they neared the airport his body tightened, the sweating got worse, and one hand dug into the other.

'What terminal, pal?'

'Uh, I'm not sure. I've got an afternoon flight for Amsterdam.'

Mark named the airline.

'Got it. Know them all now, I do, all the flights, all the terminals. Like an extra bit of knowledge, that is. Business or pleasure?'

The driver didn't wait for an answer. They never did. 'You'll have a good time over there, me old son. Fit bloke like you. That'll be sixty quid.'

Mark pushed notes into the man's hand and was gone, walking into the building, like it was a place of execution. He was just in time for the check-in. The case was small enough to keep as hand luggage and he went through the alien routines as if he'd drunk many bottles of lager, not one. No one bothered him, and his passport was handed back to him with a smile.

In the departure lounge Mark checked the mobile. Nothing from Julie but maybe no news was good news. He tried to relax. The sushi food fought with the lager and repeated on him. Mark was barely aware of what was going on around him, and the nerve kicked in. This was too good an opportunity for it to miss, and the headache soon joined it. More a migraine. He knew the signs. The way pain crept over the left hand section of his head, then got the lot in its grip. Until the dizziness came and he wanted to be sick, but never was. The nerve kept perfect time. *Tap tap. Tap tap.* The bright lights of the building united into a punishing sun, and the noise around him blurred into a drone, like wasps inside a bottle, but inside his head.

Mark's flight was called. There was a flurry of activity around him, and he let everyone go on ahead of him. He could hardly see his boarding card, as a woman took it from him. He was at the back of the plane, in a seat ridiculously small, an already amorous couple of kids alongside him. The boy looked at him with resignation.. Mark thanked Christ this would only take an hour. *An hour.* Divided up into sixty minutes. Minutes divided up into sixty seconds. Mark started to count them.

Taking off was bad. His guts seemed to be coming up to his mouth. He almost grabbed the kid next to him as his hands dug into the sides of his seat. Going up against Stellachi would be nothing compared to this. Something was said to him, but he didn't hear it. Everything was drowned out by the rushing in his ears. They popped and now he was in some underwater land. The nerve was loving it. It had reinforcements. His neighbour was saying something else to him.

'I said are you all right, mate? You're as white as a sheet.'

'Yeah, all right. Just a headache.'

At least Mark thought he said this. His voice echoed in his head.

'He's pissed,' the boy said to his girlfriend. 'He'd better not fucking throw up.'

His girlfriend straightened her clothes and told him to shut up.

Mark was vaguely aware of a voice announcing something. A sugary you-are-safe-in-my-hands kind of voice. The voice that might sell you an overpriced car, or tell you you have cancer. Yet it worked. He was so headshot that this moment of calm helped. Someone came round with tea, coffee and booze. He tried the tea, and made it as sweet as he could. The migraine became devious. It had a knife in its possession, and started to cut into his skull. Working its way towards his eyes, prodding them, stabbing at them. Mark tried to rub the pain away but it was useless.

He was up to fifty minutes. Counting out each section. His vision cleared a few times, when the tight, thin capsule of the plane stood out sharply, its captive cargo in rows, all helpless and behaving normally. The boy was staring at him again, but he was more nervous than cocky now. He probably thinks I'm praying, Mark thought – I am.

Then they were landing. The sugary voice came on again. Pleased that they were five minutes early, saying that the weather was wet, and foggy. Mark's guts rushed back down, passing where they ought to be, on their way to his boots. He almost did what the boy was afraid of and wasn't sure how he got off the plane, as his own automatic pilot took over, working his legs, and propelling them along the walkway. The fresh air was a relief, it was a blessing, and he sucked it in greedily. Mark got through controls without being stopped or questioned, which surprised him. If ever anyone looked like a dead man walking it must be him this night.

Schiphol was busy. Mark managed to change some money, though the notes danced around in his hand. He sat at a table in the nearest café, and, gradually, he pulled himself together. The ground was starting to steady, not moving in front of him, and he was cold. He'd given himself a sweat bath for the last few hours, and now he was drying out in the fresh night. The coffee was strong and he put three sachets of sugar into it. He needed to come on stream as quickly as possible.

His vision was getting better, and the headache receded

to a dull throb. There was no stopping the nerve though, it had been boosted with new sensations and it kept up its own relentless rhythm, flexing the vein.

So, this was the place Lena had passed through many times. Bringing him back little gifts, always excited about her Dutch trips. Over the years she must have smuggled stuff worth millions. He appreciated her nerve. She could have been stopped at any time and if she had been, she'd be alive now. Mark doubted they'd want to kill her for getting caught, though with creatures like Stellachi nothing could be certain.

Mark stayed at the café for half an hour, then took the train to the central station. The nightmare of flying had been crowded out. He was becoming alert again, and the station was at least somewhere he'd been before. It was dark now, and the usual nightlife was about, the type that populated train and bus stations everywhere Mark had been. The type that came alive at night, attaching itself to transient movement, like sharks to shoals of fish. Street people looking for angles, quick deals, easy scores. Looking for stragglers, and the unwary. Here it was many nationalities and colours, all fetched up under the Dutch flag, but the same action was going down. A few black guys looked at Mark expectantly as they passed. Their eyes said *you want something, mister, we got it,* but Mark was not the type to approach with any confidence. There were also plenty of police about. Every so often they herded the most persistent hustlers towards the exit door, but they hung around outside for a few minutes, then came back in. No one was taking it very seriously.

Mark had stayed at a small two-star guesthouse before, the Hotel Lola. It was a fifteen-minute walk away on Niewe Keizergracht. His type of place, run by a bald-headed fat git

215

called Anton, who always looked like he needed a wash, but who also had three useful qualities – he was deaf, dumb and blind. Mark stepped out, letting the air freshen him up. His clothes no longer stuck to him, he felt like an animal released, almost invigorated, an invigorated stupid bastard, moving blindly on towards his fate.

Chapter Thirteen

Stellachi fingered the ring on his fourth finger, which was new and a little loose. He liked to twirl it around, to run his fingers over its gold, and let the amethyst eyes in the skull catch the light. Childish, but enjoyable. It was an original SS skull's head. He was calming, though his face still burned. Earlier they'd talked to him in a way he wasn't used to, and wouldn't tolerate from anyone but his paymasters. This was that clown Agani's fault, and those imbeciles he employed. They were careless, and now the blame fell on him. He'd been sent for, told about it, what they expected from him now. Four were dead, they said. The London operation would have to be rebuilt. Stellachi was told to finish it.

If he'd found the goods nothing would have been said. Stellachi was certain she'd swallowed them, girls like her always did, but he'd underestimated Lena, just as those clowns had underestimated this Richards. It would have been better to have stayed in the girl's flat and finish him also.

Albanians! Throat slitters and back stabbers one and all, no sense of honour, of history, just vile pigs grubbing around in the dirt. He should have stayed in Bucharest and never worked for them. Since they'd shot that old bastard and his wife Romania had opened up, lots of opportunities there now for someone like him, but it was awkward to get out and go back; Albanians did not like out, unless it was feet first.

Stellachi's life had been good in the last ten years. He'd seen a lot of places, made good money, more than enough for his needs. He liked to display his new fortune, to show it to the world; the suit he wore now cost a thousand euros, how much bani in the old money was that? The shoes were hand made for him, best Italian workmanship, but he didn't pay for the ring. He'd taken it from someone who'd annoyed him, which made its presence all the sweeter. These tastes were simple, he had others more complex, fools might think them extreme, and he had the lifestyle to indulge them now. He'd earned it, and was not going to let anything go.

What this Richards was doing was understandable. The man had feelings for Lena. To him she wasn't a lowlife whore, smuggler and cheat, she was his woman. Stellachi smiled to himself. She'd thought it was Richards when he'd entered the flat. Lena didn't lack for spirit, and had even tried to hit him with an ashtray. It had been necessary to silence her quickly. By the time she came to, he'd searched the flat and found nothing. Lena wouldn't say where the goods were. So foolish. Stubborn. So Albanian. Maybe she thought he'd leave her, and report back. That was even more foolish. Even when he got the long meat knife from the kitchen she wouldn't talk. It was a new experience for him. The only other woman he'd killed had stepped in front of another target, and didn't count. He snuffed out her airwaves with the palm of his hand and went to work. Nothing was found. Lena had died for her diamonds. He'd straightened up the flat, neatness was everything to him, and left her looking quite peaceful, if a eviscerated woman could ever look that. The end, as far as he was concerned. Let others find the goods. Now he'd been sent for, and told what had happened since. At least it was quite amusing about Agani.

On the black wooden table in front of Stellachi was a picture of Mark, provided by another clown, Tony. He'd taken it when Richards was coming out of a building somewhere in London, a poor shot, but clear enough for Stellachi to study. The man was large, and obviously fit. Stellachi used a magnifying glass to examine the eyes, yes, strength was there, and a certain madness. A certain madness was necessary.

Now they thought Richards would come to Amsterdam, but the man wouldn't fly. Another fool, but perhaps a more interesting one. Enough men had died around him. Those brothers had died in Wales. He'd looked it up on a map but it still meant nothing to him.

Stellachi had men watching the ferry ports. Richards would not be hard to spot, but he'd let him come on. It might be amusing, for they'd told him that a photograph had been taken from Agani's place, that one of him and Agani in Rome. This Richards must be doing the same as him, studying an image, and looking for an edge. He would not find one. Stellachi called out for Hakim. It was the boy's eighteenth birthday and they were going out.

'Here,' Stellachi said, 'I have something for you.'

Hakim stood in the doorway, smiling hesitantly. He looked younger than he was. Stellachi liked the way the boy seemed to move smoothly along the floor, quite silently, like a rat treading on silk. Stellachi pointed to a white shirt that was draped over a chair.

'It's Egyptian,' Stellachi said, 'pure cotton. Good enough to have been worn by a pharaoh. Put it on.'

Stellachi looked out from the penthouse at the abysmal night. He hated Amsterdam when summer ended. A city of fog, rain, and shabby people.

'I feel Arab tonight,' Stellachi murmured, 'I've booked a table at the Shibli, to remind you of home. The other half of your present.'

Hakim changed in front of him. The white shirt looked good on his sand-coloured torso, taut and finely muscled. Maybe I actually have feelings for this one, Stellachi thought. Maybe.

*

Anton pretended to remember him, but Mark doubted that he did. Why should he, he was just another dodgy punter passing in the night.

'You should have phoned, my friend, I might have been full.'

Anton was another of these *my friend* people, and he was watching football on a TV the size of a wall. He held a thin glass of jenever in his hand, and wore a once-white vest stretched over a spreading gut, striped track-suit bottoms and trainers. Regulation slob gear. A small earring in his right ear completed the effect. The man was pudgier than Mark remembered, and he had a friend with him, a Dutch version of Kelly, who eyed Mark up with a mixture of admiration and fear. Mark looked right through him.

'Well? You full or what?'

'For you I have a room. Last one, my friend. Amsterdam is still busy, lots of students around. It's at the top, on the third floor. Remember how steep the stairs are.'

Anton handed him a large, old-fashioned key. He wasn't joking about the stairs. The Lola was a converted town-house, very old, built for the merchants who'd served the rich in another time. The flight of wooden stairs was almost straight up, kids could have gone up on all fours. A room at the top might be a good place to defend, but impossible to escape from.

At least the shower worked this time. It was the first thing Mark tried. He had stayed here in the middle of winter last time, when Anton's old wooden windows had proved useless against the cold and the shower had packed up.

As he let it warm up he stood by the large window and looked down onto the canal which ran alongside the Lola. The voice on the plane was right about the weather. Rain beat against the window and the street below had been slicked wet. The lights of a few houseboats glimmered through the gloom as a low fog settled onto the surface of the water. The sluggish canal below threaded its way through buildings like a black snake. Amsterdam was still tonight, and autumn was coming on strong. Mark stood under the shower and got warm.

Day five, PL was coming to a close. Five days, six lives. It might be seven if Carl didn't pull through. There was a full-length mirror in the shower room, its cracked imperfections clotted with brown slime. As it cleared, Mark dried off and checked himself out. There was nothing much to show what had gone on, just a small bruise where Angelo had chopped him. His body had come through unscathed, all the scars were inside. How many times had he posed in mirrors as a kid, not that Julie ever managed to buy a full-length one. He'd postured, dreamed, railed, gone through every emotion in front of them. Like Robert de Niro on speed. Any comments about vanity from his mother brought instant rage, the kind of rage that kids brought on when denying obvious truth.

There was no message from Julie on the mobile. He thought of sending her a text, but turned his phone off. *Arrived safely* hardly seemed right, especially as she didn't know where he was or what he was trying to do. Better to try to keep himself out of her thoughts, as much as he could.

In the low light of a bedside lamp Mark studied the notebook again, and unfolded a map of the centre of the town. He put a cross on each address he found. Three of them were firmly in Porn City, not much more than a short walk away. Footsteps stopped outside. Mark got up and went to the window. It was a couple going home, the woman trying to hold her man up as he lurched over the cobblestones. They disappeared into the fog. It was thick now, the canal no longer visible, yet he could sense the water close by and hear the light chink of houseboats moving. Mark turned off the light but it was harder to turn off his mind. He was in enemy territory now. Stellachi might be outside, he might be on the stairs, he might be opening the door. Mark fell asleep with this thought.

*

Julie almost walked straight into Carl's ex. She was rushing to get to the hospital, for a nurse had told her on the phone that Carl had regained consciousness. They appraised each other. Julie dabbed at her hair nervously, and wished she'd managed to get a night's sleep. She hadn't had time to put her face on either. Unlike this woman, who looked like she'd come straight from a beautician.

'I'm Karen,' the woman said. 'I knew he was with someone. One of his mates saw you in a club. Don't worry, I'm not going to start nothing. I don't care who he's with.'

'I wasn't worried. Not about that.'

'Look, what the hell happened to him? Fell down the stairs? I don't think so. I'm thinking of phoning the police.'

'What, do you think I've beat him up? All five-foot nothing of me. Look, I'd been out shopping. When I came back Carl was at the bottom of the stairs. He'd slipped.'

'And his car's been nicked, an' all. On the same day. He's been leading an exciting life with you, hasn't he?'

Julie shrugged. Part of her wanted this woman to phone the police, then the whole story could be dragged out of her, but it was too late. Mark was going to do whatever he was going to do, and nothing would stop that now.

'How is he? Julie asked.

'He'll live. He's pulled round. Always was a strong bugger.'

'I'll go in and see him, then. Look, do what you want about the police, but Carl won't tell them any different. There's nothing *to* tell. It'll be a waste of time, and he don't need hassle right now. None of us do.'

'Oh, I know he won't change the story. He always was close, that one, never knew what the hell he was thinking.

222

No, I wash my hands of it. You can keep him.'

I intend to, Julie thought, if any of us get out of this. Carl was in intensive care, a tube in his mouth, wires trailing from various parts of his body, screens monitoring his condition. A ward sister approached her and they spoke in whispers.

'He came round a few hours ago,' the nurse said. 'Remarkable, really, most people with head injuries like Carl's take three or four days. He's drifted off again now, but the doctors are very pleased with him. He's amazingly fit for his age, and that's helped a lot.'

'What's that tube for?' Julie asked.

'To help him breathe. It'll be out in a few days if he continues to improve.'

Julie sat next to Carl and brushed his hair from his forehead, his eyes fluttered a little, then opened.

'Hiya, babes.'

'Jool. It *is* you?'

'Course it is.'

'I've been having so many weird dreams I'm not sure what's going on.'

'Do you remember what happened yesterday?'

For a moment Julie thought it might have been wiped from his memory.

'Aye, just about. I fell down the bloody stairs, didn't I. Where's Mark?'

'Gone.'

'We'll be all right now, Jool.'

'Course we will.'

'Christ, I feel tired. Like I've never slept. Went three days awake in the Falklands, but this …'

Carl fell asleep in mid-sentence. The nurse checked on him.

'No problem,' she said quietly. 'All the monitors are fine. He needs lots of rest now.'

'Can I stay?'

'Of course you can.'

Julie was not sure how long she stayed there. She was dozing herself when she was pressed on the shoulder by a nurse and offered a cup of tea. She took it gratefully. Julie wasn't used to this world of kindness. She cried softly and started to worry about Mark again, wondering if she could survive the loss of another son. She was still only fifty yet life had seemed long, and hard to spend. Those people who said it was too short must be happy people. Meeting Carl told her how she'd missed out, and now Mark was on some stupid man's game of kill or be killed. He'd always been fighting life, one way or another. The nurse came back. It was time for Julie to go. She'd take a taxi to Carl's place now to get her stuff.

It was weird standing in Carl's house. She half expected those men to bundle their way in again. The lock of the back door was bust. Looking around, it didn't seem like Carl had much to steal, but she propped a chair against the door. It would have to do, for now.

By the time Julie got back to the B & B it was dark. She sat on the bed, looking out of the window at the sky, not thinking much at all. Her head was a strange show of images, as if the last day had been freeze-framed. She saw the action rush through her private picture show, she was able to look in on herself, see herself scream in that damn churchyard, see herself try to help Carl as he crumpled onto the floor, watch the cars blow up and not believe her eyes. Not believe any of it. Then she was in that bloody forestry, so close to the old place. That was the weirdest thing of all. Mark had brought it all back there, like they were joined at the hip to the past. Julie texted her son, but didn't send the message. She didn't seem able to. Maybe she would in the morning.

Julie looked at the cheap wooden door of the bedroom, and felt very vulnerable. She took off her shoes, but nothing else, and got into the bed, pulling the sheets over her head, like she had as a little girl. Perhaps it would all go away in the morning.

*

A truck reversing woke Mark up. It was delivering booze to Anton's, backing up along the narrow street, wheels close to the canal. Amsterdam was not built for traffic. He didn't feel too bad, and had slept. His head and body were prepared for anything, there was nothing left to do other than start the ball rolling. He showered, found clean underwear and a shirt, then checked as much as he could from the window and went downstairs. There was a young French couple having breakfast, but no other guests. So much for Anton being full, the lying bastard. He just wanted him to have the crappest room.

A Filipino maid greeted him. She had a genuine white-toothed smile, and probably thought the peanuts Anton paid her was heaven. Anton's head and shoulders appeared through a serving hatch.

'Ah, good morning, my friend. And it is, eh? Fog gone, rain gone, sun out. Just how we like it in Amsterdam.'

He still had the vest on, or, if it was a replacement, it had replacement stains, brown sauce spots like tracer bullets across his stomach.

'I can see you're rushed off your feet,' Mark murmured.

'People are up early here. So much to see.'

'Huh huh.'

'Is the room all right?'

'Perfect.'

Mark ate ham, cheese and eggs. If he came through this, he might go back to what Lena had wanted him to eat. A kind of food remembrance of her.

The couple left and Anton joined him halfway through breakfast, sitting down without being asked. He had a certain odour, like cooked meat. His face looked like cooked meat. He probably knew everything that crawled in Sexland, Mark thought. Anton was the type that might spend a lot of time there.

'So, my friend, you are well? You look well. How do they say it in English? A body to die for.'

Mark half expected Anton's hand to sneak across the table. The thought of stabbing his sausage fingers with a fork was quite pleasurable.

'You are here on business? Pleasure? I always find it best to mix both.'

'Yes, business. Mine.'

Mark held a cup under Anton's nose.

'Get me some more coffee.'

Anton looked around for the maid, but got it himself. When he brought it back he didn't sit down again.

'You are not a morning person, my friend,' Anton murmured.

'That's right. Same with afternoon and night.'

Anton tittered, but he'd got the message. The front door bell rang. Anton always kept the door locked, which was another reason Mark had come here.

'I must attend to *my* business,' Anton said.

Mark's hands tightened around his breakfast knife, which would be practically useless, but he saw Anton usher an old woman into the lobby. She wore an ancient mink coat and a poodle trailed behind her on a silver lead. She looked like a retired Madame, and could have been Anton's mother. She had the same complexion, though her cooked meat was creased with a map of bruised veins. The old woman smiled at Mark.

Mark went back up to his room. It had a boarded floor with a few worn rugs on it. He prodded around, sure that something this old would have a loose fitting somewhere. He found one near the window, a piece of board he was able to prise up a few inches, enough to expose a joist. There was room here to place Angelo's notebook, the copy would stay with him. He got a coat, his map, and let himself out before Anton knew he was gone. The Dutchman was wrong about the fog. Sun was trying to cut through it but it still lay on the surface of the canals, dissecting the city like lines of smoke. The morning was crisp, and people were dressed more for the winter. The heat of London seemed a long time ago. Mark had to think what day it was. Wednesday. Day six, PL.

Wherever he went in this place Mark would be a target, moving or sitting. If his luck was holding they wouldn't know he was here. He had just the ghost of a plan, and less than the ghost of a chance – to knock out Stellachi, then bargain for his life with the notebook. Mark had never believed in ghosts. Not that it mattered; if it didn't work with Stellachi he wouldn't be around anyway.

There were a few Lena look-alikes on the street, leggy, high-heeled women who walked cautiously over the cobblestones. The alleys near the canals must be lethal places for drunks, Mark thought, or hunted men. He kept away from people as much as possible, heading across town for Stellachi territory, trying to get his bearings and use the map only when he had to. He was aiming straight for the address Angelo had underlined. _Stellachi – Sexland_. Maybe it was the man's own club, that would figure.

Mark stood in an alley way and looked out on Dam Square. There were still a lot of tourists around, kids mostly, and a few lines of Japanese, clicking or camcording everything. The Royal Palace reminded him of one of Julie's Christmas decorations, one of the few that survived his rages and the moves of many uncles. She'd get it out year after year, and put it on the mantelpiece. The place looked like it belonged on a chocolate box, lots of fancy brickwork, maybe a hundred windows, set off by a spiked tower. Julie would love it here. She thought a beach on the Gower was exotic.

Mark took the Damstraat off the square and was soon amongst the crap. A shop was opening up, much like that camping place in Cardiff. The knives in the window caught Mark's eyes. All sorts, for all purposes. He went in and bought one. A fold-up job with a bone handle that fitted into an inside pocket. Maybe its blade couldn't deflect bullets, but at least he didn't feel so naked now. It was early, this place did not really come alive until nightfall. In daylight it was stripped of its cover, and looked bored with itself, as if sex was out of fashion, no longer exciting, just necessary. There was probably more weird stuff now, Mark thought, jaded wankers looking for ever more extreme action. Even at this time of day a few guys came onto him, asking for or offering crack or charlie. Charlie, such a friendly name, for an entrance to hell.

Mark located *Sexland*. Its neon sign was worn and tarnished but it was still on, flickering defiantly as the sun tried to oust it. Above was the backlit image of a girl fingering a breast with one hand. She was tall and deep red, the colour of blood, made to catch the eye, and she caught his. There were apartments above the club, de-luxe crud, by the look of them. An old man was sweeping up outside, attacking last night's waste, as he had a thousand times before. It looked like the brush was fighting back. He could have been Anton's father. Same grubby look, but the lechery on this one's face had turned into a memory, his face was leather rather than cooked meat, his eyes glazed, and the hair at the sides of his head was dyed jet black, like two wings. He noticed Mark watching him, stopped brushing and came over.

'Help you, mister?' the old man said.

He still smelt of last night. Mark was reminded of Kelly,

another reason to be here.

Mark tried to check out every area, but it was hopeless. Too much stuff was going down here. If he wanted anonymity he should have left it until dark, when the place would be jumping with bug-eyed punters. He was standing out in the street, for Godsake, Stellachi might be watching him, laughing his evil head off. Something inside was pushing Mark on to a rapid conclusion. He wanted out, one way or another. He was not nervous, nerves had been left in the Welsh churchyard.

'Don't you speak English?' the old man asked. 'Everyone who comes here speaks English. The whole world speaks English.'

The old man repeated his question in Dutch, then German, leaning on his brush, enjoying going through his repertoire.

'English,' Mark muttered.

'Sure. Knew it straight off. The club doesn't open yet, come back tonight. Hey, you want girls? Boys? Both?'

He fumbled in his overalls and produced some cards.

'She's good. The best. Not too much money, and this one - you'll never forget it. This one's a pretty boy. Very nice.'

Mark took the cards. The door to the club was open, but he doubted that there was a way up to the apartment. He noticed a separate entrance. There was a number on the door, the same one as in the notebook. He thanked the old creep, having acted like a young one.

'Might come round tonight,' Mark said.

'Sure. You have good time. Very good.'

Someone was watching him from the apartment window. It wasn't Stellachi, it was just a kid, someone not much more than fifteen or sixteen, Mark thought. He didn't hang around, he didn't want to make it *that* easy for them. He walked quickly down the first alleyway he saw and wished he hadn't. It needed its own sweeper, because it was encrusted with dog crap, maybe some human, and a supporting cast of junk food remnants, vomit and what he thought might be blood, but possibly could have been ketchup, trod into the stones. Discarded syringes littered the ground, like the spears of minute people, and he had to walk carefully. The place could have been the crazy design of some modern artist, out of his head on the ultimate trip. A thought came to Mark that Lena might have been part of this secret world but he crushed it out. He didn't want to go there. Ever.

Maybe that kid was on the phone right now, maybe he didn't know anything. Mark didn't think Stellachi would be the type to spread news around, but he would be careful, after the events in Wales and London. Mark saw that all the clubs had rooms above, perhaps the moneyrakers didn't want to be too far from their honey pots. All the fancy stuff was in the front, nothing much had been done with the bits out of public sight. There was a service entrance to Stellachi's place, locked up, but also a fire escape. A metal stairway tacked onto the back of the building, the type that would stretch down if you reached up for the end. Mark did so.

The kid in the window could be anyone, a cleaner, Stellachi's rent boy, a baby assassin for all he knew, but unless they were drawing him into a trap, Mark doubted if anyone knew he was here yet. Moving his large frame as lithely as he always had, he reached the second floor, where there was small balcony filled with plants. He stood here for a while, and could hear music playing inside. Foreign stuff, African maybe, too sharp for this time in the morning, but it helped with his cover because the window he tried did not want to move at first.

The knife was proving useful already. Mark unfolded it and looked for any weakness in the window frame. It was old and wooden, the type that always had a weakness and

230

the knife found it near the latch. Wood splintered under his probing and access was his. He looked in on a small bedroom that didn't look as if it was used, and was inside before the face in the window appeared in an open doorway. Mark hit it once, hard, and it fell down on the floor without making a sound.

He stepped past the boy into the main room of the flat. It was a large, and full of everything except Stellachi. He checked through the other rooms, two bedrooms, and a bathroom the size of a small house but he knew no one else was here. If Stellachi had been at home Mark would have copped a bullet as soon as he was on the fire escape. This place was similar to Agani's penthouse, not so in-your-face but the same *I've got money* statement in everything that was here. There were hand-drawn sketches of studs on the wall, all black and white in silver frames. Stellachi's pin-ups, some naked, some in white underwear. All bronzed, with health-club bodies. In the master bedroom was a large picture of the man himself showing off his own frame. Stellachi was a bit smaller than him, but only because he was in great shape, perfect muscle tone, and not an ounce of excess weight. The shape Mark used to be in, before Lena taught him other things. This man was obsessed with himself.

Mark checked outside through wooden blinds. The old man was still sweeping, the street filling up with the curious, and the shops were coming to life, but he saw nothing to worry him. He quickly searched through drawers and cupboards, looking for anything, but mainly a gun. No such luck – the knife and his fists would have to do.

The kid was coming round as Mark knelt over him. He'd split his lip and bloodied his nose. He was older than Mark had thought, but not by much. As he moaned and opened his eyes Mark lifted him up like he used to do with Daniels, this one was about the same weight, which was no weight at all.

Half dragging, half carrying him, Mark took him to the main room and threw him onto the sofa. He was fully conscious now and started a panicky jabber in an unknown language.

Mark let him rave on for a minute, checking the window again, and, making sure the main door was locked, he turned back and showed the kid the knife. The boy tried to shrink away, drawing his knees up against his chest and trying to wipe the blood from his face. Most of it was dripping onto Stellachi's cream leather furnishing. It would be a kind of calling card, Mark thought.

Mark caught hold of the boy by the throat with his left hand and pressed the knife against his cheek with his right. He shut up straight away and if anyone could be stiff and tremble at the same time, this one could.

'Stellachi,' Mark said, 'where?'

The kid's eyes rolled whiter and more strange language rushed out of him, which Mark slapped to a halt.

'English. Come on, you can speak it.'

'English? No, not so good.'

'Oh, I think you can, sonny. I don't have a lot of time, so you'd better learn it fast. Where's your friend? *Mr* Stellachi?'

The boy closed his eyes. He seemed to be praying. 'You're him.'

'What?'

'The man. The one who killed Agani, and the others.'

'That's right,' Mark said, 'I'll ask you one last time. Where's Stellachi?'

'I don't know. I never know things like that.'

'Who are you?'

'Hakim.'

Mark didn't respond, and kept the knife pressed to the boy's face. It loosened Hakim's tongue more.

'Hakim, I'm the houseboy. I cook, clean, for Mr Stellachi. He's good to me.'

'Aye, I bet. That's why you're pissing your pants with fear. You're more afraid of him than me, even though I'm standing over you with a blade.'

Hakim's blood was running onto the knife, making it looked used. Mark wiped it on the leather which made the boy wince. He put it away and let Hakim sit up straight.

'Where?'

'He went out early, before I am awake. I don't know where, but he'll be back soon. Any minute.'

'You were watching me from the window,' Mark said. 'You've been phoning people.'

'I always watch from the window. Mr Stellachi does not like me to go out without him. I didn't know who you are. Many people come here. Lots of them look like you.'

'The stairs down, where do they lead to?'

'You can go into the club or out onto the street. Mr Stellachi never goes into the club. He hates it.'

Hakim stopped and coughed into his hand. There was a gap in his top teeth and the remains of one in his palm. Hakim looked at it tragically.

'You can get a gold one,' Mark said.

'You don't understand, Mr Stellachi, he doesn't like …'

'If I were you I'd be more interested in what *I'd* like. Who's in the club now?'

'Only the cleaners. Everyone else will be in bed.'

'How come you are up so early?'

'Sometimes I don't sleep so well.'

'How old are you?'

Hakim shrugged, and was cut off by a ringing phone.

'Leave it,' Mark said.

'But …'

'*Leave* it.'

The phone stopped after fifteen rings. It was probably Stellachi.

'I must always be here. I must always answer,' Hakim

233

said. 'He will be angry.'

It was a pity about the phone. Mark might have stayed otherwise, try to kill Stellachi, here and now, but the Romanian would be alerted. He'd guess there was only one reason why little Hakim couldn't answer. Time to go. Time to find another plan. Another ghost.

Mark dipped a finger in Hakim's blood and wrote *call me* on the suite, adding his mobile number. The congealing blood stuck to the leather quite well, and he liked the effect. Then he ripped out two of the pages he'd copied from the notebook and gave them to Hakim.

'Give these to your boyfriend,' Mark said. 'Don't get them messed up.'

Mark almost felt sorry for Hakim, he was just another lost kid, fetched up in the wrong place, with definitely the wrong man.

What Mark had already seen here made all the stuff back home tame, and the estate just a playground for mouthy, disaffected punks. Here he was amongst something else entirely, the real thing; if the real thing meant depraved crazies, all out to make their smear on life. And wedged in between were the Hakims, the girls, the junkies, and all the punters who fed this world. Mark felt dirty.

'Where's your mobile?' he asked Hakim.

The boy pointed to the desk. There were two there, Mark took them both, then cut the cord of the landline. Time to get out, before the cavalry arrived. He left the apartment and went out the front way, past the old sweeper, who, if he was surprised, didn't show it. Mark glanced up at Stellachi's window as he walked down the street. Hakim was standing there, holding his face. He was grateful to still be alive, but he was definitely more worried about Stellachi's return. You should have stayed home, kid, Mark thought, better ripping off tourists in the marketplace than being ripped by a brute like Stellachi.

234

Mark's journey back across town was a mixture of care and abandon. His eyes were on constant alert but he made no attempt to conceal himself now. There was no point, Hakim would have been down those stairs to the club as soon as he left, spilling the beans.

He passed the Old Church. Someone was playing the huge organ inside, heavy sounds that seemed to rumble deep from the guts of the building and stay in his head as he skirted the Hash Museum and was back on the edge of The Dam. He went into the first brown café he saw. Although outside the smoking district, its air was still full of dope, but Mark couldn't be bothered to go anywhere else. Maybe it would help calm him down. He sat at a table near the door and watched his hands shake, veins standing out like blue ropes. A few students were at the back, giggling and already well gone, and an old black guy drooled over a hookah by the toilet doors. His face was carved ebony, and in the hazy light it looked like he was kissing a snake. It would always be murky in here, even on a sunny midday. As his eyes grew accustomed to the gloom a good-looking girl appeared at his table. She was tall, slim-thin, with button breasts in a tight top. The girl looked very fit, and after his short, sweet time in Sexland this was a figure that shone with health. Mark smiled back at her, and ordered soup, beer and a veggie-burger. Best eat now, when he could. Strange how he could still smile, how the lips formed one of their own accord, despite the torment up top.

Mark checked the mobile again. This time Julie was there. *Am in a B & B near to the hospital. Carl holding his own. Should be OK. X* The oversized X was the best she could do, Mark knew that. Julie wasn't able to ask him to get in touch, she couldn't afford to take the risk.

The burger was good. He remembered how Shane had quickly got a taste for the meat version, hanging around the table on tottering legs, like a bloody penguin, waiting for whatever Mark offered. Julie used to get annoyed. He's too young for that junk, she'd cry, as if they had healthy futures mapped out, as if they had *any* futures mapped out.

The loss of Shane was like an anvil on his back. Now he too was close to disappearing for good, maybe going down to a watery grave like Lena, and Julie would have the rest of her life to wonder what had happened. He'd given her plenty of stuff to make images with in the last few days, there was no mystery with him, just your everyday tale of murder, mayhem and revenge. *Retribution*, a big word he learned the meaning of recently. It had been in one of Lena's magazines and he'd looked it up behind her back, then shown off with his knowledge. A suitable return, that's how it was explained, especially for an evil act. There'd been a lot of them in the last few days. Was he here looking for a suitable return, or just bloody-minded selfish revenge? The type that had almost got Julie and Carl killed. Maybe Agani should have been enough, and the brothers a bonus for Kelly, but it was too late now. He'd started a bloody ball rolling, and was running with it in the heart of Amsterdam. Eating healthy food. Stellachi would have goons looking all over for him now, cursing them for missing him at the ferry ports. Then he'd see the blood on that sofa and start on Hakim. *I have flown*, Mark thought. I did it. He could hardly believe it, and trembled with the memory now. Lena had been worth that, but he doubted if anyone would be again.

Mark drank the last of the beer, holding onto the bottle tightly, trying to regain control of his hands. The slim-thin girl was watching him wistfully, he had enough of his senses left to notice that. He nodded to her and left.

Outside a pale sun was being overhauled by yesterday's cloud. It was mid-afternoon, and it looked like it would be foggy again by nightfall. In ten minutes he'd tracked back to Anton's and was opening his front door. Anton wasn't around. He'd left the TV on though, an English channel, the volume just loud enough for Mark to hear some idiot going on about houses. Mark wanted another shower. He needed one. This was foremost in his mind as he trudged up Anton's Everest stairs and pushed his bedroom door open.

There was a blur of movement in the washroom mirror and Mark grabbed at his knife. Too slow, much too slow. He was on the floor, looking at it sideways, his nose crushed. Even at this angle he recognised Stellachi. Sitting on the bed and taking off white leather gloves.

Chapter Fourteen

Julie agonised over Mark's text. She wanted to say more, the need to know he was all right made her feel cold and her stomach tighten up, she was on the verge of throwing up all the time. When she'd seen him standing on the doorstep of her flat all the old emotions had come back. Joy at the sight of him, immediately laced with suspicion. Last night she'd slept fitfully, in short snatches, jerked back to life with flashbacks of the churchyard business. That ape grabbing at her, the cars exploding, Carl lying amongst the trees, looking very dead. She'd been sure they'd killed him. At least that hadn't happened, but she was feeding off crumbs. Small windows of light in the dark passageway that was Mark's world.

Julie stood by the window in her nightie, watching dawn appear. How often had she seen Mark do this, scratching his arse and staring blankly out at the hillside, as if it might have answers. In his own private, locked-door world, and oblivious to her presence. Sometimes, when he was late back from a job, she'd come downstairs and find him like this. They were the only times she'd see him up that early, mostly he'd surface mid-afternoon, full of sleep and foul mood. Again Julie wondered if she should have gone to the police, but it was too late now. Mark was gone. Chasing a finish. He'd been doing that since he was fifteen. It *must* be her fault. After Shane vanished she'd had a lot of support from the social worker, but she couldn't call it help because there was no real help, not for something like that. Shane is not your fault, the woman said, and you can't keep taking responsibility for Mark. The woman kept saying that none of it was her fault, but Julie had never really believed it. Every time she'd gone down to Cardiff, seen the shops, and what was in them, what other people could afford to buy, she felt it was her fault. Every time she blew it with a new man, usually some tosser who couldn't provide the time of day, let alone anything else, it was her fault. Mark hadn't had a chance, so she thought that Shane was her punishment. Now all this had happened. Maybe the punishment wasn't over.

The B & B had a nice garden. Julie watched early morning birds flit around, a robin shouting the odds at bigger birds. It was one of the few she could name. It hopped around on the wall outside her window, puffing out its red chest like something from a Christmas card. She imagined herself owning a place like this. A garden, near the sea, a man coming home at the same time every night. A routine. Happiness for her would be something unchanging, even uneventful, but safe, and always there. She'd love every boring minute of it. It was starting to be a little like this before Mark knocked on the door. Having somewhere to go five days a week, even if it was work in a factory, then meeting Carl. He'd made the weekends less of a trial. Carl was a good bloke. No angel, but not useless either, an ordinary kind of man, *normal*, that word the Richards had never done. Not that Carl's actions this weekend had been anything like normal, but that's what happened when people met Mark - even after one bloody day.

Julie showered and dressed. The taxi was picking her up at nine. She'd become one of the guy's regulars now, his next customer after the school run. She wanted to spend as much time with Carl as she could. It was what normal people did.

*

'Get him up.'

Stellachi's voice was quite high. He sounded more like

the owner of a boutique than a killer. Mark thought Angelo had come back from the dead, for the man who dragged him up looked remarkably like him. Three men were in the room. One stood against the wall behind the door with an automatic in his hand. Not much of the wall was left because this man was almost as wide as it.

'Put him in the chair.'

Blood was pouring onto Mark's shirt and he tried to blink clear his vision. He hated shots to the nose, it was impossible to control the eyes. *You stupid, stupid bastard*, he mouthed to himself. He should have been more careful about this place, and about Anton. Stellachi was ahead of him, and deserved to be.

'I've just had a call from Hakim,' Stellachi said. 'I hope you left the apartment in good order. So you *flew* in. That was hard for you, wasn't it? I'm quite impressed, Mr Richards, phobias are hard to dismiss. You must want me very badly.'

This guy's English was better than Mark's own. Just the faint trace of an accent. 'I think I will call you Mark,' Stellachi said. 'It's a nice name, very Biblical. Mark, did you really think you could come so far, and not be taken? True, we did not expect you to fly, and if you could have flown into my apartment maybe you might have had a chance. But you had to take a train, and you were seen.'

Stellachi threw a photograph towards him. Mark recognised it. One from the early days with Lena. He remembered Kelly taking it outside the Queen's Head, his boozers hands fiddling with the camera, telling them to say *cheese* in his best Irish accent for Lena.

'We had many of these printed, just like the police do. For us, you are famous, my friend. You didn't really have a chance, did you, Mr Mark Richards?'

Stellachi was on his feet now, walking around like a model. Charcoal Armani suit, white polo neck, matching gloves. Mark almost expected him to be carrying a cane. Stellachi nodded towards the man by the door.

'That's Adam, *my* first man. He laughs at my gloves, thinks they are a woman's things, but not to my face, of course.'

Stellachi folded the gloves and placed them on the bedroom table, checking it carefully first, and flicking something from its surface.

'Pigsty,' he muttered to himself.

Mark didn't see it coming. The Romanian had great eye-to-hand co-ordination, and special timing. The punch flicked into his head like a wasp sting, it didn't seem to have much force but it rocked Mark back in the chair and closed his right eye. He felt Stellachi's ring imprint itself on his cheekbone. Mark thought of getting up but wall-man Adam had got close to him now, and had the gun sticking in his back.

Maybe I have only seconds to live, Mark thought. *Then it will be all over. Thirty strange years end here, in some poxy Dutch hovel, surrounded by evil arseholes. My glorious exit from a glorious world. But doesn't part of me want it? To be out of it all. No more struggle. The big sleep. Who knows, the way some call it, I might be meeting up with Lena again, even Shane. Living in happy land. No mysteries. No pain.*

Stellachi was watching him closely. He beckoned to the other man who stepped forward and handed Mark a towel.

'Clean yourself up,' Stellachi said.

Stellachi walked around the room. Mark expected another blow at any moment, or a bullet in the back of the head.

'So, this is interesting,' Stellachi said. 'I've killed men face to face, and they all showed fear. Sometimes it was masked by anger, by *their* attempts to kill me, but it was always there. You are different, Mark, aren't you. I can see it in your eyes. You are ready.'

Stellachi came closer and Mark felt the gun push deeper into his shoulders. A flicker of Stellachi's eyes and he'd be dead. Stellachi's voice dropped to a whisper, and Mark could smell his sweet breath. Some drink he couldn't place.

'Don't give up so easily, Mark. Give me a little pleasure. How do you say in English – we are fellow travellers. A pity about the girl, and what she has caused. It might have been good to get to know you.'

Mark lunged at Stellachi's throat. He thought he was quick, but Stellachi was quicker. Mark grabbed at air, then plunged down into darkness.

'Don't kill him,' Stellachi shouted.

Adam stood over Mark, the gun bloody in his head.

'Don't kill him,' Stellachi repeated, more softly. 'Oh no, Mr Mark Richards, nothing so easy for you. Bring him.'

Stellachi put on his gloves, straightened his suit and left them to it. Downstairs he beckoned to Anton, who was doing his best to make himself invisible in a doorway. Stellachi pushed a few hundred euros into his hand, taking care not to touch the man. He pointed to his tongue.

'Wag that and I'll come back, cut it out and make you eat it. You know I will, don't you?'

Anton nodded, so hard, drops of sweat flew from his forehead. Stellachi stepped out of the way quickly, then was gone. Mark followed, supported down the stairs by Adam, the other man carrying Mark's case.

*

'How you feeling, luv?'

'Not too bad. Got the mother and father of all headaches though.'

Julie touched Carl's forehead gently.

'Hardly surprising. Just imagine you've been on a bender.'

'Well I have, in a way. We all have.'

'Aye.'

'Any news?'

'I don't expect any. Not from Mark. He'll be following Shane now, vanishing into thin air.'

Julie pushed at her eyes with the backs of her fingers and was quiet for a minute or so.

'I'm surprised you still want me around.'

'Don't be daft. After what we been through? What else we got, *who* else have we got?'

'You got two kids.'

'Aye, thousands of miles away, and they always followed their mother anyway. I didn't even have a birthday card off either of them. Look, Jool, I'll need you to look after me, wait on me hand and foot, do my every bidding. The doc says you might have to do it for the rest of my life. It'll be a bloody first from any woman I've known.'

'Oh aye? I've just spoken to him. He say you'll be up and on your feet in a few weeks. Maybe back working in a few months.'

'Oh well, worth a try. Working, why doesn't that thrill me?'

Julie smiled.

'See, Jool, you can still do that.'

Carl did the same.

'Christ, it's good to have that tube out,' he murmured. 'The hole in my throat will heal up on its own, apparently. I'm not used to talking in a whisper. We were meant to survive, Jool. We'll get through this.'

'I don't know if I *can* go on, Carl. How much more am I expected to take?'

'Look, I can't change anything that's happened, but I *can* be here for you, right now. I know a knackered old soldier is not much of a substitute for losing a son, and maybe another, but …'

'You should have come along twenty years ago.'

'Well I'm here now. Look, I do need you, Jool, I realised that when the ex came to see me. There was nothing there any more, for either of us. I think she thought I was going to croak and that there might be a bit of money around.'

'I saw her in the corridor.'

'Oh. You spoke, like?'

'Just a few words. No problems.'

'You must have surprised her, good-looking woman like you. I don't think she thought I'd ever hook up with anyone again.'

'Good-looking woman! Those bastards after Mark put twenty years on me.'

'I don't see no sign of it.'

'Even on your bloody back you're a charmer.'

'Aye, for you. So, are we going to stick it out?'

Julie placed a hand over Carl's. As she traced the veins and the drip going in, she could sense the strength still in the man. Strength that had saved her and Mark. Strength that had never been offered her before, and which she needed.

'Jool?'

'Yeah, I s'pose. Give it a try.'

*

Adam had not told Stellachi about Hakim's phone call. He'd been too afraid, as Hakim had been too afraid to phone Stellachi direct. Stellachi felt the type of rage that had always made him sick. It started in the pit of his stomach, then rushed to his head, where it collided with many images. Old demons reared up at him, and there was only one way to still them. He flicked open his own phone, jet black against his gloves, and pressed the chrome numbers.

This Richards was interesting. A pity that he had been taken so easily. That was the trouble with hate, it clouded your judgement, especially if you were not used to it. If you were born with it, that was another matter. It became an ally that allowed any action. It became an excuse that set you free.

So, Mark Richards had got to the apartment. Hakim told him, his voice small and distant, afraid of every syllable it uttered.

'And he has papers, from a small book.'

'What are you talking about?'

'Papers. Lots of names, the big people. Your name, phone numbers, figures, our address.'

'*Our* address?'

'Yes, here. I couldn't stop him. He was powerful, like you.'

'Hakim, Hakim, I don't keep you to *stop* people and he's not powerful now, is he? And the apartment?'

Hakim was quiet for twelve seconds. Stellachi counted each one.

'Speak to me, Hakim.'

'He hit me. I bled. I'm cleaning.'

Stellachi turned off his phone. He imagined his furnishings soiled, the place turned into an abattoir. He felt sick again, and need rose up in him.

'Take him to the usual place,' Stellachi said to Adam, 'and be careful with this one.'

Stellachi kicked Mark, hard to the head.

'That will help you sleep, my friend. Rest while you can.'

Hakim stood by the window, watching for Stellachi. The tourists were out in force now, as the light was fading. Like the creatures of prey they were, Hakim thought. This had been his world since the age of ten. It was hard to remember anything else, before Stellachi. He had images of being amongst many children and of the mother who gave him away, but they had faded, and were getting harder and harder to recall. Better not to now. He remembered the hunger though, first in the belly, then the mind, hunger for everything, but most of all kindness.

Even the summers were cold here. He hated the water all around, and could not understand why so many came to see the boring lines of inky liquid. Canals made the city hard to move around, and, in winter, they brought down the fog that was cloaking them now. Sometimes they froze over, to lie like bloated, grey veins across the city.

From the window Hakim saw Stellachi, his elegant clothes marking him out as he glided down the street. Hakim always thought of him as gliding, so lightly did he move. The Romanian was a beautiful man. When Stellachi came for him, his mother said he would provide the kindness. With his white, shining clothes, standing so healthy and tall, he looked like someone sent by Allah. At first Stellachi was kind, if kindness could ever be provided in a cold way. Until Hakim was twelve, when it began. He was still here, one did not get away from a man like Stellachi. Hakim was eighteen years old and trembling with fear as he heard a foot on the stairs.

Mark thought it better to play groggy, though his head had cleared enough to know his life hung on a thread. These guys were on a higher level than Agani's crowd, he'd gone up a division. Adam and the other man dragged him to a car, he was pushed into the back, a gun on him at all times. He still had the towel, Adam pushed it against Mark's face.

'Don't bleed on the seat,' Adam said, 'Mr Stellachi doesn't like it.'

They were being open about names because they thought it didn't matter, in their eyes Mark was already dead. They were taking him back to the red lights, he felt the car's tyres crunch on the cobblestones. It would be jumping now that it was dark and all manner of creature out. They skirted a canal and Mark saw club lights reflected in the water, turning it into a dirty rainbow. The car stopped behind a canal-side house, in a narrow street that was poorly lit. He

246

couldn't see much but felt the dig into his kidneys from the butt of the gun. It was a blow meant to weaken and it did. He was pulled out of the car and pushed through a doorway, down slimy steps, and into a cellar. The silent man was a strong bastard, strong enough to lift him off his feet and throw him into a corner of the room. He cracked a shoulder against a wall and crashed down.

'You can stay here with your thoughts until Mr Stellachi comes for you,' Adam said, as he slammed shut the door.

All was black at first. Mark held out a hand and could not see it, then its outline appeared and slowly he made out the shape of the room. It was dank, close to water, but a faint line of light was coming from somewhere. He traced it with his eyes. There was a large wooden hatch in the wall above him, and the light was coming from a crack in this. Mark realised he was in an old warehouse, once fed by canal traffic. He smelt something too, Chinese food. Perhaps he was in Chinatown, it perched on the edge of Pornland. Sex usually led to other appetites.

Mark got up shakily. Feeling his side, and his head. The knife was gone, but they didn't have the notebook. Stellachi would be finding out about that now and it would be a problem for him. The notebook might be Mark's ace in the hole, a grubby, dog-marked ace, but all he had left to play. A boat went by outside, it felt just the other side of him and he could hear music and the laughter of people.

Mark felt his way around the room, looking for anything. Its walls were rough stone and the floor was uneven. He stumbled a few times. It must have been hundreds of years old, but it had not been used for a long time, at least not for the goods that used to be swung through the wooden doors above him. Other victims had been thrown in here before him, he was sure of that. This was a last resting place for the condemned. Mark did not want to imagine how Stellachi dealt with people, but he determined one thing. If his ace in the hole turned out to be a busted flush, somehow he'd get his hands on Stellachi and do some damage. He wanted to smash that face, it would be a good last thing to do. He looked again at the small crack in the cargo doors. A crack might mean a weakness.

Hakim held the torn out pages in front of him, and tried to hide behind them.

Stellachi took them, looking with disgust at the bloodstains. Hakim had changed his shirt and cleaned himself up. He'd vainly tried to wash off the blood from the sofa but had only succeeded in diluting the stains and making them bigger. As he'd rubbed and soaked, tears of dread dropped from his eyes. He'd learnt very quickly that everything must always be spotless in Stellachi's world, nothing out of place. Colours of depth and richness, the ones he'd grown up with, had no place here. His master liked pale, and white, almost no colour at all.

Whatever Hakim had been expecting did not happen. The pages *had* saved him. Stellachi sat at his desk and pored over them. He stretched his hands and clicked each finger joint as his thoughts ran hot. He cursed those cretins in London. This had been copied from a notebook Angelo must have had, and he'd let Richards take it from him. Stellachi hoped Angelo burnt alive for a long time in that car, and that he was burning now. He stretched and tried to calm himself, looking with interest at the slight tremor in his hands. He called to Hakim, who was trying to melt into the other side of the room.

'Come here.'

Stellachi clicked his fingers at the floor and Hakim sat down at his feet. The Romanian ran his fingers through Hakim's short black hair and murmured a few things. At times like these, Hakim was not sure if he was talking to himself or not.

'So, my little Arab boy, this Richards is troublesome. He's quite good-looking, in a rough sort of way, don't you think? What does he expect this book will gain him? His life?'

Stellachi took off his jacket and leaned back in his white polo neck. His complexion was so pale he almost merged with it. He pulled up a sleeve and ran a finger along a thin, blue scar, from wrist to elbow. Hakim knew he always did this when disturbed. It was the one imperfection on his body, the one time Stellachi had got careless, and had warded off a knife blow with his forearm.

'So, what will we do with this man, eh? And all because of a woman. An Albanian at that.'

Stellachi's hand tightened in Hakim's hair, and tugged at it.

'You don't know what I'm talking about, do you?'

Stellachi thought the value of the notebook would depend on three things. Where it was, if anyone had been charged with its safekeeping, and whether that person had been told to take it to the police if Richards disappeared. This man was smart, smart enough to have made such a plan, if he'd had the time. Maybe the original book would be back in his homeland, this Wales.

Richards had come to Amsterdam to kill him, nothing else, and he thought the notebook was his ticket back, what he'd use to deal with the organisation. Having it come into his possession was his good fortune. Angelo had been too stupid to keep much in his head, so he wrote it all down, names, numbers, transactions, and kept it with him. Even the most dim-witted police force would be able to piece it all together, in time. Stellachi would have taken the book from Angelo in London if he'd known of its existence. But then again, Richards was unpredictable, like him. He might have done nothing with the book. Stellachi would have to gamble, as he had done all his life. For a brief moment he identified with Mark, and wondered if he felt the same pain. His never went away, sometimes it was masked, almost quiet, other times it raged. Stellachi could still smell Lena as he came up behind her. *Guerlain*, quite a good scent, for a whore.

Stellachi's traced the line on his arm a few times, then started to twist Hakim's hair. The boy stiffened and willed himself not to cry out. It stopped quickly and Stellachi patted his head. Hakim felt like the pet he was.

'No, this Richards is nothing, and I have him,' Stellachi muttered. 'See to my bath. The right height, the right temperature.'

Hakim got up and walked away, but inside he was running.

Something scuttled over the other side of the wooden hatchway. A rat probably. Mark envied its freedom, its brief snatch of on-the-edge life. Stellachi would either take a chance that no one else had the book and kill him quickly, or try to have a few games with him, head and body, until Mark cracked, and spilt his one bean.

It was getting cold in the room, but night sounds were increasing outside as the district business got into full swing. Sometimes a snatch of laughter, sometimes an angry voice, a pleading voice, as money for bodies changed hands constantly. For all he knew Stellachi's club might be very close; he could hear music, old stuff from the seventies being pumped out. It drifted across the water at various volumes. Maybe he had until morning, maybe not.

Mark started to check around the room, feeling each rough piece of stonework. I'm in another fucking film, he thought, the one where the hero looks for a way out, and always finds one. Maybe it was Hollywood after all, for his busted-nail hands found a loose stone. This part of the wall had been rebuilt, with a type of house brick he could recognise. Shoddy modern workmanship might be coming to his aid. Gripping its loose end, he was able to work the brick back and fore, but could not move it much further. Mark took off his belt and used the buckle to scour the blown mortar. The brick moved again. After half an hour it came away. In his now bloodied hands he had man's most primitive weapon. His first thought was to try to brain whoever came through the door the next time it opened, but all that would get him was a quick bullet.

Night-cruise boats were going past frequently now, floating gin palaces, each one noisier than the last. He looked up at the wooden cargo doors above him and sized up the brick in his hand. The doors were large, the brick small, but there was that small crack.

In the time it took a boat to pass the warehouse Mark was able to get six or seven blows in on the wooden doors above him. At full stretch he targeted the gap where the light was, using the brick as a miniature battering ram. It also battered his fingers every few strikes. At this rate he doubted he would be able to hold a gun, if one ever came into his grasp again. A few times his timing was out and the sound he was making was exposed. He tensed, waiting for someone to come but no one did. *Voulez-vous coucher avec moi* rang out from the other side of the canal, as the DJ racked up the old song allowing Mark to increase his pounding. He'd just about lost all feeling in his right hand when something cracked, and he saw more light. Mark reached up as far as he could, thanking God for his height and pushed with all the strength he had left. There was more cracking and the doors pushed apart. Not much more than a few feet, but it was enough. He had room to haul himself up and squeeze out, to find himself standing on a ledge above the canal. Another boat passed and a few girls spotted him. They waved their glasses and shouted encouragement to him in English.

'Going for a swim?' one of them shouted.

I can't swim, Mark thought, but then I couldn't fly either. He was out, with no passport and no money. He could find the British Embassy. Say he'd been robbed. He could tell them the whole crazy tale, make some bored clerk's day, but something inside wouldn't let him. It had never let him. A door marked trouble had always been open for him, and each time he'd crashed through it. As quickly as his torn hands would allow, Mark edged along the slippery brickwork of the canal wall, until he could drop down into an alleyway, startling a few cats. They slunk away from him with blazing eyes.

Stellachi lay in his bath. The water had to be warm, not hot. Hot was like coffee, it irritated, rubbed up his nerves. This was like bathing in that place in Sicily, floating, letting the current control him, and the sun absolve. Hakim fussing with the food on the beach, his thin body brown and taut. Away from everyone, especially the vile tourists. They'd go there again next spring, when this business would be finished. Maybe he'd buy a place.

Hakim brought in a tray. He poured out the tea slowly from the silver teapot, adding a small spoon of honey, letting it dissolve and merge with the mint leaves in the glass. Stellachi sat up in the bath as Hakim handed him the glass. Stellachi flicked up foam at him, playfully. This was when Hakim feared him most.

'So, what do you think we must do with Richards, eh?'

Hakim knew he wasn't required to answer. Stellachi often had one-sided conversations with him, like the old women in the cafés did with their dogs. A phone rang. The blue one Stellachi only used for the big people. Hakim handed it to him.

'All is well?' a voice asked.

'Yes. Absolutely. I have him.'

'Good. Make sure he disappears quickly. We want no

repeat of London.'

'I understand.'

Stellachi's mood changed. He slapped the phone back into Hakim's hands.

'Get my robe.'

Stellachi sat by the window, deep in thought.

Below, the street was still busy. This was the cesspit he worked in. Stellachi could see some of the girls displayed in their glass houses. One of them always reminded him of his mother. The same hawkish features, the face lined too soon, trapped by her hopeless need, and the inability to satisfy it. He imagined a rifle in his hands, shooting at all that disgusted him. Seeing the harlots die with amazement on their faces, their windows turning red, shooting the pathetic voyeurs that thronged the street now, so that they too dropped like startled rabbits. Shooting those people who'd offered him money on the streets of Bucharest. The old men who took him to large houses full of stolen wealth. He'd killed one of them once, slitting his throat at the age of seventeen, watching the old fool's blood cascade over his fancy furniture, and feeling alive for the first time in his life. It *was* worth living after that. It was the start of it. The payback for being born.

'Hakim, bring me the dark blue suit, white shirt and the new blue tie.'

Stellachi decided to kill this Richards, without any further delay. To hell with his stupid little notebook. How could the man think to threaten him with something like that? Richards was out of his depth, and he would die for it. Twenty years of experience, from that first slit throat, to the Albanian girl, told him to take a chance with the notebook. If he was wrong, so what? He'd worked for these jackals long enough, and he liked the edge a gamble like this brought on. *He* was not Agani. Stellachi felt his body tremble, and felt a little breathless. Hakim handed him the clothes and he dressed slowly, checking each movement in a mirror as tall as him.

'Do you like Mexico?' Stellachi asked.

Hakim shrugged.

'Of course, what would you know of it? Maybe we'll go there after this. Yucatan, it will be hot, and empty. You will have to be careful, Hakim, lots of nice boys there. I might exchange you.'

Hakim would not mind this at all. At times like these, he thought that even death would be a release. He had began to imagine Stellachi dead, that a man such as this Richards would come along, and be stronger than him. Sometimes he imagined killing Stellachi himself, but chased the thoughts from his mind, so alarming were they. Another phone rang. Stellachi clicked his fingers and Hakim ran to answer it. It was Adam, the huge man that Stellachi often used. The man was frightened, something in his voice that Hakim hadn't heard before. Stellachi took the phone from him.

'Well?'

'He's gone.'

'Tell me.'

'The Englishman. I went to check on him, like you said. He was gone. Those old doors had been forced open. Smashed with something hard.'

'As you will be.'

Adam went into a flood of Albanian which Stellachi could not follow and did not want to.

'Shut up. Adam, you will find him. He has no money, clothes, no anything. You *will* find him, won't you?'

Stellachi put down the phone in the middle of Adam's assurances. They wouldn't find him, this Richards was too good, and he, Stellachi, would not have to, for the man would come looking for him again. What else could he do? Stellachi was not displeased, this made it more interesting.

'Hakim,' Stellachi shouted, his voice vibrant and full of

hope, 'I think we will have a guest soon. We must make him welcome.'

Stellachi hummed an old tune to himself, something he'd heard the gypsies play when they came to the village. He opened the draw which contained his personal armoury. He fingered his favourite, the 9mm Luger, an ancient piece, but it had never let him down and he liked its history. Each chip in its metal casing told a story. Alongside two others was the seven-inch dagger Agani had given him. Its ivory handle matched his shirt, good workmanship, for Albania. Stellachi pressed it against his chest, felt its chill through his shirt. He'd always been a knife man, it was much more intimate, and satisfying. No need for noisy explosions and mess. He'd like to use it on Richards. Stellachi held it up against the light, and flicked patterns at Hakim's face. The Arab boy's wide eyes tried to hide, it was what they did best. His way of confirming his place in the order of things.

'Hakim, I'm hungry. Go across to Wan Sing's and get my usual, but order enough for three. And pour me a glass of the driest Amontillado before you go. The special bottle.'

'For three?'

'Yes, three.'

Hakim was slow to obey.

'Why do you hesitate? Ah, you think this Richards might be out there, the bogeyman waiting for you, eh? Don't worry, *you* are not wanted by him, otherwise you would be already dead.'

Stellachi snapped his fingers again. He could do this so strongly it always reminded Hakim of a whip cracking. As Hakim left, Stellachi savoured the pale sherry, moving it with his tongue around his teeth and pressing it into the hollows of his mouth before he swallowed. There goes my bait, he thought.

Mark *was* in Chinatown, and the first thing he saw was a

pyramid of glazed ducks, piled high in a restaurant's window. Mark couldn't believe he could feel hunger at a time like this, but he did, and his stomach lurched with the many smells that surrounded him. Feeling around his pockets to see if any coins had been left he found one or two euros, not much good for anything, other than a cup of coffee.

He kept to the shadows as much as possible. Plenty of others did the same in this part of town. They'd taken his jacket and his shirt was stained and bloody. He touched his head gingerly. He'd had worse. Stellachi has just wanted to quiet him down, that bastard didn't want him banged up too much. Not yet. Mark flexed his hands, they still moved well enough but his nails were smashed, and all his fingertips bloody.

They'd be checking up on him regularly, until Stellachi came for him. He might have just a few minutes of surprise left. He looked around to get his bearings, and found he was only a few hundred yards from Stellachi's place. Mark hardly dared think this was a piece of luck.

Mark bought a takeaway coffee with his coins, then faded back into a side alley. The coffee was too hot, but he drank it straight away, letting it scald his throat. He needed its support, for it was a cold night to be standing in the midst of your enemies in a bloodied shirt. A prostitute started to approach him, then saw his state and turned away.

Mark couldn't remember what fucking day it was, or how long it had been now, Post Lena. He couldn't even remember Julie's mobile number. Maybe that was just as well, because he might be tempted to phone her on reverse charge. For them to exchange voices one last time. That would be pathetic, and a final dagger into her heart.

The closer Mark got to Stellachi's place, the more the need for care. Maybe Stellachi wouldn't be there and he could wait for him. Again. Maybe pigs flew to the moon on pink pork wings.

He got to the rear of the club without trouble. The music that pounded in the front was muffled here, just the low thud of the bass, and the suggestion of movement from the dancers inside. From the glimpse of the club he'd had coming down Stellachi's stairs, Mark couldn't understand how the man could live here. He should be over the other side of town, amongst the fine town-houses and tulips, but there was no reason why anything about Stellachi should make sense. This made trying to second-guess his actions difficult. Back on the estate, in the closed-in valley, Mark had been Stellachi, the unpredictable *Psycho Eyes*, but that counted for little here.

Mark was on the fire escape again. He couldn't believe he'd got this far. All the luck he'd never had in his life was coming now. Maybe they didn't know he was out yet. Stellachi should have killed him straight off. His mistake.

There was a noise at the entrance to the alleyway and Mark froze against the wall. A couple of kids staggered into sight, the boy pawing at the girl with drunken hands, she half pushing him away, half pulling him onto her. All Mark needed. The girl saw his outline and said something to her boyfriend.

'What's your game, mate?' rang out at him, in best south London tones.

Mark would have to go to plan B, the one that didn't exist.

'Just having a piss,' Mark answered, in his best valley voice.

He abandoned the fire escape idea, and walked past the startled couple, expecting Adam and his friend to appear at any moment. They didn't, but Hakim did. Walking past the alleyway entrance with a carrier bag of food in his hand. Instant action came from instant decisions and Mark made one. He stepped up besides Hakim pressing a finger against his neck then digging it in.

'Good, you've got food. I could use some,' Mark said.

Hakim began to squirm.

'Keep walking. If you try anything I'll put a bullet into your brain.'

They were outside the club. A doorman was fussing with a few customers in the street and they were past him and up the stairs in seconds. This was like the raid on Agani's penthouse all over again. Easy. Willing him on. They stopped outside Stellachi's door. Old wood laced with a fancy ironwork design. It looked like it could withstand a siege, but it didn't have a spy hole. Stellachi didn't think he needed one.

'Is he here?' Mark whispered, digging his finger in harder.

'No, he's out looking for you. They know you got away, somehow.'

'No, I don't think so, Hakim. Eating all this yourself, are you?'

Mark gave the large bag a nudge with his knee. It smelt good and Mark took it from the boy. It would have to do as a weapon. *Deadly killer overcome with flying sweet and sour, hah hah.* He was going from the desperate to the bizarre, but he *was* still going.

Mark bent down to Hakim's level and whispered in his ear.

'If you want to live, do exactly as I say. Open the door slowly, walk in, and tell that bastard you are back. If you do it calmly, you can fuck off back down the stairs.'

The English guy was a madman, Hakim thought, but then they all were, all the men he'd come into contact with through Stellachi were the same. Powerful, violent men, all twisted and looking to control and to hurt. Maybe this was what being powerful meant.

Hakim opened the door and Mark stepped in with him. It

was almost dark, just a few red candles in silver holders burning on a table. The place reeked of incense and Mark felt Hakim tense in his grasp. There was slight movement to his right. Stellachi whispered out of the darkness.

'My gun is six inches from your head. Don't make me use it. There's been enough mess here from you. You can give the food back to Hakim now. It's good to see you again, my friend.'

Mark could not say he was surprised, not after the week he'd had. Stellachi moved in front of him, and switched on a main light. Mark blinked, and saw Lena's killer again, standing the same height as him, but a bit leaner, and as sharply dressed as a knife. He felt Stellachi's eyes all over him, and there was just the hint of a smile on the man's face as he checked out Mark's state. Stellachi held a Luger in his hand – Mark recognised it from all the old films he'd seen.

'Come in,' Stellachi said. 'How do they say it in Spain, '*mi casa es su casa*.'

He also said something to Hakim and the boy took the food into the kitchen. A table had already been laid amongst the candles.

'Do you like the fragrances?' Stellachi said. 'I am burning two, *Khamriah*, Hakim's favourite, and *Misk Al Ameer*, my choice. They combine so sweetly, like lovers.'

They reminded Mark of cheap hairdresser's salons in the valley.

Stellachi was casual and on full alert at the same time. He had about seven years on Mark but was probably at his physical peak.

'So, here we are. Amongst us, you have become a minor celebrity, Mark, and I want to thank you for disposing of that useless trash in London. Much appreciated, but unfortunate. These matters always lead elsewhere, and for you, they have led to me.'

Stellachi went through his fingers routine and Hakim

259

appeared with a tray of drinks, shaking it so much that the glass of beer had spilled some of its froth.

'Careful, Hakim, we don't want our guest to think we are untidy, eh? Keep the food warm, I'll tell you when we are ready. I took the liberty of ordering for you, Mark. I knew you would be along.' Stellachi took up his glass. 'I thought you'd prefer beer,' he murmured.

Mark drank the beer. He had gone over this moment so many times in his head that a bullet was no longer anticipated. It was already in him.

'Cheers,' Mark said.

Each man appraised the other at eye-level. Mark thought about throwing the glass in Stellachi's face, and charging him, but he could never be fast enough. Not with this man.

'Can I sit down?' Mark asked.

Stellachi gestured to the sofa with his left hand and Mark sat next to the stain.

'Yes, unpleasant, isn't it? You gave Hakim quite a fright.'

Stellachi sat down at the table and made a point of putting the Luger down on it. Maybe he's a frustrated cowboy, Mark thought, certainly the man liked a bit of show, to play games and he was totally confident.

'So,' Stellachi said, 'here we are. Less than a week ago you had a woman and we had four men in England. Now they are all gone. A pity.'

Mark could see Stellachi entering the flat in London. Lena would have thought it was him, coming home early. She would have run to meet him, in that excited, girlish way of hers. He felt his hands tightening, forming fists. He worked hand to control his right hand, or it would have shattered the glass it held. Stellachi nodded and said something in another language. He seemed to be talking to himself, his eyes half shut, but Mark knew they saw everything.

'Yes, hate has you in its hold,' Stellachi said. 'A powerful emotion, very admirable, but you knew about it before, didn't you? Before Lena. It's always been in you, I can smell it. I know that smell. A man like you should work for us,' Stellachi continued. 'No, I'm not going to make you an offer, too much has happened for that, and the woman would always be between us, but I do want to talk about these.'

Stellachi tapped the copied pages of the notebook. He kept his left hand close to the Luger. He's a southpaw, Mark thought, or maybe two-handed, which didn't make things easier. Stellachi's voice changed, it became colder, and raised in pitch.

'Did you really think you could bargain with this? That it would save you?'

Mark drank the beer as coolly as he could and tried to smile a little. This man liked to talk. He must have talked to a lot of people he'd killed.

Your name is there, this place, all the slime you deal with,' Mark said.

'Do you think a stupid policeman could understand this?'

'If he's pointed in the right direction, and I've made sure he will be.'

'So.'

Stellachi's hand curled around the gun, the skull's head ring on his little finger catching the candlelight, then he relaxed again. This man doesn't know what he's going to do himself, Mark thought. That makes two of us.

'Hakim,' Stellachi said, 'you can serve the food now.'

Mark sat opposite Stellachi at the black table, the Luger just on Stellachi's side of no-man's land. He's giving me the sniff of a chance, Mark thought, encouraging me to go for it. Mark found that he could eat, within a few feet of Lena's killer. It was good food and his stomach welcomed it, as he concentrated on his next move. Each moment was evaluated, every minute he weighed up the chances of an attack. This was a matter of wills. A game for killers.

'The duck is good, no? Some say it's too greasy, but it's an underrated fowl, I always think. Wan Sing's is the best in Amsterdam.'

Hakim opened a bottle of wine, fighting hard to control his shaking hands, and served both men. Mark wanted to duplicate Stellachi's every move. He wasn't sure why, beer and wine would hardly sharpen up his senses, but he needed to. Maybe it was a matter of honour, whatever that word meant. Luck, chance, even destiny had got him to this point. He was still alive.

Chapter Fifteen

'The doc says he's amazed by my recovery,' Carl said. 'Best part of me to get whacked, my head. Never was much in there.'

Carl was able to sit up now, still tubed up and plugged in, but Julie could see colour returning to his face. The worst was over. She pushed a few stray hairs away from his face, like she'd used to with Mark, when he'd been young enough to let her.

'I hope my hair grows back over the scar,' Carl murmured. 'At my age you can't be too sure. They say it won't be too long before I can come out, Jool, if I've got a good carer, of course. I have got one, haven't I?'

'Looks like.'

Julie lowered her voice, but there was no one around. Carl still had a room to himself.

'What did the police say?' she asked.

'Just told me what happened to the car. I did my best wide-eyed bit, stuck in a lot of *good God*s.'

'I thought they might have thought it funny, you being so hurt at the same time.'

'They didn't seem to. Nah, they don't expect 'owt. Why should they? I'm just an old builder who happened to fall down the stairs and had his car nicked on the same day. What are the papers saying about it?'

'It's on the front page of this one. Look.'

Julie held up the paper she'd brought. It showed the remains of the two cars, still smoking, the church looming dark behind them.

'You read it to me, Jool. I can't focus too well, yet.'

'Mystery of Mountain Tragedy,' it says.' They are saying no one knows who the men in the cars are, and, guess what?'

'What?'

'They think those bastards are the only two involved. The explosion made so much mess, they are not sure who was driving what.'

'That's good, Jool, very good. Any word from Mark?'

'No. He's not answering his mobile.'

Julie's eyes started to fill up and Carl managed to move a hand towards hers.

'He's a survivor, Jool. Take my word for it, you've reared a tough 'un there.'

Carl believed this, but not enough to think that Mark really had a chance. He'd have to get better quick, Julie would need him. A nurse came in to check on the patient and it was time for Julie to go.

To kill time, Julie walked through the town to the seafront, where she sat on the driest looking bench and looked out at the sea. It was a bright, breezy day, and the sea was chopped up into small waves. Julie fixed her eyes on one grey-blue rocky point. It was better for her this way, for the sea made her restless, it being so free. She noticed that the waves broke at this same spot each time, spraying foam as they endlessly repeated their display. Far more constant than anything had been in her life. She wondered how many years they had broken at the same place, maybe it was hundreds. Thousands. Hundreds of thousands. Not very long ago she'd sat at a similar place with Carl, thinking ahead. She thought what had happened with Shane had been a one-off dose of disaster that was her lot to endure. Now Mark had provided another one. There was something about her first-born that seemed to make him a magnet for trouble. He'd been out of it for a long time, almost enough to give her hope that it was for ever. Almost.

Seabirds wheeled around her, twisting on air currents, free like she'd never been. Sun caught on white breasts and orange rimmed eyes checked her out as a source of food. There were different types of birds and she wished she knew the names of some of them. School had come and gone, something to be endured, and Mark had followed her example. *You've reared a tough 'un*, Carl had said, but she'd hardly done that. Dragged up, more like, her best never much better than hopeless. An elderly couple smiled at her as they passed her bench. They had a toddler with them, blond like Shane had been, laughing as he pulled at the old man, dancing around him on wobbly legs, but in safety. Grandparents. Mark had missed out on them too. Time went on so quickly; it seemed just a short while ago that Shane was this age, even Mark. Thirty years ago, and just yesterday.

Julie checked her mobile again. Still nothing. Mark would have phoned by now, she was sure of it. He would have phoned if he could. She shivered at this thought as the wind got up and started to bite, but she stayed on the bench and went through every possibility in her head. She'd thought the old estate grim, and some of the people who lived there grimmer, but nothing like those two who'd come for her and Carl. In the main, the people she'd grown up with had been shaped by the way life had dumped on them. Life was always a matter of luck, and on the estate it had been in short supply. She'd known many decent women who'd been pulled down, their only crimes poverty and worthless men. One led to the other in an inevitable chain.

Julie watched the changing colours in the sky, it was bigger here than in the valley, more open. By the time the birds had left it had gone from blue to gold to orange. It was time to go back to the hospital, check on Carl again before going back to his place. He might be the only man left in her life.

*

Stellachi smelt like a woman. He lived in a woman's flat, and Mark was trapped in it.

'So,' Stellachi said, 'would you like something to round off the meal? How about brandy? I have something very special here.'

'Why not?'

Snapped fingers made Hakim appear with two bulbous glasses. Stellachi took a bottle from the shelf behind him and poured some into a deep glass. He swirled it around, smelt it, held it up against the soft light, then pushed the glass across the table to Mark. Mark almost made his move, while Stellachi had one hand busy. He could probably have reached him, but would have a few bullets in his chest as a reward, and his grip would fall away into nothing.

'I read you, my friend. Looking for that slightest of edges, eh, the one that will make you think you can do it. Quite a few others have thought the same.'

Stellachi poured out his own drink.

'You need glasses this size to tease out the flavour,' he murmured, his voice dropping to such a level that he seemed to be talking to himself. 'Some find it too warming, but I acquired the taste a long time ago, when I was working in Paris. You have been, I think?'

'You like play-acting, don't you?' Mark waved a hand around the flat. 'All this crap. It doesn't change anything, it doesn't change what you are.'

'Mark, we are not going to have rough words, are we? Name calling? Surely we are above that when drinking five-star brandy?'

'No, you are below it.'

Stellachi smiled his thin smile, but Mark saw his fingers whiten around the stem of the brandy glass.

'… In this bleak world of random moments … I read that

266

somewhere, in English. Do you think the world bleak, Mark? Is this a random moment?'

It had started to rain outside. Hard. It beat against Stellachi's windows, and each drop that trickled down turned red from the neon sign outside. Like blood.

'Do you hear how it rains?' Stellachi said. 'It's good that it comes often here. To wash the filth off the streets.'

Stellachi got up and stood by the window, gun in hand. He seemed to be dreaming, hardly aware of Mark at all. On the edge of maybe his last ever move, Mark thought back to his first real fight on the estate. It had been in weather like this, with a boy older and bigger than himself. The first time that rage really kicked in, a red blur that made actions hard to remember, and impossible to control, but he remembered the blood on his hands, and that bruised and battered kid limping his way home. *Psycho Eyes* was born that night. It had been a bit hairy for a few years after that, a succession of hard boys, then hard men looking to challenge him. All failed, until he was left alone, his reputation secure, his life anything but.

'Sit back there,' Stellachi said, gesturing to the sofa.

Mark saw that the sofa was soft and deep, but the chair Stellachi chose was hard, and easier to spring up from. He made his move as Stellachi sat down, throwing the brandy glass in his face and following it with a dive. He was trying for Stellachi's throat but grabbed at air, and was struck across the side of the head by the Luger in Stellachi's hand. As he hit the deck he felt his old friend, blood, this time running down his cheek.

'Quick, Hakim, get him up. No mess.'

Stellachi backed away against a wall. Lit by the lighting there, he looked like a white ghost, as he casually brushed broken glass from his suit, and clucked his tongue at the brandy stains. There was a small spot of blood on his forehead, which got bigger, like a red island. He's too good,

Mark thought, too fucking good. Too fucking good for me.

Hakim pulled at Mark's shoulder, crying and shaking with fright. 'Sorry, mate,' Mark whispered, as he grabbed the boy by the neck and got behind him.

'Mark, Mark, so predictable. Do you really think you can use this creature as a hostage? Do you really think that?' Stellachi levelled the gun at Hakim's heart. 'For its time, the Luger is a remarkable piece. Its bullets are able to pass through modern stone quite easily. Hakim is not made of stone.'

Hakim was trying to scream but just a whimper came from him. He managed to mouth something in Arabic and Stellachi answered in the same tongue.

'He's begging for his life,' Stellachi murmured, his voice getting even quieter. 'Such a guttural language, full of whining complaint. I tired of it long ago. Let him tend to you, Mark, you are bleeding all over my floor. Perhaps we can talk about the notebook after all.'

Mark let the Arab boy go. There was not much point in doing otherwise. More language was exchanged between master and slave and Hakim left the room, to come back with a moist towel. Mark saw that the boy had wet himself too, his silk trousers stuck to his groin but Stellachi did not seem to notice. Perhaps it was a regular occurrence. Hakim dabbed at the side of Mark's head, trying to cry as quietly as he could.

Stellachi went to his desk and picked up a small bag. 'Here are your things Mark, passport, not much money. A photograph of Lena. *L...e...n...a.*'

Stellachi said her name slowly, teasing out each letter as he twisted the photograph in his fingers. Stellachi stopped playing with the photograph and placed it back carefully inside the passport.

'Where's the notebook, Mark? Maybe it can save you. It's not important to me whether you live or die. I can even

268

forgive your intrusion here. I could arrange for you to disappear. If I say you are dead, no one will check, I can assure you of that. They know me too well. You know, I rather like you. You remind me of my rougher self, the one I left behind on the streets of Bucharest. You are in good shape, I like that in a man. No unnecessary flesh, like the fat pigs who wander this city.'

Stellachi's face had softened. It made him look even madder. Mark knew there was not the slightest chance Stellachi would let him go. No matter how important the book was, it was more important for the Romanian to kill him. This junkie of death could never let a fix go. He was just talking. Doing whatever his crazy mind told him to, and enjoying the show.

At least he'd been right about the notebook, it was keeping him alive. Mark couldn't believe they hadn't given the hotel room more of a going over. If he'd found the hiding place for Angelo's book, so could they. Stellachi's thinking was loose because he was unhinged, in love with his own power, and the people who worked for him were governed by fear. He'd cut up Lena on a whim. Thank Christ he'd gone back to Amsterdam straight after, or Julie and Carl would be dead now.

The last week hadn't been one of ideas, or real plans, just gut reaction, and desperation. Mark felt he didn't have anything else to try. Maybe he should go back to his first thought, being blown away trying to smash Stellachi's face. To see the Romanian's jaw busted before he went down, and everything faded to black. It was not much of a payback for Lena, but his senses were wasted, stripped bare by the last few days. His head was beating him up, there was nowhere else to go and the nerve knew it. It joined forces with Stellachi to drum at the side of his head. He felt the vein flex against his temple, it was insistent, wanting him to make another move.

'Well, we've had a good meal, drank superior brandy, even if some went over me. So, what do you say?'

'You're wrong about the hate,' Mark said. 'I only have it for you. Yours covers the whole world. Even this poor sod.'

Mark waved a hand at Hakim, who stood against the other wall, his eyes showing white as he tried to lose himself in shadow.

'Ah, you are trying to philosophise, Mark. Don't go there. You are not cut out for it.'

'The notebook is a long way from here.'

'I don't doubt it.'

'So what are you saying? That you'll keep me alive until I produce it, then let me go. If you think I'd believe that you are crazier than you look. And you look pretty crazy.'

'You are trying to rile me. Not possible, Mark. Come on, what else can you do? How do you say it in English – you've given it your good shot?'

'Best shot.'

'So.'

Mark sat back on the sofa. He was so tired. Of all of it. At sixteen he'd stood on his hilltop, *his* hilltop, looking down on familiar territory, knackered territory most of it, littered with the remains of industry that had been first forced upon it, then stolen away again. Where he came from and where he belonged, despite no father, no money and no prospects. Back then he still thought he was alive, and that life felt real. Before Shane. Before Lena.

Mark closed his eyes, aware that Stellachi was still talking but not listening to him. Then his senses were jerked back into life, stretched out again, like an elastic band about to snap, thrown into a scene that topped everything that had come before in this hellish week.

Chapter Sixteen

Hakim ran at Stellachi. Something glinted in his hand. Then it was in Stellachi's chest, up to its hilt, the intricate inlays winking silver as the handle quivered back and forth. There was no sign of the blade. Stellachi was pushed against the wall by the force of Hakim's thrust. He looked at the boy in amazement, and the thin smile returned to his lips. Stellachi's free hand was on the dagger, but he didn't try to pull it out. His eyes were turning glassy as they turned towards Mark.

'Life is full of surprises, my friend.'

He levelled the gun at Mark who tensed for a bullet that didn't come. He was sure that Stellachi was still able to shoot, it only took a touch on the trigger, but the Romanian let the gun fall with a soft thud onto the white carpet that was turning red. Stellachi's white polo-neck was also turning red, a stain that spread out around the knife. He sank down slowly to sit against the wall, still looking at Hakim.

'So, the worm turned.'

Hakim could not believe what he had done. He looked at his hands, pushed them against his face, trying to block out the sight of the man he'd killed. Now both Stellachi's hands clasped the knife, as if preparing for a position of death, yet Mark still half expected him to pull it out with a flourish, even to spring up again like some immortal devil, but no, Stellachi died, looking at the mess he was making on his floor.

Mark checked his pulse to be sure, as Hakim began a low-pitched keening to go with his shaking. The boy had sunk to his knees and was trying to hug himself.

'You'd better make yourself scarce,' Mark said.

'Where I go? I don't have money. He did everything, controlled everything.'

'Up until a minute ago.'

Hakim managed to approach Stellachi's body now. He touched his head, and lightly stroked his blond hair, but in the way one would stroke a snake.

'They'll kill me,' Hakim muttered. 'It's Allah's will, for *I* have killed. For all the years with him, I have killed.'

Mark put the copied pages back into his pocket and checked the street. Just a few stragglers about now, pounded by the rain. Even the window girls had clocked off. Hakim looked up at Mark, with the same bewildered face Mark remembered on Daniels the glue-sniffer, snot-nosed and afraid of his own shadow, his life ending at fifteen, in fear. Hakim was equally lost, but he had another chance.

It was an instant decision, the only type Mark ever seemed to make.

'Get some overcoats,' Mark said.

'What?'

'Get a coat for him, and one each for us. Stellachi must have lots of them. Come on, you want to live, don't you?'

Hakim did. His face turned from despair to eagerness. Mark knew Hakim would attach himself if he could, like a pup changing owners. Mark was not so sure if Stellachi had wanted to live. He'd go over this moment many times in his mind, but would never come up with an answer why the man hadn't used the gun. Perhaps he wanted to check out in mystery, he was vain enough. Maybe he had other reasons. There was surprise locked in Stellachi's death mask, but perhaps relief also, even admiration, in his final frozen stare. Mark put his hands over Stellachi's, and pulled out the dagger. It had gone straight through the heart. Hakim wailed softly as he did so.

'Don't faint on me now,' Mark murmured. 'Help me get

the coat on him.'

Hakim came back with three dark and expensive coats. Mark managed to put one on Stellachi. He took Stellachi's Rolex off, and handed it to Hakim.

'Here. These go for ten grand. You might get half of that if you sell it on. Use the money to get away.'

Looking at Hakim's wild-eyed face Mark doubted that he could get away from anything, but he owed the boy.

'Come on. Put your coat on, we're going downstairs.'

Mark put on the other coat, then checked through his stuff in the case Stellachi had brought to the flat. He pocketed his passport and the money, which Stellachi hadn't touched. Mark didn't want anything else. They dragged Stellachi up, Mark holding the body between himself and Hakim. They'd be three drunks on a night out, it was all Mark could think of. If they could get Stellachi into a canal it might save Hakim. Whether they'd still come after him was another matter, but Mark couldn't think about that now. He was alive and Stellachi was dead. Lena's killer was dead, which meant it was over, for him. Mark shut his eyes for a moment and brought Lena back, that first radiant time he saw her. He hoped she could rest easy now. He hoped he could.

The weather helped. Rain slashed at them as soon as they got outside. There was still music coming from the club, but it echoed onto an empty street. The doorman was sheltering somewhere.

'Walk,' Mark whispered to Hakim, and they stumbled along the street.

If any of Stellachi's goons appeared now it was all over, but Mark didn't think they would. All the luck missing from his life was arriving now. It had gone into overdrive. It didn't make any sense that he was alive, it didn't make any sense he'd survived in the valley churchyard, but he had. Now he'd been saved by a terrified Arab rent-boy, but one whose fear had been conquered by hatred. Stellachi had talked about its power, and it had killed him.

Mark feared Hakim would lose it any moment, and bolt, leaving him propping up a dead man, so he tried to hold on to him as well as Stellachi. The Romanian still looked elegant, even with a leaking hole in his heart. They staggered into the alleyway that fringed the warehouse which had been Mark's prison. A brothel on the corner was shutting up shop. Its door opened and Mark was looking down at a dwarf, being shown out by a woman twice his size. She patted his head as if she was sending a small child to school. It was an amazing sight, but it fitted into this night. Anything could happen, anything was possible. The dwarf saw them.

'All right?' he shouted, in an English accent, his eyes still gleaming with adventure. 'I see you three have had a good night.'

Mark smiled and nodded, holding on tight to Hakim. The dwarf hung around for a moment, but when no one answered him he wandered back out into the main street, whistling tunelessly to himself, not minding the rain as he jauntily picked his way over the cobblestones.

Leaning Stellachi against a wall, Mark noticed that his face was no more ashen in death than in life, but the stare was unchanging now. He closed Stellachi's eyes with his spare hand. Stellachi's thin smile was frozen on his lips, it was the last thing Mark saw as he tumbled him into the black water. The body went down quickly in the heavy coat. On your way to hell, mate, I hope, Mark thought. You'll be at home there.

Hakim slumped against the wall and started to whimper again, Mark did not think the kid quite knew what he'd done. No one else would ever believe he'd managed to kill Stellachi either, which might be his salvation. Hakim tried to sit on the ground but Mark held him up.

'You'll have to pull yourself together. Go back and clean up that place. Do a good job - you're used to it now. Keep the watch hidden and use it when you can. When others ask, say Stellachi went out to find me. That's all you know. *He went out to find me.*'

'I can't … I can't.'

'You *can*. You're going to have to, if you want to stay alive. Right, off you go.'

Mark pushed him firmly away, then caught hold of him again, for a second.

'Oh, I almost forgot, thanks.'

Hakim was gone, scuttling away, head down into the driving rain. If the luck hadn't played itself out Hakim would get back and get to work on the mess before anyone came calling. Mark couldn't afford to think any more about the boy – he needed to get away himself, he needed to get home. If he disappeared now, and Stellachi didn't surface for a time, or not at all, maybe his masters would be satisfied. Maybe they would let it go now. It was a lot of maybes.

The notebook could stay under the floorboards in Anton's doss house, he wasn't going back there. If he was found and he had it on him, it would be worthless. It was almost three in the morning. No one was around, his only company was the odd neon light still on, red, blue, yellow, one a stuttering pink, lost without its punters.

Mark wouldn't fly again, that would remain a one-off. He tried to see the layout of the city in his head, he'd walked around it enough the first time he was here. He needed to get out to the suburbs, get a train from there, away from the airport, the ferry ports and the main stations.

Paris. The name came to him, then images of the place, Lena's face plastered all over the memories. Pain came back with it. It had been crushed out by action, but now it crept back into him. He stopped to rest his back against a wall for a moment, to fight against exhaustion. It was a good move, for Stellachi's two goons cruised past in a Volvo, Adam sitting like a rock in the passenger seat. They didn't see him, but might have done if he hadn't stopped. 'Thanks, Lena,' he muttered.

As he left the district Mark wiped the dagger handle clean of prints, then stabbed it into a wooden alleyway door. He stabbed it in with all his force, shooting pain through his battered hand.

Mark walked the three miles to Rai station before dawn. Orange light was squashing out the night and the rain had stopped. He could have been picked off easily by a passing car but the Volvo didn't show up again. No one tried to stop him, no one got in his way.

From Rai he connected to Schiphol but never left the railway platform. In the way he'd perfected in the valleys, he made his large frame as inconspicuous as possible. No one gave him a second glance. They would all be looking for Mark the flyer. His luck held and he was in Paris the next night. His money was almost gone but his credit card, the one Lena had insisted he had, got him there. Stellachi's coat was his entry card into the hotel, the same one he'd shared with Lena. People only looked at the outside, and the coat was rich. He hid his hands as much as possible and had washed on the train. Mark thought about phoning Julie from the hotel, but decided against it. He didn't want her to hear his voice until he was with her. Just in case.

In his room Mark sat under the shower, checking out his array of bruising, and wincing as the water softened his smashed fingers. Drying off, he looked in the mirror at the face of a killer. It would always be the face of a killer but nothing unusual stared back at him. His face showed relief more than anything. He was too tired to care if he was truly safe. He had some food sent up to the room, ate it, then slept for twelve hours.

The way Mark approached Julie on the hospital concourse was almost normal.

'How is he, then?' a voice behind her said.

Julie turned, and had to blink hard at the man silhouetted by the sun.

'Oh my God, I thought I was hearing things.'

Julie looked up at Mark for some time, as if not daring to believe he was actually there. Then she looked around nervously.

'It's all right, Mam. I haven't brought trouble this time.'

Julie buried her head in Mark's chest. Hesitantly, he ran a hand over her hair but no words came to him. She didn't need any.

In Paris Mark had sat in the café at the top of the Eiffel Tower, drinking coffee and checking out a city washed by warm autumn, sun. Lena was everywhere, and it was necessary that she was. This was the best he could do in memory of her. When he'd left the city, he felt cleaner, able to remember the good things.

Mark took the Eurostar to Waterloo and a train straight down to Swansea. He slept fitfully, and faces of the dead looked in on him. Kelly shuffled up the street, bad teeth, bad smells, but a decent eagerness. Tony bounced through the air, his gelled-up hair still in place. Agani clutched at his separating head with jewelled hands, and the two brothers burnt. Yet Stellachi was absent. He, truly, had been rubbed out, even if Mark still wore the man's overcoat. Underneath it his clothes were foul, though he'd bought a shaving kit and had used it.

'Jesus, look at the state of your hands,' Julie said.

Mark tried to hide them in his pockets. 'No worries. They're a sign that it's over.'

'Is it? Is it, really? What the hell's been happening? God, I got so much to ask you.'

'Not now, Mam. You don't want to know, really, and you haven't answered *my* question.'

'What?'

'Carl, how is he?'

'Oh, he's good. He's making real progress.'

'Did they ask anything awkward?'

'Not really. We stuck to the story. I'll be starting to believe it myself soon.'

'What about our adventure at the church?'

'That's died down in the papers. They think there was one man in each car but they can't identify them. Carl says he'll even get insurance money for his Mercedes.'

The tears came now. Mark was surprised she'd held off for so long.

He felt her body rise and fall against his. People scuttled past them, slightly embarrassed. They'll think we've had terrible news, Mark thought, but it's all good.

'Come on, take me in to see him.'

Carl woke up as Mark pressed a hand to his shoulder.

'Bloody hell, it is you, Mark?' Carl blinked, and looked around the room.

'I thought I'd croaked, and you were there to meet me. So, you made it, then? Hey, there's no one on your tail, is there? I'm in no state to …'

'No, relax. It's over.'

Julie sat the other side of the bed and Carl held them both by the hand. His eyes started to water.

'Fuck it, this is all a bit too much, this is.'

'He's back, Carl,' Julie whispered.

'Aye. I can see that.'

'You must be a tough old geezer,' Mark murmured.

'Not like you, son. Not like you.'

'Stop it, you'll start me off again,' Julie said.

They sat with Carl without anything else being said. When Carl fell asleep, Julie touched his face lightly.

'You're really into him, Mam.'

'I s'pose I am. That all right?'

'More than all right. Come on, let him get his rest.'

'Will you come back to my place with me, Mark? I want to get a bit more stuff. I didn't want to go back there on my own.'

'Of course I will.'

They took a train to Cardiff and a bus out to Julie's flat. It was a nice evening, the sun falling below the sea line in a yellow haze.

'Look at that,' Julie said, 'everything so calm. Normal.'

'I'm not sure we're ready to do that word, Mam.'

'Mark, we *will* be safe now?'

'I'm as sure as I can be that only those guys who burned in the car knew about you, and they only found out about Carl when they followed me down here. That knowledge burnt with them.'

Julie accepted this hesitantly and Mark wished he could have total belief himself that it was over. Time would tell.

Julie shuddered as she opened her door.

'I wouldn't want to stay here too long,' she said, 'not now.'

'Have they said when Carl will be out?'

''Bout another week. They can't believe how he's come on.'

'As I said, he's tough. How much money have you got, Mam?'

'Only about ten quid of yours left, but I'll be paid from the factory tomorrow. How about you?'

Mark fumbled in his pockets.

'About three-sixty.'

'Three hundred and sixty?'

'No, three pounds bloody sixty pence.'

'Nothing changes, eh?'

'Oh it does, Mam. It has.'

He thought she was going to cry again but Julie sat quietly in a chair.

'Gimme your money,' Mark said, 'I'll pop out and get us something to eat.'

He returned with two fish suppers and two cans of beer. Julie was standing by the gas fire. She had Lena's doll in her hand.

'Did you put this here?'

'Yes. It was Lena's. I took it from our flat in London. The doll, and this photo.'

Mark found the Paris photograph and handed it to Julie.

'Well, she was a looker, all right.'

Julie moved to hold the photograph closer to the light. She should have put the doll down first but as she fumbled with the photograph she dropped the doll onto the laminated floor. It was china, and broke easily.

'Oh God, I'm sorry, love.'

Mark wasn't listening. He was looking at the black felt bag that had been exposed, and the cluster of diamonds that spilled from it. A white line of them that rolled to a halt and caught fire in the hard overhead light.

'Jesus Christ,' Julie whispered, 'are they what I think they are?'

Mark picked up the bag and the loose gems. He lined them up in the palm of his hand.

'They're not from Ratner's,' he murmured.

Mark took them to the table and counted them out. There were twelve, none of them small.

'Hold out your hand,' Mark said.

He placed the largest on Julie's open palm, she was shaking so much she had to close it quickly, to stop the diamond from falling. She kept it closed.

'That one should be worth fifty grand, at least.'

'This gets more unreal all the time.'

'It's real all right, and it will change everything.

'Specially for you and Carl.'

'I don' know, it's more trouble.'

'This isn't trouble. Not after what we've been through.'

'These are dirty, though.'

'No, they're not. They are clean, Mam, and they are ours. Lena died for these. The way I'm looking at it now she died for us and I think we've paid for them, don't you?'

Julie put her face close to the diamond, it made her eyes shine like a young girl's.

Mark realised his head was free of pain. Nothing was crushing it any more, and the nerve no longer flexed against the side of his head.

'I can't fucking believe it,' Julie whispered again.

'Mam, don't swear.'

Also by Roger Granelli

Risk

"Roger Granelli vividly conveys the squalid and sometimes violent realities of the life of a man who has hit rock bottom."
Triple BAFTA-winning writer Elaine Morgan.

"Genuinely gritty stuff. Risk quickly becomes as addictive as the addictions it is portraying..."
Suzy Ceulan Hughes, www.gwales.com.

James Read is a troubled man in his forties. A gambling addiction has destroyed his life, career and marriage. After a period living on the streets he ends up in a hostel, where he meets Colin, a Falklands war veteran with schizophrenia.

The novel is played out against the backdrop of Colin's crazed mind and insane plans. As James's life begins to recover, so the danger that Colin represents begins to escalate. Colin becomes James's nemesis and pushes him toward the limit of endurance.

ISBN 9781906125103
£7.99

Also Published by Accent Press

Losing It   ISBN 9781906125943   £1.99